Arthur's thoughts were so clear he might as well have spoken them aloud. This was not the cramped loft in the Running Fox. The dormitory here was spacious. There was no excuse for them to be sleeping within reach of each other. Unless…

To remove any doubts as to her desires, Clare dropped her comb and held out her hand. 'I think we shall both do very well. It's beautifully warm by the chimney.'

Arthur dropped his cloak and sword on the pallet and sat down beside her. He set the lamp to one side. 'Clare…' His voice was thick. Reaching out, he picked up a strand of her hair and wound it round his fingers. His eyes went black. 'It's good to see your hair again. Those veils…' he shook his head '…I prefer you without them.'

Clare set her hand on a broad shoulder and gave a little tug. Their lips met. The contact remained gentle until Arthur turned more fully towards her and gathered her to him. Clare closed her eyes and pressed against him, opening her mouth to his tongue. His masculine, earthy fragrance surrounded her.

His breathing ragged, he pulled back. Clare felt a soft touch on her cheek. He was shaking his head.

'Clar   L   u.'

'And

D1079179

UNVEILING
LADY CLARE

Carol Townend

Published in Great Britain 2014
by Mills & Boon, an imprint of Harlequin (UK) Limited,
Eton House, 18-24 Paradise Road, Richmond, Surrey, TW9 1SR

© 2014 Carol Townend

ISBN: 978 0 263 90934 0

Harlequin (UK) Limited's policy is to use papers that are natural, renewable and recyclable products and made from wood grown in sustainable forests. The logging and manufacturing processes conform to the legal environmental regulations of the country of origin.

Printed and bound in Spain
by Blackprint CPI, Barcelona

Carol Townend has been making up stories since she was a child. Whenever she comes across a tumbledown building, be it castle or cottage, she can't help conjuring up the lives of the people who once lived there. Her Yorkshire forebears were friendly with the Brontë sisters. Perhaps their influence lingers…

Carol's love of ancient and medieval history took her to London University, where she read History, and her first novel (published by Mills & Boon®) won the Romantic Novelists' Association's New Writers' Award. Currently she lives near Kew Gardens, with her husband and daughter. Visit her website at www.caroltownend.co.uk

Previous novels by the same author:

THE NOVICE BRIDE
AN HONOURABLE ROGUE
HIS CAPTIVE LADY
RUNAWAY LADY, CONQUERING LORD
HER BANISHED LORD
BOUND TO THE BARBARIAN*
CHAINED TO THE BARBARIAN*
BETROTHED TO THE BARBARIAN*
LADY ISOBEL'S CHAMPION **

*_Palace Brides_ trilogy
**_Knights of Champagne_

AUTHOR NOTE

Arthurian myths and legends have been popular for hundreds of years. Dashing knights worship beautiful ladies, fight for honour—and sometimes lose honour! Some of the earliest versions of these stories were written in the twelfth century by an influential poet called Chrétien de Troyes. Troyes was the walled city in the French county of Champagne, where Chrétien lived and worked. His patron, Countess Marie of Champagne, was a princess—daughter of King Louis of France, and the legendary Eleanor of Aquitaine. Countess Marie's splendid artistic court in Troyes rivalled Queen Eleanor's in Poitiers.

The books in my *Knights of Champagne* mini-series are not an attempt to rework the Arthurian myths and legends; they are original romances set around the Troyes court. I wanted to tell the stories of some of the lords and ladies who might have inspired Chrétien— and I was keen to give the women a more active role, since Chrétien's ladies tend to be too passive for today's reader.

Apart from a brief glimpse of Count Henry and Countess Marie, my characters are all fictional. I have used the layout of the medieval city to create my Troyes, but these books are first and foremost fictional.

DEDICATION

To Kate Tremayne with love and thanks
for years of friendship and writerly chat.

Chapter One

*January 1174—Lodgings in the merchants'
quarter of Troyes, in the County of
Champagne.*

It was mild for January, and the shutters were
open to make the most of the light. As Clare
helped Nicola to move from her cot to the bench
by the table, she was given a warm smile. Clare's
heart lifted—Nicola was weak and ill, and her
smiles were precious.

'I see you had a visitor while I was at market,'
Clare said.

Nicola grunted and eased back against the
planked wall. 'So I did, and it wasn't just any
visitor, it was a nobleman. A nobleman with a
gift. It's of no use to me, but you and Nell might
enjoy it. I wanted to tell you before I told Nell.
There's no point in getting her overexcited if you

refuse to take her. I know how you fret every time you leave the house.'

'A gift?' Clare settled a blanket around Nicola's knees. Whoever Nicola's mysterious visitor had been—Count Lucien, perhaps?—he had clearly done her good. Nicola's eyes were brighter than they had been in months, she almost looked happy. Clare waited, Nicola would soon confirm the identity of her visitor—since Geoffrey's death, there had been no secrets between them. 'You are comfortable? If you're in a draught, I can close that shutter.'

'Lord, no, leave it open, there's little enough light at this time of year.'

Clare removed the simple linen veil she invariably wore when going to market, and hung it on the hook, over her cloak. A strand of copper-coloured hair swung forwards. As she hooked it back into its plait, she glanced at the fire. It was burning low. A thin blue haze wound up to a vent in the rafters. 'Shall I build up the fire?'

'Clare, I'm fine. Save the wood until evening.'

Nodding, Clare lifted a basket on to the table and began to unload it. Flour. Cheese. A handful of withered pears. Onions. Dried beans. And, thanks to the generosity of Geoffrey's liege lord, Count Lucien, some salt pork and dried fish.

'No eggs?' Nicola asked.

'The price was madness. I'll try again tomorrow, although I fear they won't be cheap until spring.' She glanced at Nicola. 'Well? What is this mysterious gift?'

Nicola fumbled in her purse and slapped a coin on the table.

'Money.' Despite herself, Clare's voice was flat. 'Lord d'Aveyron has been here again.'

Every time Clare thought of Lucien Vernon, Count d'Aveyron, she couldn't help but remember Geoffrey's folly. His recklessness. Geoffrey had made some devil's pact with a gang of thieves. Clare knew he had done it to help his mother—before his death he had confessed the whole. She also knew that Geoffrey had lived to regret it. He had tried to make amends, but the moment he had tried to wriggle out of the arrangement, he had signed his own death warrant. The thieves had killed him.

Clare knew about Geoffrey's dealings with outlaws, as did Count Lucien. Nicola, on the other hand, did not—she lived in happy ignorance of her son's fatal lapse of judgement. And as far as Clare was concerned, that was exactly how it should be. Nicola wouldn't learn of Geoffrey's shame from her—in her fragile state, it would likely kill her. Thus far, Count Lucien hadn't breathed a word about Geoffrey's transgression, but Clare dreaded his visits. Geoffrey had been one of Count Lucien's household knights, and she was afraid that one day, the Count would let something slip...

'There's no need to look like that,' Nicola said, sliding the coin towards her. 'The Count is a good man, and he honours Geoffrey's memory by keeping an eye on his mother. This isn't money. Look closely.'

Setting the pears in a wooden bowl, Clare reached for the coin and saw that it wasn't a coin at all. It was larger than a penny and made of lead rather than silver. 'It's a token.'

'Yes.'

A picture of Troyes Castle was stamped solidly on one face; on the other was the image of a knight charging at full tilt. Clare's stomach tightened and she put the token back on the table with a decisive snap. 'I hope that's not what I think it is.'

Some of the light went out of Nicola's eyes. 'That token gives entry to the stands at the Twelfth Night Joust—the seated area near the ladies. Clare, I thought...' Nicola paused '...I *hoped* you'd want to go. Particularly if you had a seat on the ladies' benches. You'd be safe there.'

Clare stared at the coin and repressed the urge to take a swift step backwards. The Twelfth Night Joust. Ever since the year had turned, the town had been talking of little else. 'I can't go.'

'It would do you good. The only time you leave the house is when you go to market. I thought—'

'Nicola, I go to market because we would starve if I didn't, I don't go because I like it.'

'You're afraid to go abroad, even after all this time.'

Clare's chin went up. 'Wouldn't you be, if you were me?'

Nicola shook her head and sighed. 'Yes. No. I don't know.' Her gaze sharpened. 'I do know that you're young and you can't hide for ever. I thought you were happy here.'

'I am, but—'

'This is your home—you are safe in Troyes.'

'Thank you for the thought, but I don't want to go.' Clare tapped the token with her finger-nail. 'Nicola, you could get good money for this, people are fighting to get their hands on them.'

Nicola's eyes filled. 'Nell would love to see the Twelfth Night Joust—you know she adores watching the knights. They remind her of Geoffrey.'

Clare narrowed her eyes. That was a low blow and Nicola knew it. 'Nell can go with someone else. Speaking of Nell, where is she?'

'Taking yarn round to Aimée's.'

'Couldn't Aimée take her to the joust?'

Nicola made a pleading gesture. 'I would much rather she went with you. Clare, please. Nell's a child and I'm afraid that when she is grown she will have forgotten Geoffrey. I want her to be able to remember him. If she sees a joust, it will strengthen her memory.'

'Strengthen her memory?'

'When you get there you can tell her about him. Explain what's happening. Let her see she can be proud of her brother—an ordinary boy, who received his spurs. I want her to be able to remember him, the brother who didn't forget his mother in her hour of need.'

On the table, the lead token gleamed like a baleful eye. Regret and sorrow held Clare's tongue. This was becoming awkward. Nicola's pride in her son was almost all she had and Clare wasn't about to take that away from her. She felt herself weaken.

Geoffrey had made many mistakes in his life, but as far as Clare was concerned he was a Good Samaritan. He'd given her—a complete stranger—a roof over her head. He'd trusted her to look after his mother. For all his flaws, Geoffrey had loved his mother dearly and Clare knew he would want her to honour his mother's wishes.

Taking Nell to the Twelfth Night Joust was, on the surface, a small favour. On the surface...

'Nicola, what if the joust distresses her? There might be bloodshed.' Clare repressed a shudder. True, the Twelfth Night Joust was reputed to be more of a show than a battle. A show put on for the ladies of Champagne. But it was still a joust. There would be fighting and Clare couldn't stand the sight of blood. It reminded her of...of things best forgotten. Pushing that dark memory to the back of her mind, she had to swallow before she could continue. 'Nell might remember that her brother lost his life at a tournament.'

'Geoffrey wasn't killed in the lists. Count Lucien explained how he was killed preventing an attack on Countess Isobel. That is entirely different, and Nell knows it. Please take her, Clare, she'd love to go with you.'

'The Twelfth Night Joust,' Clare murmured, shaking her head. 'Holy Virgin, give me strength.' What Nicola was asking was no light thing. Never mind that she didn't like going abroad, she wasn't sure she trusted herself if the violence got out of hand. An image of bloodstains darkening a man's tunic swam before her. She might faint. Or—more likely—become sick. If there was bloodshed, she was bound to draw attention to herself…

'Please, Clare. Please.'

Clare reached for the token and her heart turned over as she slipped it into her purse. 'Very well. For you, I shall take Nell to the Twelfth Night Joust.'

Nicola's face lightened. 'Thank you, my dear, I am sure you will enjoy it when you get there. Pass me my spindle and wool, would you? I don't like being idle.'

Soon the gentle rattle and whir of a drop spindle filled the room. Nicola's fingers were no longer nimble and she tired quickly. The finished yarn was likely to have many bumps and imperfections in it, but Clare knew she found solace in her work. And it wasn't as if the resulting yarn was unusable, Nicola's neighbour Aimée wove a surprisingly serviceable homespun out of it. Alexandrian brocade it was not, but the flaws gave stuff made from Nicola's yarn an unusual texture that was oddly appealing. The titled ladies Clare would be rubbing shoulders with on the stands would likely turn their noses up at such cloth, but Clare was more than happy to wear it.

As Clare watched Nicole's aged fingers twisting the yarn, she had a strange thought. If all imperfection was eradicated from the world, it would be a much poorer place.

Sir Arthur Ferrer, Captain of Count Henry's Guardian Knights, stood in his green pavilion while his squire laced him into his gambeson and sighed. All these years he had waited to have his own pavilion and now that he finally had one, what should he find? He missed the company of his fellow knights. He missed the banter and he missed the rivalry.

'Holy hell,' he muttered, shoving his hand through his dark hair.

His squire, Ivo, looked up. 'Too tight, sir?'

Arthur flexed his shoulders and smiled. 'No, it's perfect. My thanks, Ivo.'

Since the Winter Fair had ended, the town had emptied and there were fewer troublemakers to deal with. None the less, Arthur was conscious of a growing sense of malaise. He couldn't account for it. It wasn't that he had little to do—he'd be the last to say the streets of Troyes had been entirely cleared of wrongdoers. Human nature being what it was, that day would probably never dawn, but—

The door flap pushed back. A head that was as fair as Arthur's was dark appeared in the opening.

'Gawain!' Mood lifting, Arthur gestured him in. 'Welcome.'

Sir Gawain stooped to enter and went to the trestle where he made a show of reviewing Arthur's arms. 'Saw the unicorn on the pennon and realised you'd be in here.' Idly, he picked up Arthur's damascened sword, testing its weight. 'Is this the one your father made?'

Arthur tensed and forced himself to relax. Gawain was a friend and there had been no mockery in his voice, but one could never be sure. 'Yes.'

'It's a fine sword, it has wonderful balance. Will you be using it?'

'Not today, I'm holding it in reserve for a real fight. Are you competing, Gawain? I didn't see your pavilion.'

'I'm sharing Luc's, which is a mistake. It's hellishly crowded.'

'If you can stand some less exalted company, you are welcome to join me.'

'My thanks, I don't mind if I do. Give me a moment, while I find my squire.'

Ducking out of the pavilion, Gawain vanished. He was back, squire in tow, before Arthur had belted on his sword.

'I've yet to speak to Luc,' Arthur said, as Ivo cleared space on the trestle for Gawain's arms. 'How do matters stand at Ravenshold? Is all well?'

Sir Gawain was steward of Count Lucien d'Aveyron's nearby castle, Ravenshold. It was a position Arthur had occupied until recently, when he had resigned to join the Guardian Knights.

'Well enough.' Gawain spoke lightly, but his mouth proclaimed him a liar—it was turned down at the corners.

Arthur looked thoughtfully at him. Gawain looked as though he hadn't slept in days. 'I hear Countess Isobel is to be Queen of the Tournament.'

'Aye, she's handing out the prizes,' Gawain said, staring moodily at the turf. 'Can't remember if I've asked you this already, Arthur, but you haven't seen Countess Isobel's maid, Elise, have you?'

'Elise? I don't think I know her.'

Gawain swore softly. 'Dark girl. Shy.'

'It's not like you to mislay a woman.' Arthur would have said more, but something in Gawain's expression stopped him.

Arthur had never seen Gawain look so down in the mouth. Surely he was not pining for a maid?

Impossible. 'What you need, my friend, is a visit to the Black Boar. They've got a new wench, name of Gabrielle—'

Gawain laughed. To Arthur's ears the sound was a trifle strained.

'You've learned her name? She must be good.'

'I tell you, Gawain, she's a wonder. Very imaginative. The food's as bad as ever, but they've just taken delivery of a barrel of wine from Count Henry's vineyard. I've yet to taste better.'

Gawain nodded. 'The Black Boar this evening? Very well.'

'Usual rules?'

'Aye, the man with least points at the end of the joust must pay.'

Arthur grinned. 'Good man! I look forward to lightening your purse.'

Clare gripped Nell's hand as they were ushered into the stands. Across the lists, the walls of Troyes Castle rose up like a rock face, glistening with frost. The sky was clear, the air crisp. Count Henry's colours—blue, white and gold— were flying above the castle battlements amid a swirl of pigeons. Guards were stationed up there. A number of men had squeezed into the crenels— the gaps between the merlons—and were peering down at the field.

'This entitles you to a seat on the front row, *ma demoiselle*,' the boy said, as he took the

token from Clare. He was wearing a blue tunic
with a diagonal white band and golden embroi-
dery brightened the cuffs of his sleeves. Count
Henry's colours again. This must be a castle page.
Other pages in matching tunics were performing
similar duties.

Clare squeezed on to a bench with Nell jiggling
about at her side like a fish in a hot skillet. Fear-
ful that Nell might crush the gown of the woman
next to her, Clare caught the woman's eye and
murmured an apology.

Somewhat to her surprise, the woman gave
Nell an indulgent smile. 'It's her first joust?'

'Yes.' Clare was reluctant to talk to strangers.
They tended to exclaim about her odd eyes and
sometimes that led to questions she was unable
to answer. So she smiled and turned her gaze to
the field.

The knights' pavilions were clustered in groups
at either end of the lists. A forest of pennons rippled in the breeze—blue, green, red, purple…
The knights on her right hand represented the
Troyennes, whilst the team on her left was made
up of visitors—Count Henry's guests with a few
volunteers from his retainers to swell the numbers. A cloying sweet perfume filled the air, fighting with other smells—with human sweat, with
wood smoke, with roasting meat.

Nell dug her in the ribs. 'The blue tent is Lord
d'Aveyron's, is it not?'

Nodding, Clare drew Nell's attention to the pennon fluttering above the blue pavilion. 'Can you see the black raven on Count Lucien's pennon? Knights have different colours and devices so they can recognise each other when their visors are down.'

'Yes!' Nell's forefinger began stabbing in all directions. 'The pennon on the next tent has a wolf on it. And, look, there's a green one with a unicorn. Whose is that? I like unicorns.'

'I don't know the knight's name, but I've seen his colours about town. Maybe he is one of Count Henry's Guardians.'

'Geoffrey had a blue pennon with wiggly white lines on it,' Nell said, wistfully. 'He told me that white stands for silver.'

Clare gave her a swift hug. 'His friends will be jousting today.'

Nell lapsed into a brief silence, but she was already smiling again, eyes eagerly darting this way and that, taking it all in. The teams were mustering at either end of the field.

'Here come the horses! Look, Clare, they have colours, too.'

'The destriers are caparisoned to match their knights.'

Nell's face was rapt. She looked so happy, Clare's chest squeezed to see it.

'My brother was a knight.' Nell was on her

feet, still jiggling, clinging to the handrail. Her voice rang with pride. With happiness.

Children were extraordinary, Clare thought. They often coped with death far better than adults. At least on the outside. By God's grace, Geoffrey's death would not affect his little sister too badly. *I am glad I brought her, she needed to see this. Nicola was right to insist that we came.*

By the lance stands, Arthur took up his reins and patted Steel's white neck. There was nothing like a joust to sharpen the mind. The ennui that had gripped him earlier had vanished, as it invariably did when he took to the saddle. There would be no bloodshed today, or very little. There would certainly be no guts. Count Henry had decreed that this Twelfth Night Joust was entirely for the ladies. Still, even a milk-and-water event like this was better than nothing, it was all practice.

A light tinkling sound pulled Arthur's gaze towards one of Count Henry's household knights. The knight, Sir Gérard, was making up numbers on the team opposite. Bells? Surely not? But, yes, tiny bells were attached to his horse's mane. Arthur held down a laugh.

Sir Gérard was a favourite with the ladies in the Champagne court. As the marshal signalled, and the trumpets blared for the knights to line up for the review, Gérard let his horse prance and curvet in front of the main stand—the stand upon which Countess Marie de Champagne and Countess Isobel d'Aveyron were seated.

The ladies cooed and sighed at Gérard. Arthur exchanged glances with Gawain and looked heavenwards. Gérard had flirtation with noblewomen down to a fine art and he was not one to waste the chance to strut about before a stand full of them.

Countess Isobel was wearing the elaborate crown that proclaimed her Queen of the Tournament. The crown was counterfeit—like the Twelfth Night Joust it was all show and little substance. Coloured glass winked and flashed with Countess Isobel's every move, and fake pearls gleamed. Notwithstanding her false bauble, Countess Isobel looked beautiful. Fair as an angel. Poised. Lord d'Aveyron had every reason to be proud of his new Countess.

A drum roll had the crowd shouting with anticipation, reminding Arthur that this was a show for the people, too. He glanced at the townsfolk pressing up to the rope that ran along the other side of the lists.

'Count Henry should have been a merchant,' he murmured.

Gawain frowned. 'How so?'

'He knows a joust will draw traffic and trade back to Troyes. No sooner does the town empty after the Winter Fair than he organises this. Clever.'

The bells tinkled in the mane of Sir Gérard's

horse. The ladies tittered. At the edge of his vision, a blue scarf flickered in the stands.

'Sir Gérard, wear my favour, if you please.'

'No, sir, pray do not. Wear mine!'

'No, no! Wear mine!'

More giggles floated from the ladies' stand.
The tinkling bells sparked in the winter sun. Arthur shook his head at Sir Gérard and reminded
himself that this was entertainment for ladies.

Just then, even as the trumpets blared for the
review, a man ran to the front of the ladies' stand.
As Arthur guided Steel into his place in the line,
he watched him. The man was well dressed, in
a fur-lined cloak and a tunic that stretched too
tightly across a wide expanse of belly. A merchant, most likely. His hood was down and a bald
patch on the back of his head gleamed. Whoever
he was, he should not be on the field. A page had
seen him and was shouting at him.

'Sir! *Sir!* Clear the field!'

The merchant took no notice, he was making straight for a girl in the front row. She was
simply dressed and looked vaguely familiar. The
girl was sitting a little to one side of Countess
Isobel in her glittering crown, so she must have
some connection with Count Lucien, but Arthur
couldn't place her.

The trumpets blared. Arthur kicked Steel's
flanks and started down the lists. As the herald

began calling out knights' names and ranks, Gawain took the place at his side.

Arthur glanced back at the stand. Two castle pages were standing at the merchant's elbows, urging him from the field. Brushing them off, the merchant had taken the girl's hand and was speaking to her. Arthur's gaze sharpened. The girl pulled her hand free and put her arm round a small child. Oddly, the gesture struck him as defensive rather than protective. Whatever was being said, the girl didn't want to hear it.

'*Sir Arthur Ferrer!*' The herald's cry jerked him back to the business in hand.

Arthur lifted his arm in salute, and the crowd roared. Sir Gérard might have the favour of the ladies, but Arthur liked to think he had the common touch. By the time he had finished his parade about the lists and had reached the main stands, the pages must have won their tussle with the merchant, for there was no sign of him.

Shaken, Clare hugged Nell to her and stared blindly in front of her as the knights rode past. Luckily, the knight with the unicorn on his pennon was approaching to salute the Queen of the Tournament and Nell was watching him, stars in her eyes. Clearly, Nell had chosen this knight as her champion and Clare's interaction with the merchant had passed unnoticed. A knight on a white charger, caparisoned in green silk, was far more interesting than any conversation Clare might have with a stranger. Thankfully.

The merchant—his name was Paolo da Lucca—had slipped back into the throng on the other side of the lists. It had been kind of him to warn her, but Clare had hoped never to see him again. With one little phrase—'slavers have been seen in Troyes'—he had frozen the blood in her veins.

Slavers. Will I ever escape?

It would seem not. The last time Clare had seen Paolo had been when he had given her passage on one of his carts carrying merchandise out of Apulia. On that occasion, Paolo had been bound for Paris and they had parted ways outside Troyes, where—thank the Lord—the young knight, Sir Geoffrey of Troyes, had found her. Clare didn't like to think what might have happened to her if Geoffrey hadn't found her. She'd had neither money nor friends and Nicola's lodgings had become home, her first real home. Clare's eyes prickled. If slavers were in Troyes, she would have to leave.

I want to stay!

The thought of leaving Nicola and Nell was unbearable.

Nell was shaking a strip of Aimée's home-spun at the knight in the green surcoat. Favours of every colour of the rainbow were fluttering in his direction, but, amazingly, the knight had noticed Nell.

Clare felt his gaze wash over her and his destrier turned towards them.

'He's seen me!' Nell was quivering with excitement. 'He's coming over!'

Nell danced up and down, waving Aimée's cloth in the manner of a high-born lady offering her favour to her chosen knight. 'Sir! Sir knight! Take my favour!'

Clare sighed. A great knight like this would surely ignore a little girl? He would take the silken favour of some noblewoman behind them and she would spend the rest of the day mopping up Nell's tears.

To her astonishment, the grey—Clare seemed to recall that knights referred to white horses as grey—halted at the barrier directly in front of them. Harness creaked. The knight's green pennon snapped in the breeze; the unicorn on his shield was dazzlingly bright.

'Sir knight?' Nell said, her voice doubtful as she stared at the flaring nostrils of the destrier. She held out the scrap of cloth. Simple, ordinary homespun, slightly ragged at the edges.

The knight—his visor was up—inclined his head at Clare. He was so close, she could see his eyes—they were dark as sloes. He smiled at Nell and whisked the strip from her fingers. The destrier shifted and drew level with Clare.

'My lady?' the knight said, leaning down and proffering his arm. 'Do you mind assisting?'

I am no lady. Nevertheless, Clare nodded and wound the strip of fabric round his mailed arm. The knight stared thoughtfully at her. 'My thanks.' He was looking at her eyes—everyone did.

Spurs flashed and knight and charger surged back on to the field. Behind them, someone sighed.

'Sir Arthur never takes my favour,' a woman said, in aggrieved tones. 'And now he takes a child's!'

Clare felt a pull on her skirts.

'He took my favour! He took my favour!' Nell stared after him. 'Is he one of Geoffrey's friends?'

'It seems likely. I think he's a Guardian Knight. He's very important!' Clare recalled Geoffrey mentioning a knight by the name of Arthur who had at one time been steward of Ravenshold. This must be he. It was possible Count Lucien had asked him to look out for them.

'I wonder who he is,' Nell said.

'If you listen to the herald, you will hear the names. He was announced as Sir Arthur Ferrer.'

The trumpets blared and other knights paraded by. More favours exchanged hands. Count Lucien was riding towards the stands to greet his wife, the Queen of the Tournament.

'Look, Nell, here is Geoffrey's liege lord.'

'He will take Countess Isobel's favour,' Nell said, confidently.

Murmuring agreement, Clare let her gaze wander beyond the knights to the crowd behind the rope on the other side of the lists. Was Paolo da Lucca among them? She saw faces she recognised, but not the merchant's. She should have asked more about the slavers, but she had been too stunned to think straight. And now she had no way of finding him. She had no idea where he was lodged, she had missed her chance.

Vaguely, Clare was conscious of Count Lucien riding past, of him giving Nell a little salute. Nell squeaked and jiggled. Her cheeks were bright with excitement. Clare returned the Count's smile. It had been kind of him to find Geoffrey's sister a place on the ladies' stand.

As the knights lined up at either end of the lists, in preparation for the first tests of horsemanship, Clare scoured the townsfolk opposite.

If only she could find Paolo.

She sighed. She felt settled in Troyes. She was weary of looking over her shoulder, weary of wondering when she would feel the tap on her shoulder that announced that her days of freedom were over.

It would seem that she was as much a slave as she had been when she had arrived. Would she ever be free? Some days, all Clare had were her doubts and, sadly, this was just such a day. Whatever she did, however hard she tried to blend in, she would never succeed. People couldn't help but notice her eyes.

Mismatched eyes, one grey, one green, were hard to hide.

Chapter Two

Arthur steadied Steel and stared down the lists. Thus far, the contest was even. His team—Count Lucien's Troyennes—had won as many points as Sir Gérard and the Visitors. They had come to the last few deciding bouts of the individual jousting. Mindful of the ladies, lances were blunted—there would be no mêlée today. Count Henry had decided that Countess Marie was too delicate to watch one. The word went that she was with child.

Arthur was eager to see who he had been drawn against for the next few passes. When Sir Gérard rode on to the field and his squire hefted his lance from the stand and handed it to him, Arthur grinned. It would be amusing to see how Gérard reacted when he was unhorsed and his pretty armour muddied. It was a reasonable ambition and Arthur had the best of three tries to realise it.

The marshal hadn't given the signal to engage, and as Arthur waited, he could have sworn he heard the faint tinkling of bells from the other end of the lists. Out of the corner of his eye, he saw the little girl whose favour he had taken shift impatiently on the ladies' stand. He blew her a kiss. *This one's for you, little one.* The girl crimsoned. She was gripping the handrail as though her life depended on it. What a sweetheart, she really wanted him to win.

For a moment, her companion's striking, mismatched eyes swam before him. They were most uncommon. One grey, one green. He had never seen their like before. Except…at the back of his mind, a wisp of a memory called to him.

Wait—surely I have seen those eyes before? They remind me of…

The memory slipped beyond reach. Elusive. Yet he knew he had seen those eyes before. As he tried to hunt the memory down, the marshal bellowed.

Arthur gripped his lance and put everything out of his mind save the joust. Trumpets blared and Steel leaped into a gallop. This first pass must count, Sir Gérard was about to be unhorsed. Steel thundered over the ground. Conscious of the ladies in the stands screaming for his opponent, Arthur kept his eye on his target. Ten yards, five…

His lance glanced off Gérard's shield and splintered into a thousand shards. Gérard's lance had missed Arthur entirely and Gérard, distracted no doubt by the screaming ladies, rocked in the saddle.

'My point, I believe,' Arthur muttered.

Steel pulled up sharply at the other end and whirled about. Arthur was handed a second lance and a heartbeat later he was tearing back towards Gérard. Clumps of turf flew every which way. Gérard had been wrong-footed by that first pass and his shield wavered. The silver bells trembled.

Arthur gave no quarter and his lance connected with Gérard's shield. It was almost too easy. Gérard flew from his saddle and hit the ground with a thud. As his horse raced away, the light chiming of bells lingered in the air.

Half the crowd groaned, the other half roared. Best of three meant that it was over for Sir Gérard, who sat up with a groan, wrenched off his helmet, and tossed it aside. Gérard might be popular with the ladies of the court, but he was less popular with the townsfolk. It was Arthur the townsfolk were cheering.

Arthur lifted his visor and raised a hand to acknowledge the cheers. Behind the ropes, the citizens of Troyes stamped and whistled and yelled. And Arthur was not without supporters on the ladies' platform either. His little lady was fairly screaming with excitement, jumping up and down like a cat on coals. The young woman with the mismatched eyes was smiling down at her. Briefly, she looked across at him, and lifted her

hands in applause. Mismatch. It was too far away
for him to see those curious eyes, but the wind
lifted the edge of her veil, revealing hair that shone
bright as copper in the winter sunlight. Again a
shiver of recognition ran through him.

*Who is she? I have not met her, yet I know those
eyes. Who is she?*

By the time the Queen of the Tournament rose
to her feet to award the prizes, Arthur had worked
out where he had seen the young woman before.
He had seen her at Geoffrey's funeral.

Sir Geoffrey had been one of Count Lucien's
household knights and, before his untimely death,
Arthur had known him well. The lad had been
killed, ostensibly while protecting Lady Isobel,
at a tournament held at the Field of the Birds. The
young woman on the ladies' stand had attended
Geoffrey's funeral. The last to leave after Geoffrey had been interred, she had stood, head bowed
over the grave, a slim auburn-haired woman in
rough homespun. Throughout the funeral rites,
she had looked as though she had been on the
verge of making a run for it. A nervous, shrink-
ing violet, Arthur had thought. He had not been
near enough to notice her odd eyes at Geoffrey's
funeral, so it must have been her hair that had
given him that sense that he had met her before.
It was the same girl, no question. According to

Lucien, she wasn't related to Geoffrey. Had she and Geoffrey been lovers?

The peculiar exchange Arthur had seen earlier pushed into his mind. What had that merchant said to her? It had clearly upset her. Had the man been threatening her? If so, why? Arthur would give a day's pay to know what had passed between them. Was it in some way connected with Geoffrey's death?

Count Lucien harboured doubts as to Geoffrey's honesty. Before Christmas, he had mentioned that he suspected Geoffrey of involvement in the theft of a relic from the Abbey. Arthur hadn't paid much attention at the time and he should have done. A gang of outlaws was known to be working the area. This girl could have links with them. If so, as Captain of Count Henry's Guardians, it was very much Arthur's business. Count Henry wanted Champagne cleared of outlaws. The Guardians had been established for that very purpose. Arthur's first duty was to keep the roads and highways safe for honest folk.

The Winter Fair was over and tomorrow the town would settle down after the tournament. It was the perfect chance to root out the thieves, once and for all. If the girl had any connection with them, Arthur must know of it. As soon as he might, he would seek her out and judge for himself whether she was involved. Count Henry would expect no less of the Captain of his Guardian Knights.

A trumpet blast cut through the babble of the crowd, jerking Arthur out of his thoughts. The field was awash with blue pennons and Countess Isobel was preparing to hand out the prizes. Her husband, Count Lucien, had won the individual prize and his team—the Troyennes—had won the team prize.

As Count Lucien rode towards his countess in her glittering crown, Arthur lifted his voice along with the rest. It was good to fight on the winning side. He and Gawain would be celebrating when they visited the Black Boar.

Late the next morning, Nicola was dozing on her cot by the fire. Clare had sent Nell to deliver another batch of wool to Aimée and the child had been gone some while. No more than mildly concerned, for Aimée had two girls of her own and Nell enjoyed visiting them, Clare glanced through the shutters to see if the children were out in the street. Nell usually reappeared in time for the noonday meal.

She caught movement on the left, a quick flash of green. Someone was approaching the house. Her fingers curled into her palms, and although she was braced for it, the sharp rap on the door had her leaping out of her skin. Heart jumping, Clare set her hand on the planks and peered through a knot-hole.

'Who's there?'

A cream-coloured tunic stretched across a wide chest. A silver cloak pin held a green cloak in place. 'Good day, *ma dame*. Sir Arthur Ferrer at your disposal.'

Nell's champion. Clare glanced at Nicola and heard a light snore. Nicola usually had trouble sleeping and Clare was loathe to disturb her. Sir Arthur was surely no threat. Last night she had learned that he had indeed been sworn to Count Lucien before he had taken charge of the Guardians. Sir Arthur had known Geoffrey. She could surely speak to him outside the house, it would only be for a moment. Telling herself this knight couldn't possibly know what had brought her to Troyes, she lifted her cloak from its peg and unlatched the door. She was unveiled—no matter, this wouldn't take long.

'Good morning, Sir Arthur.' She gave him a quick curtsy. Sir Arthur's hair was brown, thick and glossy. He was wearing his sword, but there was no sign of his squire or the grey destrier. At a guess, he had walked from the garrison as it wasn't far. 'My apologies for not inviting you in, sir, but there's only one chamber and Nicola is sleeping.'

'Geoffrey's mother?'

'Yes, she sleeps so poorly, I don't want to wake her.'

Clare paused, hoping he would state his business at once. With a sinking heart, she saw his dark gaze shift from her eyes to her hair. Swiftly, she pulled up her hood. Lord, but her looks were such a curse. If there was anything that proved that God must love irony, it was her colouring. *He gives me every reason to want to escape notice and then curses me with dramatic red hair and odd eyes.*

'Did Count Lucien ask you to visit, sir?'

His eyes held hers. 'What is your name?'

'I am called Clare.' If Clare had ever been christened, she had never known it. Clare was the name she had chosen for herself after she had fled Apulia.

'Clare,' Sir Arthur murmured, studying her eyes. He shook his head. 'I thought your name might mean something, but...'

'Mon seigneur?'

A muscle flickered at the side of his jaw. 'I am a knight, mistress, not a lord.'

'Sir?'

'Never mind.' His thumb tapped the hilt of his sword. 'Your accent is unfamiliar, you were not born in Troyes.'

'No, sir.'

The dark eyes looked at her. Then, to her astonishment, he crooked his arm at her. 'You will walk with me a while.'

Clare hesitated. She was reluctant to walk abroad with a knight from the garrison, she didn't trust men, but she recognised a command when she heard one. Telling herself that a knight once sworn to Lord d'Aveyron would hardly carry her off in broad daylight, she laid her fingers lightly on his arm and he drew her down the street, towards the square. She began to pray.

Dear Lord, let Paolo have been mistaken. If the slavers were in town and saw her...

'I cannot be long, sir. Nell might come back and—'

'Nell?' The handsome face relaxed. 'The little girl who gave me her favour?'

'Yes.'

'We won't go far. There is a matter I must discuss with you out of earshot of Geoffrey's mother.'

There was a thudding in Clare's ears as her fears rushed in on her. Was this about Geoffrey? Or had Sir Arthur discovered her secret? Had her master in Apulia discovered her whereabouts?

Slavery was not permitted in Champagne. It was the reason Clare had come to Troyes. But she had learned from what had happened to Geoffrey that injustices still abounded. She lived in dread of the knock on the door, of the moment when she learned that the slaver known as the Veronese had found her.

I will never go back. Never!

'Sir Arthur, you…' she took a deep breath '…you are Captain of the Guardian Knights, are you not?' Nicola had told her as much last eve, when Clare had brought an overexcited Nell home. The child had talked non-stop about 'her knight, Sir Arthur'. It was a wonder any of them had got any sleep.

Sir Arthur nodded and Clare kept telling herself that she had nothing to fear from him. It wasn't easy convincing herself. This man was a stranger and, until Geoffrey had brought her to his mother's house, strangers hadn't shown her much kindness.

The square opened out in front of them, it was almost deserted. A few hens were scratching in the dirt outside the tavern; two women were folding sheets in front of one of the tall, wood-framed houses; and a boy was staggering under the weight of a huge bucket, slopping water as he went.

'Were you married to Geoffrey?' Sir Arthur asked, bluntly.

Clare blinked. 'No.' Geoffrey had been good to her, more than good. He had offered to marry her, thinking marriage to him would protect her in the event that the Veronese ever found her, but he had understood her reluctance. Marriage was, to Clare's mind, only a small step above slavery. In any case, Sir Geoffrey of Troyes had no business marrying a runaway slave. Even if she had wanted to marry Geoffrey, she would have refused him. As she would refuse any man. Marry? Never.

'He was your lover?'

Squaring her shoulders, Clare met that dark gaze directly. 'I fail to see why I should answer that, sir. It is none of your affair.'

His lips twitched in amusement and her breath caught. When he lost that stern expression, Sir Arthur was heart-stoppingly attractive.

'Perhaps you are in the right. My apologies, *ma dame*—or should I say *ma demoiselle*?'

'As you wish, sir.'

'*Ma demoiselle*, it shall be then, *ma demoiselle* Clare. At yesterday's tournament, a man approached you at the stands. Would you care to tell me what he said?'

'He… I…I do not know him well, sir.'

'That tells me nothing.' The dark eyes never left her. Sir Arthur drew his eyebrows together. 'It seemed to me you were afraid of him.'

Clare bit her lip. Instinct was telling her that she could trust this knight, but that didn't mean she was ready to confess to being a runaway slave.

And it certainly didn't mean she was ready to tell him what had happened between her and Sandro…

'I believe the man to be a merchant from abroad,' Sir Arthur was saying. 'I would be grateful if you could tell me what he said.'

'His name is Paolo, Paolo da Lucca, and he is indeed a merchant. He said nothing of note.'

Sir Arthur's face became stern. '*Ma demoiselle*, I should like you to tell me what you know of him.' The broad shoulders lifted. 'Otherwise, what must I think but that you are hiding something?'

Briefly, Clare closed her eyes, but when she opened them Sir Arthur was still there. Watching. Judging. She scuffed a stone with the toe of her boot, and wished she were a convincing liar. 'I am not hiding anything.'

'Does this Paolo da Lucca know of Sir Geoffrey's involvement with thieves?'

'You are speaking of the relic?' Clare asked, as it dawned on her that she might have misinterpreted the motives behind Sir Arthur's questions. His questions had nothing to do with the fact that there had been slavers in Troyes—he suspected her of having dealings with outlaws!

'Indeed.' The dark eyes narrowed. 'Was he threatening you?'

'No, sir.' Taking a deep breath, Clare lifted her eyes to his. 'I…I have known Paolo for some months. He is a kind man and he was not threatening me.'

'What did he say?' The dark eyes were thoughtful. 'I know Geoffrey was in touch with thieves.'

Clare felt herself frown. 'Count Lucien swore he would keep that quiet. Sir, you must understand that Nicola can't find out, she is so proud that her son was knighted—it would kill her if she learned of his fall from grace.'

'Never fear, Count Lucien has been discreet. And, apart from last eve when I brought the subject up with him, this is the first time I have questioned him on the matter. The Count made a point of stressing your wishes that Geoffrey's good name should not be tarnished.'

They were facing the tavern on the far side of the square. The Black Boar. It had a dubious reputation. One of the tavern girls was sitting on a bench outside, a bright yellow cloth over her knee. She was sewing, or pretending to. In reality she was displaying her charms, of which there were many. Her eyes sparkled, her smile was bold and her lips had been coloured in some way. The neck of her gown was subtly laced to reveal full breasts. She dimpled at Sir Arthur and deftly inched up her gown to display a slender ankle and a shapely calf.

'Good morning, Sir Arthur.'

Sir Arthur grinned. 'Good morning, Gabrielle.'

She knows him?

Gabrielle's gaze washed over Clare. 'Will we see you later, sir?'

He lifted a dark eyebrow, still grinning. Clare didn't know where to look. Despite her shameful past, she was innocent. In truth, her flight from Apulia had been precipitated after her owner's son, Sandro, had attempted to force himself on her. She shivered and stared at her hand, half-expecting to see it stained with Sandro's blood. She could never act the whore, not for any man.

Sir Arthur cleared his throat, replaced Clare's hand on his arm and steered her firmly past the tavern. '*Ma demoiselle*, I should like you to tell me what you know of the thieves. Count Henry is determined to run them to earth.'

Clare tipped back her head to meet that dark gaze, and was conscious of a faint stirring in her stomach. It wasn't strong enough to be fear, but Count Henry's Captain did make her nervous. Her mouth was dry.

'I know next to nothing.' Clare's mind whirled as she wondered how much to tell him. She had best say as little as possible—enough to make him go away and leave her in peace. 'Geoffrey kept things close, but I know he wanted to make amends. He was ashamed of what he had done.'

'And so he should have been. It's a disgrace that a knight should have dealings with thieves.'

Clare bit her lip. Sir Arthur was one of Geoffrey's peers and she wanted him to understand what had driven Geoffrey to lose his honour. He had not done it lightly. 'Count Lucien may have told you Geoffrey's mother, Nicola, is ailing. Medicaments are costly.'

'Money ran out?'

Clare nodded. 'Geoffrey loved his mother, he wanted the best for her.'

Sir Arthur swore. 'Damn it all, the lad borrowed money from me before, he could have done so again. I wouldn't have refused him.'

'He didn't like being indebted.'

'Pride?' Sir Arthur sighed. 'That rings true, Geoffrey hated admitting to any weakness.'

'There's nothing more I can tell you, sir,' Clare said, looking pointedly back the way they had come. 'If that is all, I should be getting back. I can't leave Nicola for long.' *And if slavers are in town, I can't risk being seen!*

'All in good time, *ma demoiselle*. I haven't finished. It's likely you know more than you realise. For example, when Geoffrey spoke of the thief, did he mention any names?'

Clare drew her head back. 'Sir, I fail to see the point of this. I thought the thief had been killed? Count Lucien said he was murdered.'

Sir Arthur nodded. 'So he was, but he was unlikely to have been working alone. Who killed that thief? Why did they kill him?'

Clare's stomach knotted. She didn't want to think about this, she had enough to worry about with how she was going to look after Nicola if the Veronese had come to Troyes. How was she going to get to market? The Veronese might see her! She glanced over her shoulder—the last thing she needed was to be drawn into Geoffrey's troubles. Geoffrey was dead, for which she was deeply sorry. But so was his murderer.

'In my view, justice was served when the thief was killed,' she said, quietly.

'And that's enough? What if more people are hurt? Do you want that on your conscience?'

The determined glint in Sir Arthur's brown eyes warned her that he was not going to let this rest. The good Captain suspected that she could help him and it was not going to be easy to dismiss him. *There must be something I can tell him...*

'Geoffrey mentioned another man, but he gave me no name. Only...'

Sir Arthur was standing so close, Clare could practically count his eyelashes. They were long and dark, and when she looked into his eyes, her heart skipped a beat. The Captain of the Guardian Knights had beautiful eyes. In this light they were not as dark as she had first thought. The brown was flecked with grey.

'Only...?'

'It was something Geoffrey alluded to when he told me that he was going to make amends for what he had done.'

He looked sceptically at her. 'You insist that Geoffrey intended to break with the thieves?'

Her chin went up. 'Sir, I can see that you disbelieve me, but I swear it's the truth.'

'If so, it's possible he was killed for trying to renege on his agreement,' Sir Arthur said, slowly. 'And not because he was barring his way to Countess Isobel, as Count Lucien suggests.' He stared pensively down a shadowy alley. It was getting cold, a water trough was edged with ice. 'It doesn't tell us who murdered the thief, though. Or why.'

'I've been wondering about that. Could he have been killed by another outlaw, angered that the relic had slipped from his grasp?'

'He could have been.' Sir Arthur folded his arms across his chest and looked questioningly at her. 'You have something else to add…?'

'It might not be of use, but Geoffrey did mention meeting someone in a cave.'

His gaze sharpened. 'A cave? Where?'

'I am sorry, sir, Geoffrey mentioned a cave. That is all.'

'Pity.' Shaking his head, Sir Arthur offered her his arm and they retraced their steps.

Soon they had reached the head of Clare's street, where the tall, wooden houses leaned haphazardly one against the other. Crooked and humble. But home.

'*Ma demoiselle*, I should be grateful if you would to inform me should you remember anything else.'

'Yes, sir, of course.' Clare smiled, but in truth she had no intention of seeing this man again. All she wanted was freedom to live her life in peace.

'And if either you or Nicola need help, you mustn't hesitate to send for me. Leave word at the garrison gate—' He broke off, shaking his head. 'Where did you say you were from?'

Clare's heart missed a beat. The dark eyes might look kind, but she wasn't going to admit to being a runaway slave. Men, as she had learned to her cost, reacted badly when they found out. Even the best of them tried to take advantage. And Sir Arthur, as that little exchange with the girl outside the Black Boar had proved, was no better than the rest. This was a man who enjoyed women.

Geoffrey had been different. Geoffrey, God rest him, had never tried to take advantage of her, which was why she had loved him. Geoffrey would have her loyalty till her dying day.

'I spent many years abroad, sir. I do not rightly know where I was born.' She gave him another bright smile. 'It seems likely I am baseborn.'

That dark, unsettling gaze ran over her, lingering in a puzzled way on a wisp of hair winding waywardly out of her hood; studying her eyes, first the grey, then the green.

She gave a light laugh. 'I certainly felt out of place on the ladies' stand.'

'Count Lucien invited you, you had every right to be there.'

His hand slid up her arm and his fingers tightened. A frisson of awareness ran down every nerve. Disturbing. *Exciting.* And that was beyond strange, since Clare hated men touching her. He gave her the most charming of bows.

'I, for one, am glad to have met you. Although...'

he paused '…your features do seem familiar. I would swear we must have met before.'

'Likely you saw me at Geoffrey's funeral.'

'I didn't see your eyes and they are familiar…'

Clare shook her head and pulled free. 'You must be mistaken.' As she dipped into a swift curtsy, she saw Nell skipping into their lodgings. 'There's Nell, sir, I had best be going.'

'Remember what I said. Send for me if you need assistance.' He leaned towards her. 'Send for me if you recall anything Geoffrey might have said.'

'I won't forget, sir.' Twisting away, Clare hurried down the street.

The Captain of the Guardian Knights was altogether too disturbing. He saw too much. And if he thought she'd be leaving messages at the garrison gatehouse, he could think again. She wanted peace and quiet. Attention from the Captain of the Guardian Knights was the last thing she needed.

Chapter Three

The girl, Clare, lingered in Arthur's mind as he strode back to Troyes Castle. Her image wouldn't shift from his brain—a small, slight girl with auburn hair and mismatched eyes. Mismatch. Who was she? Why did he feel he was missing some vital connection? Why did he feel that he should be better able to place her?

Arthur found no answer, even though tendrils of auburn hair twined in and out of his thoughts as he went to the stables and called for his squire. That faintly accented, husky voice echoed in his mind. *'Geoffrey mentioned a cave.'*

A cave—there was a chalk cave not far from Troyes…

'Ivo?'

'Sir?'

'Patrol. Saddle up. You're coming with me.'

'Yes, sir. Where are we going?'

'I want to study the lie of the land around that cave to the south.'

'Shall I fetch your chain mail?

'I only need my sword, we shan't be making a show of ourselves. This is unofficial. Sir Raphael took the regular patrol.'

Bright auburn tresses gleamed in the winter sun, invading Arthur's every thought, as they trotted through the city gates. And not only her hair. Her eyes haunted him every step of the way. It was as though the fields and vineyards of Champagne were lost behind mist, the only reality was those eyes—one green, one grey. Mismatch.

He had seen those eyes before. Where?

No answer came while Arthur scoured the terrain about the cave. He was looking for tracks or burnt-out cooking fires. He found nothing of note but, oddly, his conviction strengthened. He had seen her before.

'It will come,' he muttered.

'Sir?'

'Ivo, have you noticed how the memory plays tricks? Sometimes when you are trying to recall something, it eludes you. And the moment you give up—' he snapped his fingers '—the answer comes.' Arthur felt himself flush. He must sound like a madman.

Ivo simply nodded sagely at him. 'Yes, sir.'

'It would be best if I put her out of my mind.'
'Most likely, sir.'

None the less, Clare's image had remained with him, accompanying him on the road that ran back to the city and into the stables. It had lingered at the back of his mind as he strode to the hall for his regular meeting with Count Henry. It even remained with him that evening as he pushed through the door of the Black Boar and Gabrielle swayed towards him, all bosom and big eyes.

'Sir Arthur! What a pleasure to see you.'

Most irritating of all, Clare's image did not leave him as he wound his arm round Gabrielle's soft waist and leaned in to kiss her.

Mon Dieu! Why could he not remember?

The answer came the next day. Unfortunately, it came as Arthur was discussing the redeployment of his men with Count Henry in the solar of Troyes Castle.

The Comte was sitting behind an array of quills and ink-pots. He had been going through his accounts, and scrolls and parchment littered the worktable like autumn leaves. He nudged a stool in Arthur's direction. 'Take a seat, Sir Arthur.'

'My thanks. *Mon seigneur*, it's my belief a gang of outlaws are in hiding somewhere beyond the city walls,' Arthur said, going straight to the point. 'And with the Twelfth Night Joust behind us, Troyes is as quiet as it gets. We can expand the reach of our patrols—widen our search to the county boundaries.'

Count Henry looked narrowly at him. 'You've heard something?'

Arthur shook his head. 'Nothing reliable, my lord. A friend tells me that outlaws could be hiding out in a nearby cave.'

'A friend?'

Arthur was reluctant to name Clare—she had made it clear she wanted nothing to do with this business. He couldn't blame her, Geoffrey had been killed. Further, the lad's death meant the women of her household had been left without a protector. 'My friend values discretion.'

Count Henry nodded and picked up his quill. 'I understand. You have enough men?'

'Yes, my lord.'

'Very well. Let me know if you find anything.'

'Of course.' Arthur rose to leave, and checked as a name came crashing in on him. A name and a pair of eyes that mirrored Clare's. 'Count Myrrdin de Fontaine,' he muttered. *Mon Dieu!* Could Clare be Count Myrrdin's daughter? A by-blow, of course.

Count Henry fiddled with his quill. 'Count Myrrdin? What of him? I haven't seen him in years.'

Arthur shook his head. His gaze was fixed on

Count Henry's ink-pot, but he wasn't seeing it. He was seeing those mismatched eyes. 'It's the eyes,' he said.

'The eyes?' Count Henry frowned, then his brow cleared. 'Ah, yes, I remember. Count Myrrdin has odd eyes. Blue and grey.'

'Green and grey, actually, my lord.'

Count Henry twirled the quill between finger and thumb. 'He was a very distinguished warrior in his day, although I've heard that he's become something of a recluse. It's years since he's left Brittany. What brought him to mind?'

'There's a girl in Troyes—I saw her at the joust. She has his eyes.'

The quill went still and Count Henry leaned forwards, a line between his brows. 'A girl? Are you certain she has Count Myrrdin's eyes?'

'She could be his baseborn daughter,' Arthur said, his conviction strengthening with every moment. 'I thought I'd met her before and took time to make the connection. But I hadn't met her, I'd met her father. She's Count Myrrdin's daughter, I know it.'

'How old is she?'

'Lord, I've no idea. Eighteen? Nineteen?'

'She can't be Count Myrrdin's get. He's not known to be profligate with women. Since his wife died, well, the man might as well have taken Holy Orders, he's chaste as a monk.' The Count set the quill back in the ink-pot and leaned back. 'I want to see this girl. Bring her here.'

Arthur hesitated. He was certain Clare wouldn't want to be brought before Count Henry. '*Mon seigneur*, is that necessary? She might be embarrassed to have her illegitimacy noised abroad.'

Count Henry's brow darkened. 'What do you take me for? I'm not about to shame the girl, I want to help her. Before he turned hermit, Myrrdin de Fontaine was one of the most honourable knights in Christendom. If this girl is his daughter, illegitimate or not, he'd want to know. Where does she live?'

'She shares lodgings in the town. In the merchant's quarter.'

'Bring her here. When I've seen her, I shall decide what's best to do.' Count Henry pulled one of the scrolls towards him and unrolled it. 'Captain?'

'*Mon seigneur?*'

'Find Myrrdin's daughter *before* you start ferreting about in those caves, eh?'

'But, my lord, the outlaws…'

The Count sighed. 'Sir Raphael can take a troop to the caves. You know the girl, you bring her here.'

'Yes, my lord.'

Clare was walking back from the market with Nell, her basket over her arm. She had spent the day trying to convince herself that Paolo had been wrong about seeing slavers in Troyes, and had almost succeeded when she saw the two men standing under the eaves of the house next to Nicola's.

Sight of them turned her guts to ice. Although Nell was still jigging along beside her, chattering nineteen to the dozen, it was as though the child had been struck dumb. Clare couldn't hear her. She couldn't hear anything except the blood rushing in her ears.

Ducking her head, she whipped round and affected a great interest in the carving on a nearby lintel. One of the men was unknown to her, but the other…the other…

I am going to be sick.

The other man was unquestionably Lorenzo da Verona, more commonly known as the Veronese. Clare hadn't known he travelled as far from Apulia as this, but it made sense. Da Verona would cast his net wide to find slaves. The fact that it was forbidden to sell or own slaves in Champagne wouldn't stop his evil business. Slaves could be taken from anywhere, as she herself knew. In Apulia where her master lived, Clare had crossed paths with slaves who had been captured in France, in Brittany, in the Aquitaine…

Slavery was a trade that knew no boundaries. Da Verona's only concern was to turn a fat profit. Clare's master—her *former* master—had bought many slaves from the man standing not twelve feet behind her, herself included. Clare had no memory of her early life. She only knew of da Verona's involvement because one day, when her master had been buying more slaves from him, her mistress had informed her that she, too, had been bought from the Veronese.

Time seemed to slow. Da Verona mustn't see her—he would seize her and return her to her master! She must leave Troyes today. Had she left it too late? Blessed Virgin, what would happen to Nicola? To Nell? How would they cope?

'Clare, you're not listening,' Nell said, twitching at her skirts.

'I'm sorry, sweetheart. I've just realised I've forgotten to buy salt. Be a love and carry the basket home, will you? I shall follow when I've bought the salt.'

Those men are talking about me, I know it. Lord knows how the Veronese found me, but somehow he knows where I live. There is no time. I must leave.

Clare had hoped to stay in Troyes long enough to ensure that Nell was cared for when Nicola died. For Nicola was dying, of that there was no doubt. Every day it was more of a struggle for her to leave her cot; every day she became more drawn, more grey. Nicola might have days left, she might have weeks, it was impossible to judge. Clare had wanted to stay with them until the end, she had wanted Nell to be able to live her old normal life for as long as possible.

'I can come with you to buy salt,' Nell said.

Blinking through a blur of tears, Clare handed Nell the basket. 'Thank you, but that's not necessary. Mama is waiting for these things. When you get home, I need you to start the soup for me.' Conscious of the men at her back, Clare went down on her haunches, so as to meet Nell eye to eye. 'Can you do that, sweetheart? Do you remember when we made barley soup?'

'I remember.'

'Do you think you can make it on your own?'

'Yes!'

'Good girl.' *Poor Nell. First she loses her brother and soon she will lose her mother.* If truth be known, Clare had prayed for a few more weeks with Nicola and Nell. Living with them had been her only taste of family life and she was greedy for more. However, it would seem that God had other plans. She swallowed hard, blinked away the blur and managed a smile. 'Off you go. Make a start on the soup. If I'm late, you can give Mama her supper. And…' she paused '…this is important, sweetheart. If you get stuck with the recipe, if something happens that worries you, go straight to Aimée. Aimée will help you, she will *always* help you.'

Nell looked at her as though she had grown horns. 'I know that, silly.'

Smile wobbling, Clare straightened and made a shooing gesture with her hands.

'See you later,' Nell said and skipped away.

Throat tight, Clare watched her go. Keeping her head down and her hood up, she walked swiftly past the two men and slipped into an alley between the houses. It was dank and shadowy, more of a gutter than an alley—the ground was soggy with moss. Her mind raced as she hurried along. She knew exactly what she must do.

She had money left over from market, Nicola would not begrudge her it. First she would find a scribe and get a note to Sir Arthur. He would see that Nicola and Nell were safe. Then she would buy bread and then she would leave.

What she didn't know was where she would go. It was January, nights were bone-achingly cold, but there was one blessing—she was wearing her cloak.

Arthur was crossing the yard in front of the garrison gatehouse when a sentry hailed him. 'Captain Ferrer, there's a message for you.' The sentry went into the guardhouse and emerged with a scrap of vellum.

'My thanks.' Arthur frowned at the vellum. He'd told Clare to send word if she needed help, but not for one moment had he thought she would heed him. Yet he could think of no one else who would contact him in this way. 'Who brought this, did you see them?'

'Local scribe, sir. Pierre Chenay.'

Arthur unrolled the scroll. It was the briefest of letters, a few lines, no more. Glancing at the bottom, he saw that it had indeed been sent by Clare. The letter began formally, it was obvious it had been penned by a scribe, though the language was stripped of the traditional flowery sentiments. She wouldn't have had money for those...

Most honoured knight,
You were kind to Nell at the Twelfth Night
Joust and I thank you for it. I hope to impose
further upon your kindness. I am leaving
Troyes. As you are aware, Nell's mother is
ailing. I think she will soon be leaving this
world for a higher place. The Count and
Countess d'Aveyron have most graciously
helped Nicola and Nell in the past, and I
am writing to ask that you will inform them
that I can no longer care for them. Count
Lucien and Countess Isobel will see to their
needs, I know.
My heartfelt thanks,
With all good wishes,
Your servant, Clare

At the bottom, next to where the scribe had written her name, there was an awkwardly

formed cross and a large ink blot. She wouldn't
be used to holding a quill.

Stupid woman, what was she doing leaving
town when Geoffrey's family had such need of
her? Had the outlaws approached her? Had she
been bullied into leaving?

Crushing the message into a ball, Arthur
shoved it in his pouch. There was a cold lump
in his belly.

'When did this arrive?'

'Not half an hour since, Captain.'

Arthur forced himself to relax. Half an hour.
She'd be on foot—she couldn't have got far in half
an hour and he'd be able to track her, whichever
road she'd taken. He was on the point of retrac-
ing his steps to inform Count Henry of what had
happened when it occurred to him she might not
yet have left her lodgings.

Arthur raised his hand to knock at the door. Inside, a child was crying. *Nell.* Lord. He knocked
hard and the crying cut off. A bolt squealed and
the door opened. Nell's face, puffy with tears, appeared in the crack.

'Sir Arthur!' Sniffling, Nell wiped her nose
with the back of her hand.

'*Holà*, Nell.' The child's woebegone face told
him that Clare had already left, but he had to ask.
'May I speak to Clare?'

'She's not here.' Nell's eyes filled. 'Mama says she's gone away. Mama says—'

'Nell?' a faint voice cut in. 'Let Sir Arthur enter, if you please.'

Arthur bowed his head under the lintel and stepped into the room. It had been a while since he'd set foot in lodgings as basic as this. Smoke from a fire at the back filled the low-ceilinged room with smoke. A kettle sat on the hearth and a small clay pot lay slightly askew among the embers, steaming gently. Clothes were drying on a crooked clothes-rack.

Nell's sick mother, Nicola, lay on a cot by the fire. And she did look sick. The light was poor, but not so poor that Arthur couldn't see that her eyes had sunk deep into their sockets. The skin over her cheekbones was wafer-thin.

Age-spotted hands plucked at the blankets. 'Sir Arthur Ferrer?'

'At your service, *ma dame*. As you doubtless heard, I am looking for Clare.'

Nicola's lip trembled. 'I am afraid you have missed her. She has…moved away.'

Nell jumped into his line of vision, fists clenched. 'No, she hasn't! She's gone for salt.' A small hand batted his. 'Sir Arthur, Clare told me she was going to buy salt.'

Arthur looked at Nicola. He wasn't used to dealing with children and, sweet though this one was, he was helpless in the face of her tears.

'We have plenty of salt, sir,' Nicola said, gesturing at a pot by the fire. 'Clare's not coming back.'

Tiny fingers curled into his tunic. 'She *is*! She *is* coming back! She forgot we had salt. She'll be back soon, I know it.'

'Nell,' Nicola's voice, though weak, held a warning. 'Shouldn't you be watching our soup?'

The small fingers uncurled and, sniffing, the child went to the fire.

'I knew this time would come, sir,' Nicola said. 'I hoped she would stay, but in my heart I knew she would leave us.'

Nell had found a wooden spoon. Arthur watched her stirring. 'Was Clare threatened, do you know?' he asked quietly. Thanks to Geoffrey's change of heart, a priceless relic had slipped out of the thieves' hands. It was more than likely they bore a grudge. Had they demanded recompense? Were they taking their anger out on Clare?

'Threatened? Why should anyone threaten Clare?' Nicola gazed thoughtfully into the fire. 'I suppose there could have been something. Clare kept her thoughts to herself much of the time. When Geoffrey brought her here, a scrawny waif whom he found on the road to Ravenshold, I had my doubts.'

Arthur stared. 'Sir Geoffrey found her on the road?'

'Yes, sir. She had nowhere to go, so he brought

her here. My Geoffrey offered her board and keep in return for looking after us.' Nicola's eyes were glassy with tears, her voice was a thread. 'She was a tower of strength when Geoffrey died, but more than that, I have grown fond of her. She stayed longer than I dared hope.'

'Do you know where she's gone?'

'No, sir. Will you…' her expression brightened '…will you try to find her?'

Arthur hesitated. 'I shall try, but I am sworn to serve Count Henry.' He moved to the door.

'You are Captain of the Guardian Knights and must follow the Count's orders?'

'I must.'

'Perhaps, sir, if you asked for Count Henry's permission…?'

Arthur reached for the door latch. *Mon Dieu*, the last thing he wanted to do was to leave Troyes, particularly to chase after a chance-met girl, even one who might be Count Myrrdin's by-blow. It was an honour to be Captain of Count Henry's Guardians—an honour that had been hard won. Being Captain of the Guardians was no sinecure. Several knights were jostling to take his place, young Raphael of Reims to name but one. If Arthur were to leave Troyes, even with the Count's blessing, the post of Captain of the Guardians might be lost to him for ever.

However, it wasn't safe for a vulnerable young woman to be wandering the highways without protection. Never mind that it was midwinter, there were rogues everywhere, anything could happen. A fist formed in his stomach. She must be found.

'That will depend on Count Henry, *ma dame*. Rest assured, I shall inform him of Clare's disappearance. I shall also inform Lord d'Aveyron.'

Nicola's head came up in a way that reminded Arthur of her son. 'Thank you, sir, but there's no need to speak to Lord d'Aveyron.'

Clare had mentioned that Nicola was unaware of the trouble Geoffrey had embroiled himself in before his death. Was it wise to leave her in ignorance? If, as he suspected, Clare had been bullied out of Troyes by a gang of outlaws—might they take their revenge out on Nicola and the child? He must speak with Count Henry again.

In the meantime, he didn't want to worry Nicola more than was necessary. He smiled. '*Ma dame*, in my judgement Count Lucien would wish to know that Clare has left Troyes. He was Geoffrey's liege lord and he has your welfare at heart. I will also send a manservant from the castle to assist you. Good day.'

Nicola looked at him before sinking back into her pillows—the exchange had exhausted her. 'Thank you, Sir Arthur. Good day.'

Back at Troyes Castle, Count Henry admitted him at once. During Arthur's absence, the parchments and scrolls seemed to have trebled in number.

'Well?' Count Henry demanded, setting his quill aside and flexing inky fingers. He looked past Arthur and scowled at the empty doorway. 'Where is she?'

'*Mon seigneur*, I am afraid I missed her, she has left Troyes.' Arthur delved in his pouch for the letter. 'This was waiting for me at the gatehouse.'

Count Henry skimmed the message before handing it back. 'Pity. I wonder where she went. Any ideas?'

'No, my lord. I have spoken to the woman she shares lodgings with, but she wasn't able to help.'

'I take it she—?'

'Her name is Clare.'

Count Henry's gaze sharpened. 'Clare. I assume Clare is ignorant of the identity of her possible sire?'

'I believe she is, my lord.'

Count Henry looked thoughtfully at the solar window, before waving Arthur to the stool. 'Sit, man, for heaven's sake. Do you really believe this woman could be Myrrdin's daughter?'

'My lord, I'd be uneasy swearing to it. All I can say is that only once have I seen eyes like that and they belonged to Count Myrrdin de Fontaine. I'd like your permission to find her and bring her back to Troyes. She cannot be safe wandering abroad.'

Count Henry picked up a fresh quill and began toying with it. Already his thoughts were straying back to his account books. 'Very well, you may find her, she can't have got far.'

Arthur rose. 'Shall I bring her to meet you?'

'Heavens, no, I've had second thoughts on that score. What would I do with the girl? When you find her, you can take her straight to Count Myrrdin in Brittany.'

Take her straight to Count Myrrdin in Brittany?

Arthur felt his jaw drop. 'Take her to Fontaine? But, my lord—'

'Myrrdin will know if she's his daughter, he can decide what's to be done with her.' Count Henry picked up a knife and started trimming the quill.

Arthur's guts were cold. 'My lord?'

'There's a problem, Captain?'

'This…' Arthur cleared his throat '…this commission may take some weeks to complete.'

'So?'

'Are the Guardians to go uncaptained for all that time? *Mon seigneur*, I urge you to reconsider. Wouldn't it be better to bring her here, when I find her? We might then send word to Fontaine.'

Count Henry scowled at his quill, tossed it aside and selected another. 'No, no, you are my best man—who better to escort Myrrdin's daughter to Fontaine? Sir Raphael can stand in as Captain of the Guardians until your return. The boy shows promise, it will do him good to be given real responsibility.'

Arthur ground his teeth together. *Not Raphael, dear God, not Raphael.* Sir Raphael de Reims was everything Arthur would never be—the younger son of an old and ancient line. Arthur Ferrer, as everyone in Troyes knew, had not a drop of noble blood flowing in his veins.

Arthur had hoped that Count Henry valued a man for his deeds and not his ancestry. *I am the son of an armourer. Illegitimate. Raphael is the son of a count. What chance do I have against the son of a count? Is this Count Henry's way of telling me I have lost my captaincy?*

Count Henry scrawled on a piece of vellum and handed it to him. 'Take this to the treasury. You will be given money to cover your expenses. God speed, Captain.' He glanced at the window. 'It'll be dusk before we know it. You had best hurry, if you intend to catch up with her tonight.'

Chapter Four

Light was fading by the time Arthur was ready to leave. He had explained the circumstances to his squire, none the less, the lad was startled by their haste of their departure.

'We're setting out at this hour?' Ivo asked. '*Before* supper?'

'We'll find an inn later,' Arthur said, yanking so hard on the girth of his saddle that Steel shifted and stamped in his stall.

He was in a dark mood. Why the devil had Clare put him in the position of having to chase after her? It was plain that something must have happened to make her run off and naturally he was sorry for it, but it would have been so much easier if she had just come to him for help, as he had suggested. Worse, he was disappointed with Count Henry for finding a replacement Captain so eas-

ily. 'Raphael, *Raphael*,' he muttered. *'Mon Dieu.'*
The Count hadn't even needed to think about it,
he had immediately known who he would pick.
It was almost as though he had been planning it.

The old doubts rushed back. *It is because I am
low-born. Count Henry seems fair and just, but
when it comes to promotion he is more likely to
advance someone of his own class than an illegitimate knight from the lower orders.*

Ivo was leading one of Count Henry's Castilian ponies, a black mare, into the yard. The
Count was insistent they took her with them, so
that Count Myrrdin's daughter, if such she was,
would have her own mount. In Arthur's view the
mare would have a wasted journey. It was unlikely that the girl would be able to ride.

Mon Dieu, he couldn't believe it—he was to
ride to Brittany. In January. As the escort of a girl
who in all likelihood hadn't so much as sat on a
horse, never mind ridden one…

'Ivo?'

'Sir?'

'You've said your farewells to your mother?'

'Yes, sir.'

'She understands you may be away for some
weeks? When we find this woman, we must take
her to Fontaine.'

Ivo's eyes glowed. 'Yes, sir.'

To Ivo this commission was an adventure. Arthur wished he felt the same.

They left Troyes by the Paris gate. Arthur had already discovered from one of the sentries on the city wall that someone answering Clare's description had been taken up by a cloth merchant anxious to catch the tail end of the Lagny Fair. She had been seen sitting in the back of a cart on a bale of cloth. Wretched woman.

Arthur urged Steel into a trot. 'We should catch up with her by nightfall. I reckon they're heading for the Stork.' Reaching into his saddlebag, he found a chunk of bread. 'Here, if you're starving, you'd best have this.'

'Thank you, sir.'

The miserable, grey evening did nothing to improve Arthur's mood. A persistent drizzle set in, and they reached the Stork a little later than he had predicted. Arthur's stomach was growling; and despite his fur-lined cloak, his clothes were sticking, cold and clammy, to his skin. Doubtless his squire felt equally miserable. Wretched woman. If it weren't for her, he and Ivo would be happily ensconced by the fire in the great hall, eating their supper.

Torches were sputtering in the yard of the Stork. The ground was muddy and rutted by cartwheels, and puddles were spotted with raindrops. Light flickered under the inn door, a small but welcome sign of life.

'Sir...' Ivo pointed '...is that the lady?'

In a shed next to the stable, a large wagon was

covered in sailcloth and Clare was sitting on a heap of straw next to it. She made a forlorn figure. If she had set out with a veil, she had lost it *en route*. Her auburn hair clung like dark weed to her skull and she was combing through it with her fingers. Her nose was pink. A threadbare cloak hung limply on a nearby hook—both Clare and the cloak looked as damp as he. Despite his ill temper, Arthur's heart went out to her.

'That's the lady. Find a stall for the horses, would you? Get the grooms to assist, and then order supper for three.'

'Yes, sir.'

Dismounting, Arthur left Ivo to deal with the horses. As he approached, those mismatched eyes widened.

She jumped to her feet. 'Sir Arthur!'

'Good evening, *ma demoiselle*.'

Pushing her hair over her shoulder, she gave him a troubled look. 'Why are you here?'

Arthur folded his arms. 'I am come to find you.'

She shifted back a pace. 'Why?'

'Orders from Count Henry.' He gave her a brief bow and looked deep into those mismatched eyes. 'I am to escort you to the man we believe to be your father.'

She went white. 'M-my father?'

Arthur waited. He was interested to hear what she said if he did not prompt her.

'My father?' Mouth working, she took that step back towards him. 'Sir, since I've already told you that I don't know where I was born and that I suspect I am baseborn, you must be making fun of me. I do not know my father. And he does not know me.'

'I believe I have worked out who he might be—'

'Sir?'

She seemed to stop breathing. Had this girl been Geoffrey's lover? Arthur longed to know. Those unusual eyes were very expressive and the hunger with which she was watching him was curiously moving. She looked wary, almost hopeful. It came to him that she was afraid. She wasn't used to feeling hopeful and it frightened her.

'It's my belief your father is a powerful and wealthy Breton nobleman. His name is Count Myrrdin de Fontaine.'

Clare looked blankly at him, as though she had never heard of Count Myrrdin de Fontaine which, given that Count Myrrdin had been one of the leading noblemen in Brittany, was passing strange.

'You've not heard of Count Myrrdin?'

Slowly, she shook her head. 'No, sir.' She glanced away. 'As I mentioned before, I have spent many years abroad. Where is Fontaine again?'

'It's many miles to the west of here, in the

Duchy of Brittany. Count Myrrdin has largely retired from the world, but in his day he was known
as a man of great honour.' He gentled his tone. 'I
do not think he would reject you.'

'Sir Arthur, most men would find an illegitimate daughter a great embarrassment, they would
be ashamed. What makes you so certain Count
Myrrdin will accept me?'

'He has been a widower for some years. He
has a strong sense of right and wrong, and if you
are his child, he would want to know of it. Count
Henry agrees with me, which is why he has given
me this commission. Incidentally, you might like
to know that Count Myrrdin has another daughter.'

'I assume she is legitimate.'

'Yes, and thanks to her marriage to the Comte
des Iles, she is already a countess—the Countess
Francesca des Iles.'

'You are certain Count Myrrdin is my father?'

Reaching out, Arthur took her by the shoulders. Even though his touch was light, she
strained away from him. He frowned and gently
turned her to face the hissing torches. 'It's your
eyes,' he murmured, looking into them. Truly
they were fascinating—the green one had grey
and silver flecks in it, and the grey one had black
speckles near the pupil. 'You have one green and
one grey, *exactly* like Count Myrrdin. It's so unusual. You're his daughter, I know it.'

Long eyelashes lowered, she shifted and Arthur released her. The instant he did, she edged away. It was like a dance. She came near, she edged back, she came near…

She fears men.

Arthur jerked his head towards the inn. 'What's the food like in there?'

'I couldn't say.'

'You haven't eaten?'

Her eyes wouldn't meet his. 'Not yet, sir.'

Arthur found himself scowling at the cloak on the hook behind her. 'You were planning to eat tonight?'

'I…I, yes, of course. I shall eat later.'

She was lying. Glad that he'd asked Ivo to order food for three, Arthur's gaze shifted to the cart and the pile of straw. 'You were going to sleep out here. Lord, woman, that's begging for trouble. Come along, I am buying your supper.'

'Oh, no, sir, I couldn't.'

He reached past her, ignored the way she shied away from him, and lifted her cloak from the peg. It was pathetically light. It would be useless at keeping out rain and cold. 'Of course you can.' With a grin he added, 'Particularly since Count Henry will be paying for it.'

She hung back. 'Sir Arthur, I can't. You don't understand, I've promised to rest here. I'm guarding the cart tonight.'

'You? Guarding the cart?'

'The merchant wanted to charge me when I asked for a ride.' She shrugged. 'I haven't much money, and when I explained, he said he'd take me if I watched over his merchandise.'

'All night?'

'Yes. He refused to take me otherwise.'

Arthur swore. 'We'll see about that.' Gripping her firmly by the elbow, he steered her across the wheel-rutted yard and into the inn.

Inside, Sir Arthur turned to Clare. 'Where is this merchant? What is his name?'

The inn was ill lit, smoky and crowded, but the merchant's son was a lanky youth with a red crest of hair, which made him and his father easy to see. She pointed. 'He's at the table by the serving hatch—the one in the russet tunic. He's called Gilbert de Paris.'

Arthur strode straight over. 'Gilbert? Gilbert de Paris?'

The merchant looked Arthur up and down, his gaze lingering for a moment on his sword. 'Sir?'

'If you want someone to guard your cart overnight, you'd best make new arrangements. This lady is no longer in a position to help you. And even if she were, it's shameful to take advantage of a woman forced to travel alone.'

The merchant looked dourly at Clare, grunted and elbowed his son. 'Renan?'

The boy grimaced. 'Father?'

'Take your supper outside, you're watchman tonight.'

The red-haired boy pushed to his feet and Clare held back a sigh. It was a relief to be out of the wet. She had been frozen in the barn.

Sir Arthur gestured her to a table a few feet from the fire and she chose a bench in the shadow of a large oak beam. She preferred not to be in full view of other customers. She preferred not to be noticed. It was an old habit and it was hard to break.

He was looking at her damp hair. 'Wouldn't you rather sit nearer the fire?'

'I am fine here, thank you.'

She remained in the shadows, grateful simply to be in the warmth. Flames flowered in the fire as Sir Arthur hung up her cloak and joined a boy—presumably his squire—by the serving hatch. She wriggled her fingers. They were beginning to tingle as the heat reached them. Her mind was darting back and forth like a shuttle on a loom.

Sir Arthur thinks my father is a count! It couldn't be true. And yet…if it was…

Was it possible that her eyes, the cursed eyes that brought so much unwanted attention wherever she went, had come down to her through her father?

My father is a Breton count! It seemed so unlikely. And yet…

It was possible. For as long as she could remember, Clare had wondered about her parents. In the end, she had come to the view that her parents couldn't have been married. Years ago, she had concluded that her father must have abandoned her mother, leaving her to give birth alone. It was common enough. And after that, anything might have happened—her mother might have died, or she might have abandoned her baby. And then, by some tortuous means which Clare had never hoped to unravel, she had ended up enslaved. Her memory began in her master's house in Apulia, a place which by any reckoning was a world away from Brittany. She remembered nothing before then.

And here was Sir Arthur telling her she might be the daughter of a Breton count…

Quietly, she hugged herself. For the first time, she was on the brink of learning the truth of her background. She had somewhere to go and reason to hope that she might be able to stop looking over her shoulder. Was she going home at last?

Of course, there was much to overcome. What would her father think of her? Sir Arthur was clearly so honourable he couldn't imagine a man refusing to acknowledge his daughter. Clare's experiences had taught her otherwise—Count Myrrdin de Fontaine could easily reject her. Not to mention that his true-born daughter—this Countess Francesca—might resent the appearance of an illegitimate sister. Countess Francesca might hate her.

Her path was strewn with obstacles, yet, for the first time in an age, Clare had hope and somewhere to go.

Sweet Virgin, let Count Myrrdin be my father. Let him acknowledge me.

Sir Arthur was making his way back through the tables, bearing a jug of wine and some clay cups. As he took a seat on the bench opposite, he nodded briefly at her. Filling a cup, he slid it towards her.

'Thank you, sir.'

Sir Arthur was good-looking in the rough-hewn way of the warrior. *Nell's knight.* His nose had a slight kink in it, likely it had been broken at some joust. His brown eyes were striking, dark and penetrating. Though Clare hardly knew him, she had already seen kindness in those eyes. Kindness was a rare quality, particularly in a knight. He had handled Nell with great tact when she had offered him her favour—a lesser man might have mocked the child.

This evening, Sir Arthur's hair was ruffled from his ride, thick glossy strands caught the light. His mouth—Clare's gaze skated past when she found herself staring at it—was nicely shaped, even if at the moment it was unsmiling. A haze of stubble darkened a square jaw. If she were to choose one word to sum him up, it would

be the word *strong*. Except it didn't do him justice. He was so tall, so *large*—the width of his
shoulders… Sitting opposite him, Clare felt tiny.

Sir Arthur was Captain of Count Henry's
Guardian Knights and it was incredible to think
that for the next few days he would be her escort. Saints, she had a knight as her escort! How
strange life was. For years she had needed help
and lately two knights had ridden to her res-
cue. First her Good Samaritan Geoffrey, and
now Arthur. *Sir* Arthur, she corrected herself.
Of course, Geoffrey had turned out to be less
than perfect, but Sir Arthur—covertly she studied him—Sir Arthur seemed to be cut from different cloth.

He tossed back his wine and poured another.
Still unsmiling.

*He is displeased. Count Henry has asked him
to be my escort and he resents it.*

The thought was upsetting. Did Sir Arthur
think it beneath him to have to guard a girl who
might be Count Myrrdin's by-blow? She dreaded
to think how he would react should he discover
that she was a runaway slave from Apulia. 'Sir?'

The dark eyes turned to her, and her stomach
swooped. His rough-hewn looks were danger-
ously appealing and she was reluctant for him
to know it.

'How long will it take for us to reach Fontaine, sir?'

He grimaced. 'This is the worst time of year for travelling, so it's hard to be precise, much will depend on the weather. But I would imagine it will take several days.'

'*Several* days?'

'Three weeks. Maybe even a month.' An eyebrow lifted. 'If you can ride, it won't take as long.'

Clare bit her lip. 'I don't ride, sir.'

'I didn't think you would, but Count Henry has lent you a Castilian pony from his stables. If you're willing to learn, you may try her out tomorrow. Otherwise, you'll have to ride pillion with me.'

His tone was so brusque it left her in no doubt that if that were to happen, he would be most disgruntled. 'Very well, sir, I will try the pony tomorrow. Sir Arthur?'

'Hmm?'

'You would rather have remained in Troyes? It displeases you to take me to Brittany?'

He toyed with his wine cup. 'I have duties in Troyes.' He shrugged. 'However, my liege lord has commanded me to take you to Brittany and I must obey.'

Her heart sank—there was no doubt, he misliked having to escort her to Fontaine. Was it because she was baseborn? Or was there more to it than that?

Beneath the table, her hands balled into fists. This man had been kind to her. And his diligence in looking for her after she had sent him that letter had been ill rewarded—he'd been given a commission he resented. 'I am sorry you have been inconvenienced.'

He glanced pointedly at her damp hair. 'It's not the best time of the year to be on the roads, as you have already discovered. Hopefully, we will complete the journey in good time.'

He stared into the fire, and a small silence fell.

Clare sighed. It was a pity he viewed her as a nuisance, but there was little she could do about it. And she was bursting with questions. She unballed her fists and reached for her wine cup. 'Sir?'

'Ma demoiselle?'

'I will be quiet if you wish it, but there is much I would ask you…'

'Please…' he gestured at her to continue '…I am at your disposal.'

'Sir, you said that Count Myrrdin is a widower. When did his wife die?'

'I am not certain, but I believe she died giving birth to their daughter, Countess Francesca.'

Clare leaned forwards. 'If I am acknowledged, Countess Francesca will be my half-sister. How long has she been married?'

'I believe she married a couple of years ago.'

'To the Count of the Isles?'

'He is also known as Tristan le Beau.'

Grasping her wine cup, Clare absorbed this.

Tristan le Beau—Tristan the Handsome. Another great lord whose name she was clearly meant to recognise. It meant nothing to her. 'And like my father he is a count,' she murmured. 'A Breton count?'

'Count Tristan has lands in Brittany and in the Aquitaine.'

So, if Sir Arthur was correct, she was to have a sister—a countess!—with lands in Brittany and the Aquitaine. She opened her mouth to ask more, but the conversation was interrupted by the arrival of the young lad whom Clare had seen earlier. He turned out to be Sir Arthur's squire, Ivo. By the time introductions had been made, a serving boy had appeared. Steaming bowls of mutton stew and several slices of wheat bread were placed in front of them.

Clare's mouth watered. She'd missed the noon-day meal, and couldn't recall when she'd last eaten meat. Her stomach growled.

'I'm starved,' Ivo said, reaching for his spoon.

Murmuring agreement, Clare bent over her stew. The questions were piling up, but she was reluctant to discuss her altered circumstances in front of Ivo. One last, practical question sprang to mind and it refused to go away.

Sir Arthur, where will I be sleeping tonight?

With his belly full and his bones warmed through, Arthur set down his spoon. Clare had looked half-dead when he had found her, a pale, bedraggled waif with her hair plastered against her head. No longer. Colour was creeping back into her cheeks and tight curls were springing up about her face, bright as copper. She had emptied her bowl and was mopping up the last drops with a chunk of bread.

'More?' he asked, quietly.

'Thank you, no.' She leaned back with a sigh. 'It makes a welcome change to eat something I have not cooked.'

Her features were finely drawn. She was pretty, in an elfin sort of way. Arthur tried to recall Count Myrrdin's face, but it had been years since he had seen him. The Count's eyes were the only thing he could recall with any clarity. Arthur had a dim memory of a bluff, heavyset man. The elfin, other-worldly looks and bright hair must come from her mother.

Thankfully, she didn't put on airs and graces. She was graceful, but not haughty. Arthur couldn't abide haughty women. She was plucky, too, perhaps too much for her own good.

'What made you leave Troyes in such haste, *ma demoiselle*? Why didn't you come directly to me? I told you I was willing to help.'

Those mismatched eyes flickered towards him before settling on the fire. 'No time,' she muttered. 'Matters became urgent.'

'Was it something to do with outlaws? With thieves?'

She hesitated. 'Outlaws...yes, it was something to do with outlaws.'

Arthur leaned back to study her. Something didn't ring true. Why did she feel threatened so many weeks after Geoffrey's death? 'You've been living openly with Nicola for some months. I fail to see why matters should suddenly become so urgent that you are forced to leave without your belongings.'

'There wasn't much to leave behind.'

He held her with his eyes. 'You left two distressed friends behind, friends who would have liked to bid you farewell. Which reminds me...' Arthur opened his purse, and counted out some silver that Geoffrey's mother had pressed on him. 'This is from Nicola. Before setting out, I went to tell her I was going after you and she asked me to give it to you.'

'She shouldn't have done that.' Clare's voice was thick as she stared at the coins. 'She has barely enough as it is.'

'She told me that this was Geoffrey's and that he would have wanted you to have it.'

She blinked rapidly. 'Nicola should have kept it.'

Arthur tried to catch those mismatched eyes. He was certain there was more to this than Geoffrey's involvement with thieves. 'Clare?'

'Sir?'

'What are you hiding?'

Fiercely, she shook her head. Bright curls swirled like a cloud about her face. 'Nothing, sir. Nothing.'

Arthur knew a lie when he heard one. He held down a sigh. It was plain her life had been troubled, likely she had many demons. In time, she might learn to trust him. For the moment, however, his best course was simply to follow orders. His task was to deliver her safely to Count Myrrdin. And if, when they reached Fontaine, she had not opened up to him, he would simply have to cut his losses and return to Troyes. Count Myrrdin could deal with her demons.

My task is to take this woman to Count Myrrdin. Nothing more.

The sooner he got her to Fontaine, the sooner he could return. Arthur had won his position as Captain of the Guard thanks to Count Lucien's recommendation, a recommendation earned through years of service. He refused to be ousted by the likes of Raphael de Reims.

Clare's face was averted. Arthur was uneasily aware he had yet to broach the matter of their sleeping quarters to her. Noble blood might run in her veins, but thankfully this was no spoilt madam—he couldn't see her demanding a maid or a feather bed. However, a blind man could see she mistrusted men. How was she going to react

when he told her they would be passing the night
in the sleeping loft with everyone else?

'*Ma demoiselle*, about our sleeping arrangements...'

She stiffened. 'Sir?'

'You understand that you shall be sleeping in
common with other travellers?' At her nod, he
let out a breath. 'I have secured the last of the
spaces in the loft. It will be cramped up there,
but I thought you would feel safer.' He gestured
about him. 'You could bed down in here, but there
will be constant traffic.' He grimaced. 'And more
draughts.'

'Thank you, sir, I should prefer the loft. Will
you be sleeping in the loft, too?'

'If it pleases you. Ivo and I should be happy
to guard your sleep, but if our presence troubles
you, we can remain here.'

'There's no need for that, I will feel safer with
you nearby. I...' she flushed '...I have never slept
in an inn before.'

It was a remark which, when uttered in that
husky, lightly accented voice, had Arthur wondering anew about her past. He had made a few
hasty enquiries at the barracks, but no one knew
anything about her before she began sharing
lodgings with Nicola. Clare's eyes told him all
he needed to know about her ancestry, but what
kind of a life had she lived between her birth and
the time she moved in with Geoffrey's mother?

It was none of his business. Gaining her trust, however, was. Thankfully, she seemed to trust him, at least enough to accept his protection in the common sleeping chamber.

'Sir...?' She twisted her hands together.

'Yes?'

'I have no bedding.'

'There's no need to trouble about that, I told Ivo to bring an extra bedroll.' Arthur got to his feet. 'We'll be up at cockcrow. Permit me to escort you upstairs.'

'Thank you, sir, you are very kind.'

Arthur was pleasantly surprised when she allowed him to take her hand and lead her to the stairway. It was a small hand, and though it was fine-boned, it was definitely not the hand of a lady. The skin was roughened with work and slightly chapped. The impulse to rub his thumb over the back of her fingers came from nowhere. He kept it in check.

'I am sorry to put you to this trouble, sir. I realise it is a great inconvenience for you to take me to Count Myrrdin.'

'It is no inconvenience, *ma demoiselle*.' And, as he caught a shy, elfin smile, Arthur almost believed it.

The noises in the sleeping loft were different to the noises Clare had grown used to in Troyes. More unnerving. The other guests took an age to settle. No sooner had everyone quietened down, when someone got up and fumbled through the flickering half-light towards the stairs. The privies were outside and the wooden steps groaned with the to-ings and fro-ings. A baby whimpered and snuffled; a woman muttered to her husband.

Lying next to the wall, Clare felt safe enough to have her back to the room. With Sir Arthur's squire, Ivo, sleeping at her feet like a guard dog and Sir Arthur bedding down between her and the other travellers, it would have been hard not to feel safe. It was reassuring having the knight's large body so close. *My knight.* Clare was surprised with herself for thinking this way—after what had happened with Sandro in Apulia, she had never imagined she'd trust a man she hardly knew. Particularly one who, as she had discovered when walking with Sir Arthur past the Black Boar in Troyes, enjoyed his women.

Sir Arthur was not just any stranger, that must account for it. Geoffrey had spoken highly of him, making especial mention of his loyalty to Count Lucien under trying circumstances. Exactly what those trying circumstance had been, Clare had never discovered, but the fact was that Count Henry was not the only great lord to trust Arthur with high office.

Sir Arthur Ferrer is trustworthy. Sir Arthur Ferrer would use his strength to protect me, he would never force himself upon me.

Clare closed her eyes and let her mind wander as she tried to relax into sleep. His name had such resonance. Arthur. Many a time she had heard it on the lips of minstrels and troubadours as they sang about the knights and ladies at the Court of King Arthur. His name alone might inspire confidence. She must be wary though, she hadn't known him long.

If it was hard to credit that Sir Arthur believed she might be the daughter of Count Myrrdin de Fontaine, it was even harder to credit that Count Myrrdin would be happy to receive her. Clare ran her finger along a crack in the plaster. Would Count Myrrdin really accept her? It seemed unlikely, but Sir Arthur clearly believed he would, he had spoken of her father's great sense of honour. To Clare's mind, he was speaking of himself. Sir Arthur Ferrer had a high sense of honour and he imagined the world shared his values.

He could be right about Count Myrrdin, but in Clare's mind he was more likely to be wrong. Count Myrrdin could well reject her. In the meantime, she was more than happy to accept Sir Arthur's company on the road to Fontaine. She was well away from the Veronese and it wasn't as though she had anywhere better to go. As for travelling in the company of a fine knight like Sir Arthur…well, she had never looked so high. At the least it would be interesting.

Once, Clare had taken Geoffrey for the soul

of honour. Geoffrey had been good at heart, but
he had compromised his principles too easily. Sir
Arthur would never do such a thing.

I must remember, I haven't known him long.

Rolling on to her back, she stared up at the rafters. The way that girl outside the Black Boar had
brightened when she had seen him! She might
have been a whore, but her smile had been genuine, her greeting warm. Sir Arthur liked women
and they liked him. Sir Arthur would never force
a woman, of that she was sure. He would be
gentle. Careful. Those strong hands would pull
the ribbons from her hair, they would stroke the
clothes from her body...

She caught her breath, dismayed by the direction of her thoughts. What was she doing? Such
imaginings were not for her.

Closing her eyes, she pulled the blanket about
her. Just before she drifted into dreams, she found
herself wondering why such a personable knight
should take his pleasure in the Black Boar.

Surely someone like Sir Arthur might have any
woman—any *lady*—he wanted?

Chapter Five

The difference was subtle, but Arthur noticed it when he shook her awake—she smiled openly at him.

'Good morning, Sir Arthur.'

Clare's smile was shy and beguiling. It lit the loft. The bedraggled, haunted waif of yesterday seemed to have melted away and the woman who'd replaced her, although obviously still frail, looked stronger. More confident. Startled by the difference—Clare had no difficulty meeting his eyes—Arthur spent the morning observing her. He watched her as they took their places at a table downstairs and broke their fast. The smile stayed firmly in place.

Was this the effect of her learning that her father might be Count Myrrdin de Fontaine? It must be. She looked as though a weight had lifted from her. Hopefully, the stain of her illegitimacy would seem as nothing—a count's daughter would surely not have to worry about her future even if she was baseborn. Arthur liked the change, it suited her.

Outside, the rain had stopped. On the horizon, a clutch of trees were silhouetted by the rising sun, and pale shafts of light shot through them. The branches cast long, spiky shadows. When Arthur went into the stable to saddle Steel, he was conscious of Clare exchanging greetings with the son of the cloth merchant who had taken her place in the barn overnight. The lad was all arms and legs, and when she spoke to him, his cheeks flushed poppy-red. After the conversation was ended, the boy's eyes followed her, lingering on her hair, her figure.

Arthur couldn't fault him for that. Clare wasn't tall, in truth, she barely reached his shoulder, but those delicate, elfin looks were very feminine. Even that homespun gown couldn't conceal a pleasing figure. Wide shoulders set off small, high breasts; her body curved in pleasingly to a slim waist, and flared out again at her hips. Sweetly rounded hips. As she fastened her cloak ties, Arthur felt a tingle of interest, deep in his loins. Firmly, he repressed it. His duty was simply to escort her to Fontaine.

He kept his dalliances with women light. Uncomplicated. Which was why he was in the habit of visiting the Black Boar. His transactions with Gabrielle were based on a simple exchange of silver—Gabrielle would never mistake their relationship for anything more lasting.

In his position, Arthur couldn't afford otherwise. Not only was he a landless knight who lived solely on the service he gave to his lord, his brother's untimely death had taught him that he had nothing permanent to offer a woman. He might have climbed up through the ranks, but life was a lottery. It had been a harsh lesson and not one he was about to forget.

He watched her as he loaded his belongings on to Steel and Ivo slung a saddle on the Castilian and led her into the yard.

'Are you ready to try the pony, *ma demoiselle*?' Ivo asked.

Clare came smiling towards the black mare—her uncovered hair was a halo of flame in the morning sun. She had tied it back in a plait that hung well below her waist and several shining twists had sprung free. An image of Clare, with her body concealed by nothing but that swirling red hair, leaped into Arthur's brain, temporarily paralysing his tongue.

She was devastatingly pretty when she smiled, her whole face transformed. For the second time in the past hour, Arthur felt a stirring of desire. It occurred to him that the journey to Brittany might not be all penance, there were unlooked-for compensations. Not only was this smiling Clare pretty enough to make him want to forget his self-imposed rule about complicated entanglements with women, but he was so drawn to her that it was tempting to turn his back on his decision never to involve himself with a woman with noble blood in her veins.

Lord, this journey was becoming far more of a challenge than he had anticipated.

Leaving Steel in his stall, Arthur went into the yard. Clare was studying the black mare, eyes wary. He cleared his throat. 'You said you don't ride. Have you sat on a horse?'

'No, sir.'

A small hand came out, tentatively stroking the pony's neck. The pony snickered and turned to look at her. Clare snatched her hand away.

Catching her hand, Arthur enfolded it in his, he couldn't resist. 'She's perfectly tame, she's curious about you.' Carefully, he carried their joined hands back to the pony's neck. A rush of feeling raced from her hand to his, a sensation so rare he was tempted to prolong the contact.

Startled, he released her and stepped hastily back. He couldn't afford to become involved with her. This girl might have noble connections. Of course, being illegitimate, she would not be strictly noble. Nevertheless, he knew without asking that she would consider herself insulted if he were to offer her the kind of arrangement he had with Gabrielle. This girl was not to be bought.

'Does she have a name, sir?'

Arthur was staring at the hand gently stroking the pony. Her sleeve had fallen back to reveal a slender wrist, a slim arm. Did she have the strength to ride all day?

'Sir?'

'Hmm?'

'The pony—what is her name?'

Arthur glanced helplessly at his squire. 'Ivo?'

'I am not sure she has a name, sir.'

Clare's smile dimmed. 'She should have a name. I shall call her Swift.'

'Swift?' Arthur bit back a grin. The little mare was known for her placid nature. 'I've yet to see her stretch to a trot.'

Those unusual eyes met his, her lips curved. 'Sir, I cannot tell you how glad I am to hear you say that. If I stay on her while she's standing, that will be miracle enough.'

Gently, Arthur manoeuvred her to the pony's side. A delicate fragrance hung about her—flowery and elusive. Feminine. 'We shall see. Come…take up the reins in your left hand. No, not so. So…'

Their fingers met on the reins and again that tingle scorched up his arm. They were standing so close, he could feel the heat of her body. He could hear the slight flurry of her breath. As he adjusted her hand, a small pulse made itself felt in his groin. He gritted his teeth.

No entanglements.

The pony shifted. 'Ivo, hold the pony's head.'

Arthur closed his hand on Clare's. 'That's it. Hold the reins like that while you mount. Once you are seated, we shall readjust them.'

Bending, Arthur linked his hands to make a step for her. After a moment, when nothing happened, he glanced up at her. She was looking down at him, biting her lip, all confidence gone.

'Oh, no, sir. I…I'm sorry, I don't think I…'

Arthur straightened. 'Yes, you can.' With a smile, he took her by the waist, ignored her squeak of protest and lifted her into the saddle.

Progress was painfully slow. Slower by far than Clare had expected. Sir Arthur had kept her on a leading rein and, despite the pace, it had taken all her concentration to stay in the saddle. Mere moments after they had set out from the inn, Clare had realised that she would have to use all her resources simply to stay mounted. She had no leisure for thinking, and conversation was out of the question. At noon, Sir Arthur called a halt outside another hostelry. She was so exhausted, she could have wept.

Sir Arthur dismounted, slung his reins at Ivo and came towards her. 'You did well,' he said, reaching up to lift her down. Clare found herself wrestling with the temptation to rest her head against that broad, mail-clad chest. Stiffening her spine, for her legs were wobbly, she forced a smile. 'Liar. A snail would proceed more quickly.'

'You stayed on and you didn't complain, that's a promising start. You are all right?' His hands were warm on her waist. When she nodded, he released her. 'Any stiffness?'

'A little.' She grimaced. 'And I suspect you're about to tell me that it's going to get worse.'

'Very likely. Come, let's see what this inn has to offer.' Sir Arthur crooked his arm at her and they went inside.

And so a pattern began to emerge. They ate at the inn. Clare was lifted on to Swift again—the irony of her choosing that name was not lost on her—and they rode. They stopped at another inn. They found lodgings for the night and then it began all over.

Sir Arthur lifted her—more stiff and aching than she would have believed possible—on to Swift. They rode. They stopped at an inn....

By the end of the second day, the leading rein had vanished.

By the third day, they tried a trot. It was hell, a silent hell, for they rode in silence. Clare was uncertain whether Sir Arthur was quiet because he resented having to escort her to Fontaine. On the other hand, he might be trying to help her. He wasn't stupid—he knew she needed to concentrate. Neither thought was particularly uplifting.

They were riding abreast along a road that was screened by trees at either hand. Brambles snaked in and out of the margins. Occasionally, Clare saw a flash of red as a squirrel whisked through the leaf mast.

She decided to try breaking the silence. 'I don't think I'm a natural rider, Sir Arthur, and I'm sorry for it. It looks as though it will be some while before you are back in Troyes.'

Brown eyes glanced across. 'Arthur,' he said. 'Since we are to be companions for so long, you should call me Arthur.'

'Thank you.'

'You are becoming more at ease on horseback. We shall make a rider of you yet.'

Sir Arthur—*Arthur*—thought she was at ease?

'If you knew how stiff I feel, you wouldn't say that,' she murmured.

However, she was quietly pleased with her progress. Only yesterday, conversation had been the last thing on her mind. Concerned that the Veronese might be following them, she had been obsessed with escaping as swiftly as possible.

Today, simple conversation would be welcome. If she could earn Sir Arthur's—*Arthur's*—regard, she might win his friendship. And this man's friendship would surely be worth having. Arthur was honourable and he took his responsibilities seriously—he would make a loyal friend. She would begin by asking him about Nicola and Nell. She felt badly about leaving them. It would be good to know they would manage without her.

'Sir—*Arthur*—I wanted to ask you about Count Lucien. Is he steadfast?'

A dark eyebrow lifted. 'Steadfast?'

This morning, Arthur had dispensed with his mail coat, Clare had seen Ivo stowing it in his pack. None the less, he was unmistakably a knight. Beneath his green cloak, he was wearing a simple grey tunic with a leather gambeson for protection. His helmet was looped round the pommel of his saddle, and his shield was slung on his left. Clare studied the unicorn while she waited for him to speak. Why had he chosen a unicorn as his device? It seemed odd that a straightforward, earthy man like Arthur would choose a mythical beast.

'Count Lucien is one of the most steadfast men I know,' he said. 'Why do you ask?'

'I am hoping that he and Countess Isobel will continue to visit Nicola.'

'They will, no question. I sent word to Ravenshold that Nicola was getting weaker. Countess Isobel is sure to visit. I also sent them a manservant from Troyes Castle.'

'That was kind, thank you.'

Harness jingled. 'Countess Isobel may offer them lodgings at Ravenshold.'

'I doubt Nicola will accept. She might be frail, but she's fiercely independent. She's lived all her life in Troyes and won't want to move.'

Arthur nodded. 'My father was the same when he grew old.'

'Your father lived in Troyes?'

'Aye.' Arthur stared at the road ahead of them.

'Your father was a knight, like you?'

Mouth tightening, he gave the tiniest of head-shakes. 'My father was an armourer.'

Clare stared—that she had not expected. Not that she had thought about Arthur's ancestry, of course, but if she had, she would have assumed his father had been a nobleman, at the least a knight as he was. 'Ferrer,' she murmured. 'You came by your name because of your father.'

He shot her a fierce look and she realised that he had not intended to discuss his background with her.

'My father was more than a blacksmith, he was castle armourer until he became too old to lift a hammer.' He stared ahead, eyes bleak. 'It pleases some to mock me for it.'

'Some people will make mock of anything.'

'Father was renowned throughout Champagne for the quality of his work. Why, even the King...' He scrubbed his hand over his face, and the fierce look faded. 'Lord, I don't know why I told you that. It's not something I normally talk about.'

She smiled. 'Why not? You are proud of your father's work.'

'I am and justly so.' He touched his sword hilt. 'This is one of his, it's the best sword in Troyes. Although to speak to some, you would think I have much to be ashamed of.'

'You? Ashamed?'

Mouth twisting, he turned the subject. 'We were speaking of Nicola, I believe. Count Lucien knows she needs assistance. Should she wish to remain in Troyes, he will ensure she may do so safely.'

'It was kind of you to send a manservant.'

He shrugged. 'Anyone would have done the same.'

Clare wasn't so sure. Arthur had been displeased with his orders to escort her to Fontaine, yet he'd paused to consider Nicola's welfare. In her experience, men wasted little thought on the welfare of others, particularly men who had been commanded to a duty they found distasteful.

'Clare—if I may call you that…?'

'Please do. *Ma demoiselle* is far too formal.'

'Clare, why did you leave in such haste? Did the thieves threaten you? You must know you can tell me without fear of reprisal, I am sworn to protect you. And when the man I think is your father acknowledges you—you will be beyond their reach for all time.'

'*If* he acknowledges me,' Clare said, lightly.

'If you are his child, Count Myrrdin will acknowledge you.'

Arthur leaned across to give her hand a reassuring squeeze, and an odd quiver ran up her arm. She felt it in her breasts, in her belly. Unsettled, she looked swiftly away.

'When I return to Troyes,' Arthur continued, removing his hand, 'it is my hope to root out the thieves once and for all. It would help if you would tell me everything you know. You can start with the cave.'

'Truly, sir—'

'Arthur.'

'Truly, Arthur, I know so little, I am not the right person to ask.' *And even if I had anything to tell you, I am not certain I would.* She didn't want him finding out about her life as a slave. She couldn't imagine how he might react. Would he look at her with pity? Or would he take her part, and redouble his efforts to rid Troyes of thieves and slavers alike?

The thought of him catching the Veronese had a chill run through her. Not for the sake of Lorenzo da Verona, never that. It chilled her because if Arthur found the slaver, he would soon discover that back in Apulia she had been accused of attempted murder. That would surely wreck any friendship between them.

Who would believe her word—that of an escaped slave—against her master's son?

Arthur's dark eyes were far too watchful. It wasn't surprising, he was trained to hunt down wrongdoers. Lifting her chin, Clare gazed at the trees ahead. Holy Virgin, what was she to do? He knew she was hiding something.

'Clare, your loyalty to Geoffrey does you credit, but I know he was involved in the theft of a relic before Christmas.' His voice was quiet. Implacable. 'Think. If you confide what you know to me, you may prevent other thefts. Or worse. And if you do not…' he paused significantly '…what am I to think, but that you yourself have been consorting with thieves?'

'I have not been consorting with thieves!'

His mouth lifted at the corner. 'In that case, you will not mind telling me what you know.'

And then Arthur couldn't say exactly what happened, for he didn't see Clare use her heels, but Swift jolted into a trot.

Clare gave a little cry and clung to the saddle. Swift was only trotting, but it was a very smart trot. For a couple of seconds, Arthur found himself grinning at Clare's appalling seat—she was bouncing up and down on the little mare like a sack of grain. Her hands seemed to be entangled in her cloak; several skeins of coppery hair went flying every which way. She was slipping slowly to the left.

Lord, she was falling. Arthur's smile faded. He gave Steel his head and was at the mare's side as

Clare slithered, all arms and legs and outraged gasps, from the saddle. She landed in an ungainly heap at the side of the road.

Ivo gave a snort of laughter, quickly muffled as Swift trotted away.

Arthur bit the inside of his mouth and dismounted. He couldn't risk catching Ivo's eye, for she did look amusing. He found himself contemplating a pair of attractive feminine legs with prettily shaped calves.

She yanked her skirts down and rubbed her head. 'I hit my head on a stone and it was your fault!'

Arthur sobered. 'You're hurt? Let me see.' He knelt at her side, peeled her hand aside and peered at her scalp. There were bits of dead bracken in her hair. Some blades of grass. Gently, he drew her plait from the back of her cloak.

Instantly, she was stiff as a board. 'What are you doing?'

'Easing the pressure on your scalp.' He frowned and gently probed his way through her hair without completely unravelling her plait. It was thick and soft as silk. Arthur was close enough to identify that scent—lavender. Releasing her—her tension hadn't eased and he didn't like to think that she found his touch distasteful— he lifted his hands away and leaned back on his haunches. 'There's no blood and I can't see any bruising. You'll survive.'

'No thanks to you.'

Rising, he offered her his hand to draw her to her feet.

It hadn't been his fault. Somehow, conveniently, Clare had evaded a conversation she found difficult by goading that slug of a mare into a trot. However, there was nothing to be gained by challenging her on the point. They were no longer in Champagne, but they hadn't entered Normandy yet, never mind Brittany—he had plenty of time to win her trust and draw the truth out of her.

That elfin face was turned his way. The wind was playing with her hair, lifting the bright strands from her plait, twisting it into long curls. Arthur cleared his throat. 'My apologies, your hair…'

She didn't move. Time seemed to slow. Arthur's senses sharpened. Overhead, a rook cawed. Steel shuffled and stamped. Clare was looking at his mouth—he wasn't mistaken, she really was looking at his mouth—and licked her lips. It was as though she was thinking about kissing him. He was certainly thinking about kissing her, even though kissing this woman should be the last thing on his mind. She had been entrusted to his care—he mustn't take advantage of her.

Recalling the way she had frozen when he had examined her scalp did the trick. He moved away. It was just as well he did, for Ivo had caught Swift and was already ambling back towards them.

Clare tidied her hair. She was shaking. It had been a serious error of judgement to goad Swift into a trot, but Arthur's questions had unnerved her. And then she had compounded matters by pretending to hit her head. Her stomach twisted. What else could she have done? She was desperate to prevent him from realising that she had links with slavers rather than thieves. Unfortunately, her ruse seemed to have failed. He was more suspicious than ever.

She felt utterly confused. She had never met anyone like him—the feelings his fingers had evoked in her as he had parted her hair had been beyond her experience. Arthur had careful, gentle fingers. Who would have thought so large a man—a knight—would have it in him to be so delicate? She'd actually enjoyed his touch, she wouldn't have minded if he'd prolonged the contact. It was most unsettling.

She gave him a sidelong glance. Those dark, watchful eyes rarely left her. He would, she was sure, mention the thieves again. He seemed convinced she was in league with them.

Clare's left buttock throbbed—it had been her bottom, rather than her head, that had landed on the stone. Frowning, she wriggled and resisted the temptation to rub the pain away. She would be bruised for certain. Not that she would admit that.

Shaking out her skirts, her hand caught in

the fabric. She glanced down—there was a jagged rip in her gown and her knee was poking through. Stooping, she pleated the fabric together with her fingers. It would be impossible to ride with any decency, her thigh would be on view the entire way.

She glanced warily at Arthur. She hadn't missed the heat in his brown eyes, he'd been staring at her mouth. He was attracted to her. Normally, she went out of her way to avoid attracting attention of any sort from men. What had happened with Sandro had put her off for life. However, she didn't think Arthur would force his attentions on a woman. This was a man of honour.

Her heart thumped. It was most odd, but the thought that Arthur might be attracted to her wasn't as worrying as she would have expected. It was actually quite…enlivening. Not that she'd ever act on it. In a way, it was a pity her experience with men was so limited. If she were more experienced, more confident, she might build on that attraction—she might use it as a means of distracting him from awkward conversations. However, she wasn't at all confident. And she certainly didn't want him to see the rip in her gown.

Swallowing hard, gripping the edges of her skirt together, she hobbled thoughtfully towards him. *Arthur is an honourable man, Captain of the Guardians. He would never force himself on a woman. I can trust him.* None the less, she kept a firm hold on her skirt.

She felt herself frown. Falling off Swift had been something of a disaster—she had a tear in her gown and Arthur would soon return to his questions. She'd have to think of other ways to avoid them, because he mustn't learn the real reason for her flight from Troyes. It was bad enough that he should think her hand in glove with thieves, but if he found out her real secret, she would die of shame.

She needed to know he valued her as a friend before she entrusted him with that particular secret. And the day would never dawn when she would be ready to confess to the Captain of the Guardian Knights that she'd been accused of attempted murder.

'Clare, we'd best make haste,' he was saying. 'The days are too short for lengthy delays and there's some way to go before we reach the next town.'

'Will there be a market there?' she asked, catching her breath as he reached for her and set her back on Swift. Deftly, she arranged her skirts to keep the rip hidden. It wasn't easy, the fabric kept gaping. Hunching slightly in the saddle, she pressed her fingers against the tear.

'We will arrive too late for any market—' He

broke off, brown eyes narrowing. 'Clare, are you hurt?'

'No, why?'

'You're sitting awkwardly. And you're not experienced enough to ride with one hand on the reins. Use both.'

'I can't.'

'Can't?'

'I…I've torn my gown.' Cheeks burning, she let go of her skirt. 'That's why I asked about a market. It's my only gown and—'

'There's thread in my pack,' he said, voice curt as he frowned at the tear. 'Ivo?'

'Sir?'

'Find the thread, will you? And a needle.'

Ivo rushed to do his bidding. To Clare's astonishment, she found herself clinging to the pommel as Arthur himself took up the needle.

'Hold still.' Large fingers brought the edges of the fabric together on her thigh. 'We can't have you exposing yourself like that, it's not seemly.'

Not seemly? This from the man whom she had seen giving the eye to one of the women at the Black Boar? A man who made her melt inside simply by looking at her mouth?

Arthur's dark head bent over her thigh. He slid a hand—in a manner so matter-of-fact it was almost an insult—up the inside of her gown. He was mending her gown! And there was nothing in the least lover-like in his manner. He was all practicality. Had she imagined the heat in his eyes?

'We can't have you attracting unwanted attention,' he said.

Those strong fingers knew how to wield a needle. The stitches were large, but surprisingly neat. He was quick, too. And despite his matter-of-fact manner, little *frissons* of sensation were shooting from Clare's thigh to her belly. 'You have done this before.'

He glanced up. 'Every warrior worth his salt knows how to mend his gear. Is that not so, Ivo?'

'Yes, sir.'

Arthur's eyes danced. 'I wouldn't attempt a love knot, but I know the basic stitches. My mother was an excellent seamstress.'

'Oh.' Thoughtfully, she absorbed this. Arthur's mother had been a seamstress. With an armourer for a father and a seamstress mother, his background was far less exalted than she had imagined. But unlike her, there was no shame in his past—there was no slavery, and there were certainly no false accusations hanging over him…

She stared at the large fingers holding the needle and her heart ached. This knight was mending her gown to spare her unwanted attention from strangers. She found herself remembering the warmth in the smile of the girl outside the Black Boar. He would be a wonderful lover.

Gripping the pommel, she stared at the dark head.

Holy Mother, what was she doing? She was imagining Sir Arthur Ferrer as her lover, she was longing to try out his kiss.

Impossible. She never had longings like this. Not for any man.

Chapter Six

'There!' Fastening off, Arthur drew out his dagger and cut the thread.

Sight of the skin of Clare's thigh had given him pause. Sad to say, his first thought had been that he wanted to see more of it. It was the colour of ivory and it was perfect. Was she perfect all over? However, the instant he had touched her, his male curiosity had turned to shame. Goosebumps, the woman was covered in goosebumps. Arthur was irritated and disappointed with himself. It seemed he had forgotten what it was to be poor. Clare had no undergown and her cloak was unlined. She must be chilled to the bone.

'Thank you, Arthur.'

'We won't reach the next town in time for the market, but if it pleases you, tomorrow we can see about finding warmer clothes for you.'

'I should like that, it is getting colder. And as you know, I do have money.'

Arthur mounted and they continued up the road. 'We can't have you greeting the Lord of Fontaine in rags. And keep your pennies, Count Henry gave me plenty of money.' He paused. 'I should have thought of it before, I am sorry.'

Whilst he had been mending that rip, Arthur had been appalled at his thoughtlessness. He'd known she had fled Troyes without a backward look. She'd left everything behind. He'd known she lived simply—of course her everyday clothes would be basic.

Yes, she needed warmer clothing, she also needed*decent* clothing. *Mon Dieu*, she wasn't even wearing an undergown! The threadbare nature of her cloak was obvious, he'd noticed as much when he'd found her at the Stork, how could he have forgotten? He had no excuse, particularly since he too had come from a humble background. He had—he swallowed down a sigh—allowed his irritation at being given this commission to distract him. Added to that had been the even more irritating realisation that he found her intriguing. Not to mention desirable. Which was utterly irrelevant. Clare was under his protection and he ought not to touch her.

It was a resolution that was sorely tested at the next hostelry, the Running Fox. Arthur had been warned the place was shabby, but it was the only inn they could reach that evening. By the time they reached it, Clare looked weary. The skin beneath her eyes had a bruised look.

The wind was raw when they arrived and they hurried in. Even though Arthur knew the inn was second-rate, he had only to cross the threshold to see that it fell far below his expectations. Inside, there was little relief from the cold. The last of the daylight was squeezing through chinks in the wattle and daub—chinks which the wind whistled through. The fire gusted with every draught. The air was thick with tallow smoke and the trestles looked as though they hadn't been wiped for nigh on a year.

Arthur tucked his gloves into his belt and exchanged looks with Clare. 'This is the only inn for miles,' he muttered. 'I am afraid we have little choice but to stop here.'

Clare squeezed past a couple of dull-eyed customers to get close to the fire, and held her hands towards the flames. They were blue, mottled with cold.

'Lord, let me see.' Arthur took her hands, they were like ice. When she flinched, he turned them over and saw that her palms were red. They'd been blistered by the reins. 'Why didn't you tell me? I have spare gloves. Come to think it, so has Ivo, and his will be a better fit.'

She gave him a quiet smile. 'It is of no importance.'

'No importance? Those blisters must hurt.'

She looked at him in a puzzled way. 'We can buy gloves when we reach a market.'

Arthur couldn't fathom her. Why had she not complained? What had her former life been like that she felt she must suffer in silence?

She jerked her head at the flames. 'At least there's a fire,' she said. 'And it didn't rain today.'

Arthur could see there was no point offering to hang up the rag that passed as her cloak until she had thawed out. Leaving her by the hearth, he went to speak to the landlord. He didn't have high hopes for the sleeping accommodation, however, they would have to make the best of what was on offer. Left to himself, he would think nothing of it, but Clare…in that thin cloak…

It wouldn't do to deliver her to Count Myrrdin with the lung fever.

'Oh, no, sir.' The landlord of the Running Fox had piggy eyes that peered out between folds of fat. 'We have no sleeping loft. You and your friends will have to bed down in here, like everyone else.' The landlord sniffed, and rubbed his fingers together. 'If you pay a little extra, I can see you and your lady get fresh mattresses by the fire. Or…' he smirked '…we have screens if you want to pay for your privacy.'

A ladder was leaning up against a soot-blackened wall. Lifting his gaze, Arthur saw there was a loft on a platform over the main chamber.

He stared pointedly at a door high in the wall. It could only be the loft door. 'Where does that lead to?'

The landlord scowled. 'Up there? That's storage, sir. There's precious little space, it's packed to the rafters.'

'Show me.'

With much grumbling and fuss, the ladder was unhooked from the wall and set below the door in the platform. A lantern was found. Arthur followed the landlord up. The loft was dark and cramped, and the ceiling criss-crossed with low beams. Stooping, Arthur took the lantern from the landlord and forced his way as far as he could. The way was blocked by an ancient mattress—the stuffing was spilling out of it. His nose wrinkled, the air was faintly stale. Musty.

Arthur wrenched the mattress aside and a spider scuttled into the shadows. Behind the mattress there was an assortment of worm-eaten packing crates; a pile of broken pots; a rusty spade head; and a couple of bill hooks. An aged wine barrel sagged under the eaves. He poked it with his foot and felt it give. He could think of no reason why an old barrel should have been carried up here. Like everything else, it was only fit for the fire. However, the roof looked sound enough, there were no gaps in the underside of the thatch. And it was warmer in the loft than it was below.

'This will do. If these are shifted to the side…'

Arthur waved at the packing crates '…there's floor space for two. I shall sleep here with the lady. My squire will sleep in your main chamber.'

'But, sir…'

As he climbed down the ladder, Arthur listened to the man's objections with half an ear. He was determined to get Clare on her own. He wanted her on her own, not because he found her attractive—no, he wanted her on her own because the more he got to know her, the more she intrigued him. He sensed dark mysteries, mysteries that, as Captain of the Guardians, he was honour-bound to explore. He was sure he could get her to open up to him, if he only he could speak privately with her.

He would swear that Clare had information that would prove useful when he returned to Troyes.

He let out a breath. He had enough self-awareness to know there was more to it than the suspicion that Clare could help him cleanse the outlaw-infested highways of Champagne. Irritatingly, he was curious about aspects of her life that were not his concern. He couldn't help wonder about her relationship with Geoffrey. Had it been as innocent as she claimed? Had they been lovers? Friends? Where had she come from before she had met Geoffrey? Where had she lived?

And—Arthur was certain the answer to these questions would be the most telling—if she proved to be Count Myrrdin's daughter, why had she left Fontaine in the first place? How could she be so ignorant of her lineage?

She's Count Myrrdin's daughter, I know it.

Unfortunately, this conviction simply led him deeper into the mystery surrounding her. Something extraordinary must have happened to separate her from Count Myrrdin. If her father had been anyone else, Arthur might have suspected him of finding a way to rid himself of an unwanted, baseborn child. But not Count Myrrdin. Not the most honourable man in all Brittany. For Clare to have no clue as to her sire's identity, she must have been taken from Fontaine when she was an infant. All babies were born with blue eyes, but they soon changed. And Clare's eyes— one glance and anyone in the Duchy would suspect Count Myrrdin of being her father.

The woman was hedged about by mystery. And when she had deliberately and oh-so-innocently fallen from that pony rather than answer his questions, his curiosity had only grown. Well, two could play at that game. She was half-frozen, and that was largely his fault. He was going to—oh-so-innocently—make amends. If they slept together in the loft, he could make sure she was properly warm. More importantly, with only him up there, she wouldn't be able to evade his questions…

'The loft is fine,' he said, glancing across at

Clare as he pressed silver into the landlord's palm. 'I would like it cleared and properly swept by the time we have eaten. Fresh mattresses, mind.'

The piggy eyes brightened at sight of the coins and the grumbling stopped. 'Yes, sir. All shall be as you wish, sir.'

'We should like wine and ale, and we'll sup by the fire.'

'Yes, sir.'

Arthur joined Clare and they found a table near the fire. He smiled blandly at her even as he wondered how she would react when he informed her she would be sleeping alone with him. He would tread softly, she was wary of men. She had pushed back her hood and her hair, that unruly hair that he ached to see loose, glowed about her like a nimbus.

'You are feeling warmer?' Lightly, he touched her hand.

'Yes, thank you.'

Ivo joined them. Carefully, eyes downcast, Clare slid her hand from his.

The food when it came was just about palatable. The pea-and-ham soup was over-salted and greasy, and the bread was at least a day old, but it was fine for dipping in the soup. There was a soft goat's cheese. It was surprisingly tasty. Clare cut generous slices and handed round the platter.

'My thanks,' Arthur said. 'We shall survive till morning.'

Ivo grimaced, fished something out of his soup and wiped his hand on his chausses. 'I am not so sure, sir.'

'Eat up, lad. Until we reach Fontaine, we can't be sure what we'll be eating.'

Outside, twilight was falling fast. Clare noticed. She glanced towards the door and her mismatched eyes swept over the cracks in the walls. Her brow wrinkled. 'Are we staying here tonight? Is there room?'

'There's space in the loft.' Arthur jerked his head at a serving boy, who was at that moment wrestling a mattress up the ladder. 'It's cramped, but it's warm and the thatch looks sound. No draughts.'

Clare smothered a yawn and nodded. They'd been in the saddle long enough to tax a veteran and Clare was no veteran, she was exhausted— she was so exhausted she hadn't realised she was going to be on her own with him.

Arthur watched it sink in after they had climbed the loft ladder.

She dug in her heels at the storage room entrance and scowled at the mattress. 'Arthur? There's only one sleeping space.'

Arthur took her firmly by the elbow, ducked his head under the beams and guided her into the loft. The latch clicked behind them. 'So there is,' he said calmly. The lantern sat—slightly askew— on top of the crumbling barrel. 'Holy Mother, that looks dangerous.' Reaching out, he plucked the lantern from the barrel and placed in on a packing case.

'Arthur?' She folded her arms. '*One* mattress?'

He shrugged, which wasn't easy given he was almost bent double under the low, sloping ceiling. 'Look around, what room is there for *two*? Don't you trust me?'

'Yes, but...but I thought Ivo would be with us.'

Arthur sighed. 'You can go back downstairs and sleep with the others in the draughts, I shan't stop you.'

Her frown deepened. 'I think I shall do that.' She lifted the door latch. 'Will you be coming down, too?'

He shook his head, cracking his skull on a beam. *'Mon Dieu!'*

Her hand went to cover her mouth and Arthur heard a distinct giggle. When the door latch fell back into place, he knew that she would not be sleeping downstairs.

Arthur looked so uncomfortable, stooped over, ruefully rubbing his scalp.

'You look like a hunchback,' Clare said, almost before she had thought. 'A gargoyle.'

'Flatterer.' His hand fell away and he gestured at the mattress. 'For pity's sake, if you're staying, can't you settle down? I'm getting a crick in my neck.'

Nodding, Clare dropped on to the bed and

shuffled to one end of the mattress. She pulled off her boots. The mattress wasn't narrow, but it wasn't very wide either.

'We...' she flushed '...we are to lie down together.'

'Yes.' With a sigh, Arthur lowered himself down a good yard from her and rolled his shoulders.

She untied her cloak. Someone—Ivo presumably, when she hadn't been looking—had brought Arthur's pack up. Blankets had been left on top of it.

'Here.' Arthur tossed a blanket at her, lips twisting. 'Wrap yourself in this, it will save your virtue.'

'I do trust you, you know.'

He shook his head and bent to ease off a boot. 'No, you don't.' The boot landed by the lopsided barrel and sent up a puff of dust. 'You would have answered my questions if you trusted me. You wouldn't have resorted to a ridiculous ploy like pretending to fall from your horse if you trusted me.'

Her breath caught. 'What questions?'

'Each time I mention the thieves, you turn the conversation.'

'I do?'

'You know you do,' he said, voice hard. He tugged off his other boot, his dark eyes bleak. 'God knows why, but it irks me, it irks me more than I can say. I want you to trust me.' He shoved his hand through his hair.

'Arthur, I do trust you.' She leaned towards him, twisting the tie of her cloak round her finger. 'Am I not here with you now? Alone. Of course I trust you.'

'Prove it. Talk to me. Tell me what you know about Geoffrey's death.'

'He was killed at the Field of the Birds, before the tournament began.'

'That I know. He hoped to sell that stolen relic on behalf of the thief, did he not? He was acting as a middleman.'

Clare bit her lip. She had thought—hoped—that only Count Lucien knew the full extent of Geoffrey's shame. Somehow Arthur had divined the truth. It was hard talking about it.

When Arthur touched her arm, she almost jumped out of her skin. 'There is no disloyalty in you admitting this,' he said. 'It's obvious what he was about.'

'Geoffrey regretted his alliance with the thieves,' Clare said softly. 'He realised what a mistake it was, but he was far too naive—when he tried to break free—'

'That's why he was killed?' Arthur's eyes were intent. 'Because he wanted to break with the thieves?'

She nodded. 'He was foolish enough to tell

them that he intended to return the relic to the Abbey.'

The dark eyes held hers. 'That's the truth?'

'I swear it.'

'They must have decided he knew too much. Lord, what a waste. But it's a relief to know Geoffrey saw the error of his ways. I always did like that lad. He had potential.' Arthur scrubbed his face. 'At least the man who killed him is dead. What concerns me is how bold the other outlaws have become. Time was when most of them would abandon Troyes once a fair was ended. They would follow the fair to the next town in search of richer pickings and they'd only come back when the fair returned. This winter it's different—a number are known to have stayed behind. Clare, why did you flee Troyes? Do the thieves have a hold over you? Did they threaten you?' His eyes held hers. 'I cannot shake the thought that something else is afoot. Please help. You might prevent other deaths.'

Clare fiddled with the ties of her cloak. On the one hand, she wanted to help him, he was straightforward and honest. She liked him, too much for her own good. As Captain of the Guardian Knights, it could only advance him in the eyes of Count Henry if he returned to his post with information about the thief and his connection with slavers. On the other hand, it was unlikely that he would be satisfied with a brief warning that slavers were at work in Champagne.

Arthur would want every last detail and she would end up being forced to confess that, up until a year ago, she had been a slave in Apulia. And from there, he would be but one step away from learning about the accusations that had been levelled against her. Attempted murder.

Count Myrrdin might be the most honourable man in Brittany, but he is a nobleman—he is bound to be proud. What will he think if he learns that his supposed daughter is an escaped slave with a price on her head?

And Arthur...

Briefly, Clare closed her eyes. She didn't like to think how Arthur would react. She slanted a look at him, sitting so calmly beside her. The man exuded power. Tonight, the lamplight softened those dark, clear-cut features. It blurred the determined line of his jaw. None the less, his attention was entirely focused on her, he was trying to read her.

I am safe with this man.

Clare dropped the tie of her cloak. It was an innocuous movement, but he noticed. This man was, she was learning, peculiarly attuned to every move she made. Voices were floating up from downstairs—the low rumble of a man's voice; a child's high-pitched laughter. She was fully conscious of the clatter and chatter of the customers below, and of a strange vulnerability in Arthur's expression. There was a kiss in his eyes. A kiss.

Her pulse quickened. Arthur wanted to kiss her. Her mouth went dry. It was nerves. The temptation to accept that kiss was irresistible...

Her cloak fell open. Her gown hadn't been cut with seduction in mind, she could never compete with that woman—Gabrielle—at the Black Boar in Troyes, but there was warmth between them. She really liked this man. Dare she take his kiss?

Scarcely breathing, she reached for his hand. She hoped she wasn't trembling. She didn't think she was, but she had never initiated contact with a man in this way and wasn't entirely certain how to proceed.

I shall be myself.

His eyes searched hers before dropping to her mouth.

'Clare?'

She shifted closer and the mattress rustled. Broad shoulders blocked out the light. She saw him swallow and it gave her pause. Arthur couldn't possibly be nervous. Not a strong, red-blooded man who was in the habit of visiting Gabrielle at the Black Boar. Of course, Clare wasn't Gabrielle, but it was good to think that she had the power to attract him. It was a heady feeling.

And she had spoken the truth earlier—she did feel safe with him, Arthur was no Sandro, he would never push her to give more than she wanted. She ached for that kiss…

Arthur's hand turned, palm up and he held it motionless as though curious to see what she would do. Shakily, she slid her fingers between his and squeezed gently.

His breath hitched and he cleared his throat. 'This is another of your ploys.'

'Ploys?' Slowly, Clare released his fingers and moved her hand on, under the sleeve of his tunic. Light though she kept her touch, she could feel the strength in his forearm—the muscles, the slight abrasion of masculine hair…

Her heart thudded. She felt fluttery and nervous—she was longing to try out his kiss, but none the less this would be the first kiss that had not been forced on her. *I like this man.* She moistened her lips and waited.

'Clare…'

His voice was husky. It sounded as though he hadn't used it in an age. In the poor light his face was unreadable, but she thought his skin had darkened. His eyes glittered like jet—she could see the grey flecks in them. She was unaware of moving again, but he was nearer than he'd been a moment ago. His mouth—she was watching it closely—went up at a corner.

'Clare, I'm warning you…'

Face aflame, she inched in, only stopping when

her breasts touched the front of his leather gambeson. A tingle shot from her breasts to her belly.

'Clare.'

And then his hand was round the back of her neck, steadying her head, and his mouth was on hers. One kiss. Two. Three. They were brief kisses and they tantalised. With each touch of his lips, the thrill in her belly intensified. She felt warm right through. He was so gentle. He smelt of leather and horse and a fresh earthy smell that was simply...Arthur.

She pressed closer, catching hold of his shoulders when he paused and she feared he was making a move to end the kiss before they'd truly begun.

No, she was mistaken—he wasn't retreating, he was raining kisses on her mouth, on her cheeks. One. Two. Three. On her neck. One. Two. Three. The tingle turned into an ache. Clare had never felt this pleasure that was pain before, but she knew what it was. Want. These small kisses were torture. They made her want a deeper, more thorough kiss. She wanted the kiss she had seen in his eyes.

Shocked at herself, she pulled back. Breathing hard, Arthur tore off his gambeson, tossed it on to the boards and took her in his arms. As her breasts pressed against his linen tunic, his lips fastened on hers and he smiled against her mouth.

'Better. Much better,' he murmured.

They were kneeling on the mattress and, with the gambeson out of the way, Clare had his tunic under her fingers instead of leather and padding. She could feel the heat of his body. Through the slighter barrier of linen, his wide, muscled shoulders were hers to touch. The skin of his neck was warm. His hair sifted through her fingers, gleaming in the lamplight. She eased back and, with a quiet mutter of protest, he allowed her to explore his chest. Strong. So strong.

If only Arthur could be her guardian knight, in truth. She wouldn't have to worry about slavers. The past could remain in the past, and she wouldn't have to worry about whether or not Count Myrrdin would accept her.

Nipping her ear, he held her firmly against him. His tongue ran round her lips and Clare found herself opening her mouth to accept a full kiss. His tongue swept in and touched hers. Though startled, she found herself responding in kind, sliding her tongue against his. It was disarmingly playful and she loved it. Her bones were melting. She ached *everywhere.*

Oh dear, she liked this man far too much...

Arthur was enjoying the restless slide of Clare's breasts against his tunic. He would kiss her for ever if it meant she kept moving against him like that. His hands ached to tear that homespun gown from her and see if her breasts were the same perfect ivory as the thigh he had seen earlier. But there could be no tearing of gowns, she only had the one.

He tore his mouth from hers. *This must stop.* He shouldn't be kissing her, she was under his protection. Her mouth—Lord—it was swollen with kisses and he yearned to kiss it again. Her breasts were straining against the fabric of her gown—they were beautifully shaped, and her nipples were pressing into the weave. For a slight woman she had the most beautiful breasts. 'Tomorrow...' he swallowed '...tomorrow we shall find you a warmer gown.' *And an undergown, even if it means I shall feel less of you. Even if I can see less of you.*

She didn't answer, not in words. A small hand curled round his neck and guided his mouth back to hers. His palms ached to cup her breasts. As for his loins, he was like a rock. Ready. Aching. Desire pulsed through him, every bit as strong as the desire Gabrielle's clever fingers had wrung out of him back in Troyes. Stronger. He had to stop. He must.

Clare moaned his name. 'Arthur.'

Even though Arthur knew this must go no further, his hand slid over a breast. Perfect, as he'd suspected. Even more perfect was the way she gave another moan and pressed into him. Simply perfect. Her eyes were closed, her eyelashes fanned prettily across deeply flushed cheeks. Her breath was coming in short gasps, drawing his gaze down. He weighed her breast in his palm, longing to see her body. He burned to touch her, flesh to flesh.

This elfin girl had aroused him with incredible ease. He couldn't fathom it. She had only been in his arms a few moments and it was obvious that Geoffrey had taught her very little. She hadn't half the skill of Gabrielle and yet...

He grimaced. He was hard, painfully, agonisingly hard. But he could do nothing about it, not without risking his honour. She was under his protection...

'It would be wrong,' he muttered, releasing her.

Mismatched eyes gazed up at him and her breath feathered across his face. Her shy smile was confirmation that this woman was not one to tumble lightly. Particularly if her father might be the Lord of Fontaine. Arthur might want nothing more than to roll with her on to the mattress and take his joy of her, but that was impossible.

He reached for the second blanket. 'Sleep now. Sleep.'

It was only after they were both cocooned in their cloaks and blankets that Arthur realised that once again, the conversation had been turned and she had avoided his questions. He grimaced up at the rafters, shifting to ease the tightness in his loins. Had the kiss been but another of her ploys, another attempt to distract him? If so, she had succeeded. She had touched him at a deep, primal level. They'd done little enough, but for a while he'd almost lost control. Their brief—some would say innocent—exchange of kisses had roused him enough to have him tearing off his gambeson like a lad of sixteen. He'd been desperate to get closer. Well, this girl was out of bounds to him, they must not get any closer.

Arthur listened to her breathing. Soft. Quiet. She had her back to him and was pretending to be asleep. He knew she wasn't asleep, but he would let her think she had him fooled. What was she thinking? Was she regretting having kissed him? Something—likely a mouse—rustled in the thatch above them. The soft rumble of voices floated up through the boards from below. A child coughed.

Throbbing with thwarted desire, he found himself painting a picture in his mind of what Clare would look like naked. Naked beneath him. She'd be soft and delicate, all feminine curves. Welcoming. It was odd how much he wanted to see—and touch—her naked skin. At the Black Boar, Arthur had tumbled Gabrielle every which way, but not once had he bothered to undress himself. It had never occurred to him. He'd had Gabrielle whilst still clad in his tunic and hose; he'd had her with his gambeson firmly in place; he'd had her with his boots on...

But Clare... Lord, he'd give a month's pay to lie with her naked and play the lover.

Arthur knew as much as there was to know about bought love. Bought love was the only sort of love a landless knight such as he could afford. Clare made him wonder about an altogether different sort of love. What would it be like to play the lover, in truth?

He studied the back of her head. Her loosely braided hair drew the light from the lamp. A coppery skein flowed across the blanket. Other colours were twisted amongst the copper—blonde, chestnut, brown. Reaching out, he was about to stroke it, when he checked himself. Lord, he must take care. Clare wasn't his lady-love. A landless knight had nothing to offer someone like Clare. He must remember what had happened to his mother—the way the townsfolk had shunned her because she had given birth out of wedlock. That was not going to happen to Clare. He rolled on to his back. He'd only kissed her, thank God. But had things gone much further, he wasn't certain he'd have been able to stop. He wanted her.

This must go no further.

Best keep his eyes on the ceiling. No—best close his eyes. Best sleep.

He was going to sleep. And as soon as they reached Fontaine, he would find a likely inn and buy himself some love.

Chapter Seven

Arthur must have dozed, for when he came to himself again, the lamp had burned out. He had dreamed he was walking in a field of lavender. Below, all was quiet. A warm weight lay on his shoulder. Clare's head was tucked against him and her arm was about his waist, the scent of lavender was coming from her hair. Arthur laid his palm gently on her head and his gut twisted.

Want? Thwarted desire? It was irritating that he couldn't pin it down.

Arthur wasn't in the habit of waking alongside a woman, that must be the trouble. He paid for the act of love and he paid well, but he had never paid to spend the entire night with a girl. It had seemed extravagant in the extreme to pay for hours of a woman's company when most of the time you would be asleep. This was the first time he had woken with a woman in his arms.

Carefully, so as not to disturb her, he rested his cheek against her head. Lavender. This waking with a woman was really quite pleasurable. When he felt a pulsing ache, deep in his loins, he grimaced. Although clearly, there were drawbacks...

After breaking their fasts, Arthur took Clare out to see what the village had to offer in the way of clothing. Ivo came with them. Their breath fogged out before them and frost crunched underfoot.

Clare cast Arthur a sidelong glance and touched her mouth. She was meant to be choosing new clothes and all she could think about was that kiss. She could feel its echo—it was as though those warm, firm lips were still exploring hers. She'd enjoyed being cradled in his arms and she'd loved the way her body had melted into his. Was this a glimpse of what it might feel like to give oneself to a man one trusted? The feeling of being able to abandon oneself to another was oddly empowering. She'd felt defenceless and she'd felt invincible all at once. How was that possible?

And why had Arthur pulled away? Had she done something wrong? Something that repelled him? Doubt sat cold inside her. She'd love to think he'd enjoyed it as much as she had, but...

His dark eyes were focused on a handful of

cottages clustered round the village well. Some had lowered their shutters and transformed themselves into stalls. Loaves of bread were for sale at one house. Another was displaying rounds of cheese. There was a potter and a blacksmith. A goat was tethered to a stake by the well head, its pitiful bleating sliced through the air. A brace of bedraggled hens crouched, fluffed up with cold, in their coop.

And that kiss lingered. It was probably just as well he'd ended it. Had it gone on much longer, she would have been certain to have embarrassed both of them.

'Look—' Ivo pointed '—there's cloth over there.'

They crossed the square and Clare forced herself to concentrate. Clothing, they were looking for clothing.

'This isn't bad,' Arthur said, fingering a blue worsted. 'It should keep out the worst of the chill.'

Clare's eyes fastened on a bright green cloth. 'I like this one, but...' she gestured at the mend in her gown '...we will be travelling and I can't be sewing on the journey. I need a finished gown.'

'A finished gown, *ma dame*?' The shopkeeper's face lit up, and he gestured at the house behind him.

Through the open shutter Clare saw the flash of a needle. A woman was sewing inside.

'*Ma demoiselle* needs three warm gowns,'

Arthur said. 'She needs a lined cloak, some gloves and the usual assortment of undergowns. But she needs them this morning.'

The shopkeeper's eyes bulged. 'This morning? *Three* gowns? My wife will see what she has.' He measured Clare with his gaze, and gestured her towards the door. 'Alix! *Alix!* A lady has come to see you. She needs finished gowns.'

Clare looked wide-eyed at Arthur. '*Three?* It seems an extravagance to buy one made gown, but three? Are you sure?'

Arthur nodded. 'If she has them.' He dug a handful of coins from the purse at his belt and dropped it into her hand. 'Buy whatever you need. Count Henry would have my head on a platter if I were to present you to Count Myrrdin looking like a beggar.'

Feeling as dazed as she had when he'd kissed her, Clare nodded. 'There's no need to wait, I shall see you back at the inn.'

The horses were saddled and ready to go when Clare came back from the seamstress. She was wearing a light blue veil and a cloak the colour of cornflowers. Her gown was a couple of shades darker.

A fist seemed to clench in Arthur's stomach as he looked at her. The veil suited her, even though it hid most of that glorious hair. A few rebellious curls still framed her face, but he preferred her without the veil. He liked looking at her hair and the veil seemed to have distanced her from him. 'You look very well,' he said. In truth, Clare looked every inch the noblewoman, but the words stuck in his throat. 'Your father will be proud to acknowledge you.'

'I pray you are in the right,' she said, holding out a bundle. 'Here are the other things I bought. I also found a comb.'

'Ivo, put Clare's things in that pack.' While Ivo was busy with the saddlebags, Arthur took her arm. 'Are you sure you have enough?'

'Yes, indeed! Fortune was with me, for the seamstress and I are almost of a size—there was plenty of choice. She even had a gown in that leaf-green on the stall.'

Her eyes were bright with pleasure, Arthur wished he had thought to do this sooner. 'The cloak is lined?'

'Yes, with English wool.' She opened it and stroked the lining, a pleased smile about her mouth. 'I can take it back if you think I've been too extravagant.'

'I wouldn't hear of it. You must be warm.'

'Thank you.' With a glance at Ivo, Clare stepped nearer and lowered her voice. 'And before you ask, yes, I have an undergown and look…'

Reaching beneath her cloak, she tugged a pair of gloves from her girdle.

Arthur took them from her and lifted a brow. 'Calfskin.'

'They belonged to Alix's neighbour. She was delighted to sell them.'

'Good, they will protect your hands from blisters as well as the chill.'

She touched his hand. 'I thank you, Arthur, most heartily. I have never had such fine things before.'

'Don't thank me, thank Count Henry,' Arthur said, turning back to the horses. He found himself wishing that it had been he who had bought them for her. Delight enhanced her looks. Her unusual eyes shone and the curve of her lips was pure temptation. He hoped that Count Myrrdin would be pleased with his pretty daughter and more inclined to accept her. *What will he think of her? Will he shower her with gifts?*

She seemed doubtful that her father would want to acknowledge her, but she didn't know Count Myrrdin. The Count was getting on in years, he no longer attended the tourneys and he'd retired from his position as adviser to the young Duchess of Brittany. A pretty young daughter would surely gladden his heart and lighten his declining years.

Arthur watched critically as Clare took up the reins and mounted—she had learned to do so without his help. By the end of their journey she'd be a fine rider.

Count Myrrdin might, of course, deny that she was his. He sighed. The Count would have to be mad to reject a girl whose eyes were the match of his, but if he did…

Perhaps I might offer her my protection. Would she marry me? The question made Arthur freeze even as he was placing his foot in his stirrup. *Lord, where had that come from?*

Marriage was not for him. A landless, illegitimate knight had nothing to offer—neither a home, nor security. He swung into the saddle and adjusted the stirrups.

But if Count Myrrdin finds her an embarrassment…

Arthur had never taken part in the games of love that were acted out at Count Henry's court. The black memory stirred. After what had happened to Miles, he had watched them as from afar. His brother, Miles, had believed that his skill at arms would be enough to overcome the stigma of his humble birth. Miles had thought that if he proved himself honourable, his background and illegitimacy would be ignored—he had paid a high price for his beliefs.

Who am I to think I can succeed where Miles failed?

Arthur had to admit that even though everyone knew that his father had been Count Henry's armourer, several ladies had made it clear that they would be happy to wear his favour. The women at Count Henry's court didn't see his background as an impediment when it came to a flirtation. A few had gone so far as to suggest an illicit affair. However, if one flirted with an unmarried woman, one risked being misunderstood. And if one flirted with a married one—Arthur grimaced—he had never liked the idea of flirting with married women.

No, because of Miles's death, Arthur avoided entanglements of any sort with noblewomen, whether unmarried or married.

It had made little odds, in any case. There were plenty of Gabrielles in the world.

Gabrielle understood him. She met his needs in ways a lady of the court could never do. Noblewomen were not for him. Arthur knew that if he were involved with a high-born lady and a misunderstanding arose, if his honour was questioned, the entire court would close ranks against him. That was as certain as day followed night. If his honour were put to the test, if his word was weighed in the balance against the word of a better-born man, Arthur knew who would be believed. And it wouldn't be the illegitimate son of the castle armourer.

Urging Steel forwards, Arthur led his little cavalcade on to the road.

Behind him, Clare was chattering to Ivo, waving a hand to show off her gloves. Ivo coughed, nodding and smiling back at her through the coughs. It was plain the lad liked her. As Ivo coughed again, Arthur frowned. Had his squire caught a chill?

'Don't dawdle, you two, we must cover more ground today.'

Clare urged Swift towards him, irrepressible curls of hair winding out from beneath her veil like dark flames. Could he marry someone like Clare? Someone who was, like him, illegitimate?

Clare would never look down her nose at me. We are equals.

It was something of a shock to realise that for the first time in his life, he was considering marriage as a distinct possibility. Ivo was not the only person to like Clare, Arthur liked her, too—even more so since she had shed some of her reserve. He certainly wanted her. What had happened between them last night was proof of that. He suspected she had kissed him as a means of turning the conversation—and it had not lessened his desire for her.

Surely someone like Clare—Count Myrrdin's love child—would be pleased if a knight offered for her? She had never enlarged upon the nature of her relationship with Geoffrey, but they must have been lovers. And, the rumour mill being what it was, it would not be long before her father's retainers coupled her name with that of Sir Geoffrey of Troyes.

Everyone at Fontaine would assume that

Geoffrey had taken Clare as his *belle-amie*. When that happened, Clare would not simply be a fallen woman, she would be a fallen love child. Her future would be shadowed by her past.

And then? If she was lucky, her father would bribe one of his household knights with a small manor and the knight would agree to marry his daughter, his tarnished, love child of a daughter. The thought of Clare being married off to one of Count Myrrdin's household knights brought a bitter taste to his mouth. Clare deserved better than marriage to a man who had to be bribed to take her. It had been surprisingly delightful waking up with her in his arms—discounting the inevitable frustration, of course. But if he were to offer her marriage, there need be no frustration. And no need for Count Myrrdin to go to the trouble of bribing a household knight.

Clare was laughing at something Ivo had said and Arthur saw the moment she caught him watching her. Her smile deepened. Arthur smiled back, even as he found himself wondering if the smile might be her way of keeping him sweet, of distracting him from discussing matters she would rather avoid?

One thing was certain, Clare knew he desired her. With difficulty, he pulled his gaze from her and looked between Steel's ears at the road. He must take care, this woman was muddling his mind. Most likely deliberately. Arthur hadn't reached his position as Captain without learning the value of caution. He ought not to rush to a decision on marriage or anything else. Not until he had learned more about her.

If, at the end of their time together, she seemed suitable and if he was still attracted to her, then he might consider offering for her.

One bitter, wintry day succeeded another. As Swift picked her way along mile after mile of glistening white road, the cold bit deep into Clare's bones. The roadside was bordered by frosted bracken. Puddles were coated with a skim of ice and ruts were hard as iron. When the sun appeared it was pale—it had no strength against a cold that gnawed like a starving wolf at every finger and toe. Clare's calfskin gloves might have been made of gossamer for all the good they did her. The cold pinched her nose and nibbled her ears. Without the lined cloak, she would be one solid lump of ice.

Ivo sneezed repeatedly.

The land was alien. More days passed. Chartres lay somewhere behind them. Places called Alençon and Vitré lay ahead. The names meant nothing to Clare, but according to Arthur they had reached the halfway mark of their journey. She was past caring. She had stopped trying to talk because every time she opened her mouth, her teeth hurt. Her lungs ached with every breath.

She was so numb she had left all thought of tired, aching muscles behind her. There was only cold.

And riding. They rode up hills and they rode down them, the horses' hoofbeats ringing loud on the frozen earth. They nodded to passing riders. The skies turned grey. Clare's fingers could barely move. She would swear that ice had formed inside her gloves. It was in her boots, too, she had lost feeling in her feet hours—days—ago...

Midwinter. Trees and shrubs were coated in hoar frost. It was fairy-tale pretty, but it made grim riding. Ice in frozen puddles snapped like breaking glass when the horses stepped in them. The only birds braving the chill were the rooks, ragged flecks swirling in a pewter-coloured sky. All the other birds must be huddled in the bushes, too frozen to fly.

No wonder that Arthur had been disappointed when he had been ordered to escort her to Fontaine. Travelling at any time of the year was not easy, but in midwinter it was purgatory. Count Henry must have been eager to wash his hands of her. They were chastening and sobering thoughts.

With the horses' breath wreathing about them like smoke, Clare adjusted the hood of her cloak and hunched into it. Thank God for this lined cloak. Without it, she would catch her death.

In the event, it was not Clare who succumbed to sickness. Towards the end of one day when, oddly, there was less bite to the wind, it became clear that Ivo was far from well. He had sat slumped and silent on his horse for hours and barely responded when Arthur took charge of the pack-horse.

'St Peter's Abbey is a mile or so ahead,' Arthur said. 'We had best stop there.'

Ivo's nose was blue and his breathing laboured. Just over a week since, Clare could barely sit on a horse; but by this time she had improved so much she had no difficulty leaning towards Arthur to touch his sleeve.

'I agree, we have ridden enough for now,' she said. 'Ivo needs warmth and rest.'

Ivo roused himself. His cheeks had the hectic flush of the slightly fevered. 'Oh, no.' He smothered a cough. 'I am very well, sir. I don't want to cause delay.'

Arthur's dark eyes turned thoughtfully towards the east where a mass of clouds was gathering above the treeline. 'It will harm none of us to rest for a while,' he said easily.

'But, sir...' Ivo gave a racking cough '...I know how eager you are to return to Troyes.'

'Not at the cost of your health. I am far more eager that my squire should be hale. A squire with lung fever is worse than useless.'

A white-robed monk ushered them into the abbey guest house. In the lodge hall, they were met with the sight of flames leaping in a large hearth. The lodge was empty and their footfall echoed round the whitewashed walls.

'You have no other guests, Brother?' Arthur asked.

'No, sir. The weather...' The monk shrugged.

Clare was staring at the chimney flue, which was stone and set against the wall. 'I've never seen a fireplace like that, but it's just what Ivo needs.'

Arthur watched as Clare led his squire to the fire and fussed over him—pulling a bench closer, pushing him on to it, chafing his hands.

'Supper will be served in the refectory,' the monk said. 'You and your squire, sir, are welcome to join us. I shall arrange for a tray to be brought to the lodge for the lady.'

Arthur hesitated. Ivo didn't look as though he would make it to bed unaided, never mind to the refectory. And much as he understood that Clare might not feel comfortable being the only woman in a roomful of monks, he didn't like to think of her eating alone. 'If convenient, I would prefer my party to eat together here in the lodge.' Unbuckling his sword, Arthur hung it on a hook on the wall.

The monk nodded. 'As you wish, sir. A novice will bring a tray over shortly.'

'My thanks, Brother.'

Clare was good with Ivo. Before supper arrived, she had him ensconced in a pallet by the fire. She heaped it high with blankets and stalked off, muttering about finding the infirmarian. When she returned, she had the ingredients for a herbal brew, which she proceeded to make over the fire. The wonder was that Ivo drank it. Likely he hadn't the strength to resist her. When food and drink arrived—a lentil broth, warm bread and ale—Clare saw to Ivo before she saw to herself.

Concerned that she would forget to eat, Arthur waited until Ivo's eyelids began to droop and drew her to the side table. 'Ivo's caught a chill, he's not on his deathbed. Your soup's going cold and, if you don't eat it soon, I might be tempted to eat it for you.'

'I doubt Ivo will be fit to travel for some days,' Clare said, picking up her spoon.

'I realise that.' Arthur winced as Ivo coughed in his sleep. 'I knew he had a cold, but this—if only he'd spoken up. I wouldn't have driven him so hard.'

'He knows how eager you are to return to Troyes. Do you have family there? I recall you saying your father was dead. What about your mother? Is that why you're so eager to return?'

'No family. They're all gone.'

'All?' Arthur's tone hadn't been encouraging, but the question was out before Clare could call it back. To her surprise, he answered.

'Father, mother, brother—they are all dead.'

For someone of Arthur's age—Clare guessed that he was in his late twenties—it was not surprising to find that his parents had died. But how sad that he had lost a brother…

'You had a brother… Were you close?'

Arthur nodded, he was staring at the ale jug. 'His name was Miles. He was knighted some years before me. He was older than me by ten years, but, notwithstanding that, we were fast friends. That sword—' Arthur jerked his head at the sword on the hook '—belonged to Miles before it was mine. Father made it.'

'Your parents must have been proud to see both sons knighted.'

'Mother only saw Miles knighted—his death all but destroyed her. She died before I received my spurs.'

Clare put her hand on his. 'Arthur, I am sorry.'

He squeezed her hand. When he bent his head and kissed her fingers, her heart gave a little jump.

'Father was never quite the same after Mother died.'

'That is understandable.' She swallowed. 'What happened to Miles?'

The dark head shook and he dropped her hand. 'It's an ugly tale and I don't like talking about it. One day, perhaps—'

There was a world of pain behind his words. Clare was opening her mouth to tell him that she didn't care that the tale was ugly, that it might be better if he talked about it, when the door swung open and the cold rushed in.

It was the novice who had brought their meal. 'I've come for the tray, if your supper is finished, sir?'

Arthur glanced at Clare. 'You've had enough?'

'Yes, thank you.'

The novice loaded the tray, leaving the cups and ale jug on the side table. 'Will you care to break your fast in the morning, sir?'

'If you please. We may have to rely on your hospitality for a couple of days. I doubt my squire will be fit to travel tomorrow.'

'Fresh bread will be ready shortly after dawn, sir. And should you need more candles, there's a supply in the box by the hearth.'

'My thanks.' As the door clicked shut behind the novice, Arthur glanced at the stairwell leading to the upper chamber—the guests' dormitory. 'You are ready to retire?'

She nodded. 'What about Ivo?'

'It would be a crime to wake him. He looks settled by the fire. Let's get you comfortable upstairs. Would you like me to escort you to the wash house first?' He gave her a rueful smile. 'The monastery won't have been built with the comfort of female guests in mind, I can stand as your guard to ensure your privacy.'

Clare returned his smile. 'My thanks.'

Clare sat on a pallet in the guests' dormitory, combing her hair by candlelight. Arthur was yet to return from the wash house, and she had dragged two pallets close together. Very close. She had put them next to the chimney flue, where they would be warmed by heat coming up from below.

Arthur had told her that they were more than halfway through their journey. The news should be welcome, but Clare's stomach was tight with anxiety. She dreaded meeting Count Myrrdin. She wanted him to acknowledge her, indeed she prayed daily that she might make a home at Fontaine, but everything was so uncertain.

How would the Count react? What would he expect of her? Her life would never be the same again and, for the most part, that had to be a blessing. If Count Myrrdin accepted her, she would never be hungry again; she would have fine clothes and a place in the world. On the other hand, her life might not change that much…

Would Count Myrrdin expect unquestioning obedience? She knew next to nothing about how the illegitimate daughter of a count was expected to behave. She might find herself in a position where she had no more control over her life than she had when she was a slave.

And then there was Arthur. She glanced at the pallet next to hers. He was yet another reason to dread reaching Fontaine. He was returning to Troyes and she knew she'd miss him. She didn't want them to part.

Which was why she had decided that tonight was the night. Such an opportunity—a whole chamber to themselves, a cosy bed—wasn't likely to present itself again. She was alone with him. Anything might happen after they reached Fontaine, but if she wanted Arthur—and she did—it had to be tonight.

Her pulse quickened. She could never have imagined trusting a man enough to have him stand guard outside a monk's wash house while she completed her toilette. Something in Arthur inspired her complete trust.

In her life, Clare had trusted only one other man—Geoffrey. When she had met Geoffrey, she had been exhausted and hungry. Sheer desperation had her agreeing to accompany him to his mother's house. As soon as she had set eyes on Nicola and Nell, she'd known she would come to no harm. But would she have been so quick to stay if Geoffrey had lived there on his own? She doubted it. She smiled sadly at a candle glowing on a wall sconce. Poor Geoffrey. He had bitterly regretted his dealings with thieves and he had never had his chance to make amends. Geoffrey had proved to be something of a broken reed.

Downstairs, the lodge door slammed. Footsteps were coming up the winding stairs. Arthur. Arthur was no broken reed. She found herself praying that the kisses they'd exchanged at the inn hadn't quenched his desire. It was possible that he'd stopped for honourable reasons. Well, she was about to find out…

Her pulse jumped. How would he react when he saw the intimate way their pallets were arranged?

He pushed through the door, a lamp in one hand, his cloak and sword in the other. Their eyes held. 'Warm enough?'

Shadows moved as he strode towards her. He broke step when he noticed the positioning of the pallets.

'Clare?'

Arthur's thoughts were so clear, he might as well have spoken them aloud. This was not the cramped loft in the Running Fox. The dormitory here was spacious, there was no excuse for them to be sleeping within reach of each other. Unless…

To remove any doubts as to her intentions, Clare dropped her comb and held out her hand. 'I think we shall both do very well. It's beautifully warm by the chimney.'

Arthur dropped his cloak and sword on the pallet and sat down beside her. He set the lamp to one side. 'Clare.' His voice was thick. Reaching out, he picked up a strand of her hair and wound it round his fingers. His eyes went black. 'It's good to see your hair again. Those veils…' he shook his head '…I prefer you without them.'

Clare set her hand on a broad shoulder and

gave a little tug. Their lips met. The contact remained gentle until Arthur turned more fully towards her and gathered her to him. Clare closed her eyes and pressed against him, opening her mouth to his tongue. His masculine, earthy fragrance surrounded her.

Breathing ragged, he pulled back. Clare felt a soft touch on her cheek. He was shaking his head. 'Clare, I'm here to protect you, not ravish you.'

'And if I want to be ravished?'

'When you meet your father, you may find he has plans for you.'

'Who knows what will happen at Fontaine?' Clare heard her voice go hard. It took effort, but she softened it. 'Arthur, I have been prey to the wishes of others all my life. This is something I want for myself.'

For an instant she thought she saw vulnerability in him. Then he smiled. 'You want me.'

'Yes, Arthur, I do.' She lowered her eyes. This was harder than she had imagined it would be, her cheeks were on fire. 'Unless you no longer… That is, the other day at the Running Fox I hoped…' Bracing herself, she glanced up. His mouth was soft. Receptive. 'Don't you want…?'

He looped his hand in her hair and tugged her back. 'I want you, rest assured.' He fitted his lips to hers and she lost herself in the warmth of his kiss. 'Of course, I want you, *ma mie*,' he muttered. 'But you are not a woman to love and leave.

I don't know what happened between you and Geoffrey…'

Clare made as if to speak, but he put his finger on her lips.

'Say nothing. When I asked you before, you told me it wasn't my business and you were right. What happened bctwccn you and Geoffrey is nothing to do with me. However, we cannot simply take pleasure in each other. You are not a Gabrielle.'

Clare's heart swelled. 'No?'

'You…' he kissed the hair wound round his hand '…you are a beautiful, desirable woman and I want you.' He went on playing with her hair, stroking it, examining it in the lamplight. 'Clare, we both know what it is to be illegitimate.'

Clare felt herself go still. 'You, Arthur? You are illegitimate?'

His mouth tightened. 'I am.'

As far as Clare was concerned, illegitimacy was not so terrible a slur. How could it be? She had been enslaved. Next to that, illegitimacy paled into insignificance. But she could see that for an ambitious knight like Arthur, illegitimacy might present some problems. Particularly since he came of humble stock.

She frowned. 'Your parents never married?'

'No.'

'Heavens, why not?'

Broad shoulders lifted. 'It would have made

their lives easier if they had married, but my mother refused to consider it. Discussions about marriage were banned and Mother rarely spoke about her early life, so it was hard to discover why she wouldn't marry Father. Over the years I picked up enough to realise that she was already married when they met.'

'An unhappy marriage?'

'Mother had been mistreated. She rarely talked about it. Father adored her and our house was filled with love and laughter. When I was a boy, it didn't occur to me to probe for details. And after Mother died—it was soon after Miles—it seemed irrelevant. It would have wounded Father to discuss it and he was wounded enough by two great losses coming so close together.' He slid his hand round her neck, catching the rest of her hair and drawing it forwards over her shoulder. 'Clare, all I am saying is that I understand what it is to be illegitimate. We cannot simply take our pleasure of each other. I won't bring another illegitimate child into this world.'

Clare bit her lip. She felt very small. Very foolish. Arthur was refusing her. It felt like rejection, though she couldn't fault him for it, he was a responsible man. She nodded.

'However...' shifting her hair aside, he kissed her neck and a warm shiver went through her '...there is something I would ask you. Clare, will you permit me to ask your father for your hand?'

Clare blinked. He wanted to ask Count Myrrdin if he could marry her?

'Well?' Arthur's brown eyes were intent. More watchful than ever.

Clare couldn't seem to take it in. One moment he was saying he wouldn't take her as his lover and now he was asking her to marry him?

'Arthur, my parentage is not yet proven and you want to marry me?'

His smile was crooked. 'I hadn't thought to marry, but you and I are both of a kind. We are equals.'

'Because we are illegitimate?'

'Exactly. I never liked the idea of marrying someone who might look down her nose at me because of my birth.'

Clare hesitated. She was at a loss as to how to respond. She was unfamiliar with Arthur's world, but surely his skill at arms and his captaincy would have been more than enough to ward off any scorn that might have attached to him because of his birth? And if that were not enough, he was kind, honourable, handsome… In short, Arthur was the perfect knight. She was dreading being separated from him, she had enjoyed his protection and it would be wonderful to have someone on her side when she reached Fontaine.

But never in her wildest dreams had she thought he would offer her marriage.

And never in her wildest dreams had she

thought she would consider marrying any man, not even for a moment.

Marriage is but a form of slavery.

Something told her that marriage to this man might be different. However...

'Sir...Arthur, I am not the best match for you.'

'I think that you are.'

She gripped his arm. She could feel the strength of it through his sleeve, strength that she needed and admired. Yet she spoke the truth when she said that she was not his match. Arthur might not cavil at marrying someone who carried the stigma of illegitimacy—but someone who had been a slave? Someone who had been accused of attempted murder? For the Captain of the Guardian Knights that would be a different case entirely. She couldn't marry him when he knew so little about her. And she couldn't tell him about what had happened with Sandro, she simply couldn't.

'You don't know me,' she muttered.

'I know all that matters.' He leaned in and pressed his mouth to hers. The kiss was hot. Slow. Deep. It heated her blood and curled her toes. It was the kiss of a man who would be her lover. Her husband. And there were more kisses in his eyes.

He cleared his throat. 'I want you, Clare. I want you as I have wanted none before. Let me pleasure you, I can do that.'

A pulse throbbed in her throat and her cheeks

warmed. Pleasure her? She wasn't quite sure what he meant by that, but it would seem he wasn't rejecting her. She felt like pinching herself—he'd asked her to marry him!

Her hands went to his shoulders. 'Arthur, I want you for my friend.'

He drew his head back and gave her a puzzled smile. 'You don't have to let me pleasure you to have me as your friend.'

'I know.' As she smiled shyly up at him, her fingers went to the ties of his gambeson. 'I want you for my lover as well as my friend. But you don't have to marry me. I trust you to take care, Arthur.'

A hand covered hers, stopping her from pulling off his gambeson. 'You don't wish me to approach Count Myrrdin?'

'I didn't say that. You must do as you see fit. I don't want you to be obligated.'

His face cleared. His hand fell from hers. 'There is no obligation.' He looked pointedly at her mouth. 'Kiss me, *ma mie*, kiss me.'

Chapter Eight

A delightful *frisson* ran through Arthur's body as she knelt up and pressed her mouth to his. Clare intrigued him. The ladies at the Champagne court had never approached him with such candour—such shy candour. It was as appealing as it was uncommon. The manner in which she had confessed to wanting him for her lover would in any other woman be proof of great experience. And yet, as her soft mouth sought his—so sensual, so tentative—there were times when all he could see in her was innocence.

He shrugged out of his gambeson, gathered her close and bore her with him on to the mattress. He would give her pleasure and then he would stop. He couldn't take her to her father and leave her worrying about the possibility of bearing his child.

Her hair tumbled about her like copper silk; it glinted like fire. Pushing a strand from her cheeks, catching the scent of lavender, he leaned over her. Her lips were parted, and her eyes, her mismatched, beautiful eyes, were looking at him with complete trust. He was utterly disarmed. And his thoughts were in knots.

Did she want him to approach her father with an offer of marriage? Or was she, like his parents, against marriage for some reason? He longed to know. What did she see when she looked at him? A friend—she had said she saw a friend. And a lover. Why not a husband?

She was reaching up, combing her fingers through his hair, breaking the thread of his thoughts with that soft touch, that quiet smile. Catching her hand, he kissed a work-worn finger. Then the next and the next. He took the last, smallest finger into his mouth and sucked.

He heard a breathy giggle. 'Arthur.'

Her free hand was wrestling with the hem of his tunic, pushing it up. Easing back, he dragged if off and tossed it aside.

Her gaze slid over the silver unicorn he wore on a chain round his neck and her cheeks flushed as she studied his chest. She sighed, once, and reached to touch him. It was the lightest of caresses. Again, and he could not have said why, he felt utterly disarmed. With infinite care, finger trembling, she traced a line along his collarbone. His groin tightened. She ran her hand over his muscles, slowing slightly to ruffle the curls on his chest. It seemed she was taking pleasure in the contact. Simple pleasure, though she must have done this before.

When she smiled, the dark burn of desire throbbed deep in his veins. Arthur swallowed and, lowering himself alongside her, found her mouth. He kissed, he nipped and licked. She tasted delicate and sweet, and set off a raging hunger in him. He would devour her if he could.

Devour her? No. He might want to devour her, but all the signals were telling him that this woman needed careful handling. She hadn't hesitated to express her desire in the manner of the most experienced of women, but he must not forget the shyness of that smile, that tentative touch...

He would be gentle. There would be no devouring, not today.

Clare's head was spinning. Longing was twisting tightly inside her. Arthur had said he would pleasure her. Whilst she was hazy on what exactly he meant by that, it would seem that at last she would know something of what went on between a man and a woman who desired each other.

The word love hadn't crossed Arthur's lips. How could it? They hardly knew each other. But just as he was the only man she'd ever yearned to kiss, he was also the only man she'd wanted in this way.

Life was changing. Anything might happen when she reached Fontaine. Some changes would be for the best, but would they all? She couldn't be sure. Arthur was right to suggest that Count Myrrdin—a great lord—would make plans for her. It was unlikely that she would be consulted. This was a man's world and she was used to that. But tonight, she had a choice. Tonight, she wanted Arthur. The feelings this knight evoked in her were unlike any in her experience. She might not understand the emotions behind those feelings—the warmth, the hunger—but she knew enough to recognise that liking and trust were vital. She couldn't imagine feeling this way with anyone else.

Only with Arthur could she be so bold.

The future was unknown, but tonight she would accept what he offered. In return, she would do her best to see that he had pleasure, too.

She ran her palm up that muscled, masculine chest, and heat rushed through her. She was melting. Arthur's answering groan made her long for him all the more. Sir Arthur Ferrer. Until she had met him, she had had no notion that a woman could want a man so much that it hurt. She had never met anyone with his particular combination of strength and gentleness. It was extraordinarily compelling.

He had come of common stock and some would name him a bastard. Even though he had risen to become Captain of the Guardian Knights, it was plain he had suffered because of his birth. How could people be so blind? So stupid. How could they not see how honourable he was? How exceptional.

At the back of her mind, she was aware there was much Arthur hadn't told her. Was his brother's death related to his humble background? Was that why he had avoided marriage?

He asked me to marry him—he can't mean it. Sir Arthur Ferrer can't really want to marry me.

Why would he, when back in Troyes he had matters arranged to suit him? Gabrielle. And, presumably, when the mood took him, other women at the Black Boar. His father had never married, why should he?

Arthur offered because he felt he ought to. Because he is chivalrous.

Clare had no wish to bind herself to any man. Admittedly, her experience of marriage was limited to observations she had made during her time as a slave. Her owner's wife, Veronica, had been little better than a slave herself. The only difference between Veronica and the slaves had been that Veronica's beatings had been less severe. For many women, marriage was but another form of slavery.

Arthur was dragging up the skirts of her blue

gown, smoothing his hand up over her calf, thigh, hip…

Her thoughts scattered. A strange lassitude had stolen over her. Her limbs felt heavy. She was at this man's mercy and, miracle of miracles, she felt not the tiniest jot of fear. All she felt was want. She shivered.

'Clare? You are cold?'

'Not at all.' She smiled and ran her hands down his back and over his buttocks. The chain round his neck flashed in the lamplight. Hooking her fingers into his belt, she gave it a slight tug.

He was quick to take the hint. There was a breathless flurry of movement—the whisper of garments sliding over skin—and before she knew it they were naked on the pallet.

His gaze ran down her and a large hand followed his gaze, stroking in the gentlest of ways— arm, waist, hip…

He swallowed. 'Honey and cream,' he muttered. Clare felt her nipples tighten. Bending close, he blew a strand of hair from her breast and bent to dot kisses on her breast. On her nipples. Holding her steady with the gentlest of touches, he used his tongue, pausing only to give a sensual murmur of approval. 'You even taste of honey.'

A sharp sensation shot from breast to womb and her gasp had him lifting his head. His smile was wicked. He knew the effect he was having on her. Eager for more from that smiling mouth, she dragged his head back to her breast. He groaned. Clare moaned.

Then it struck her, they mustn't make a noise—they were in a monastery, for heaven's sake, and what they were doing was a sin. It wouldn't do to offend their hosts.

'What if someone hears?'

Arthur lifted his head and brown eyes gleamed down at her. Dark. Hungry. 'You've changed your mind?'

'No. *No.* But we must be quiet. Ivo…the monks…'

'Ivo's asleep and the monks are in their dormitory by now. No one will hear.'

Clare frowned. 'I really don't want to upset them.'

With a sigh, Arthur reached for a blanket and drew it over them. 'You've remembered it's Sunday.'

'Sunday?' Clare blinked. For a moment she could not think what he was referring to.

'It is forbidden for a man and a woman to take their pleasure of each other like this—we have no intention of having children. What we are doing is forbidden on Sunday; even if we were married it would be forbidden. And…' Arthur's fingers moved gently up and down her breast, teasing, tantalising '…as we are not married, I expect that makes us sinners twice over. This worries you? You are religious?'

'Not especially.'

Clare's master had seen to it that his slaves had attended the chapel on his estate. The services had been a welcome respite from what had been, for the most part, hard labour in the field and kitchen. But as she'd grown older, she'd begun to wonder about the character of a priest who condoned slavery. From there it had been but a short step to work out that the slaves were sent to chapel, not for their spiritual welfare, but to benefit their master. If slaves were instilled with a sense of right and wrong, they were more likely to be obedient. If slaves had been taught to understand the hierarchy, they were less likely to rebel against their place at the bottom of the scheme of things.

She was no longer a slave. However, the shape of her life in Fontaine was as yet unmapped. Today she was as free as she was ever likely to be. In Fontaine, if Count Myrrdin acknowledged her, her life would in all likelihood be arranged for her. She had no experience of life as the daughter of a count, but she would have to do her duty.

How odd. She had prayed for freedom for years, yet she had only just realised that no one was completely free. The daughter of a count was not free. And neither was Arthur—he had managed to rise through the ranks, but he was bound by his oath of loyalty to the Count of Champagne.

His hand shifted. He was sifting her hair

through his fingers, arranging it round her neck, draping it over her breast. She wanted to please this man. Today she was a free woman, tomorrow could fend for itself.

'Show me how to give you joy,' she said, taking his hand and pressing a kiss to his palm.

He rolled over her, cupped her face in his hands and gave her a kiss that left her breathless. Burning.

Breathing in that earthy, masculine scent—*Arthur*—Clare hooked her legs around his.

'Careful, *ma mie*.' She allowed him to unhook her legs and stroke her thighs apart. Her heart was thudding as though she had run all the way from Apulia. He was her equal. Hadn't he said so?

As he moved to touch her in her secret place, she moved to touch him in his.

She hadn't done this before, but instincts were strong, her body knew what to do. She pushed against him and he pushed against her. He groaned, and laughing brown eyes met hers— the grey flecks seemed to dance. '*Ma mie*, I cannot promise silence.'

She shook her head. Silence was no longer important. His responses to her touch—he was very vocal with his murmurs and groans of approval— were astonishingly arousing. 'Touch me there…' she whispered '…again. Don't stop.'

'Nor you.'

'I won't.'

'Good.'

They were as bad as each other with their sighs and moans. She could feel his heart pounding in his chest. Her hand gripped carefully.

'Clare, yes, like that. More.'

She pressed herself against him, blind with need. In a frenzy for…for…

He was kissing her neck, giving her breasts soft little bites. His strong knight's body, so large, so beautiful, seemed to respond to her every need. Except, except…she was hurtling towards something, something she was unable to define, but she wanted—needed—to reach it. Quickly, quickly…

Then the world convulsed and for an instant she was at peace. With Arthur. It was bliss. Save for the rush of their breathing and the hoot of an owl, the world was at rest.

Arthur's tongue was playing with hers as she felt his large body shudder and she understood that he too had found his pleasure.

Clare fell asleep almost at once. Pillowed against Arthur's shoulder, cloaked in that bright hair, she looked as though she belonged there. He wanted her to belong.

She refused me. Why?

He dragged the blankets over them and stared into the shadows. They'd brought each other joy. Indeed he'd almost forgotten himself—when she'd wound her legs round his, the temptation to push home had been overpowering. A pulse beat in his loins. *Mon Dieu*, pleasuring a woman and being pleasured by her was all very well, but it simply wasn't the same. He still wanted her. Properly.

He stroked her hair.

She refused me. She likes me, but she refused me.

Arthur had never thought to ask for a woman's hand. Without lands or a manor, he didn't have much to offer in the way of security. Was that in Clare's mind, too? Had the discovery that she might be a count's daughter turned her head? Did she think she was above him?

He sighed, and wished he knew more about her. She'd told him that Geoffrey had found her on the road before he'd brought her to Troyes. It was likely she craved security. If only he could get her to open up about her past, he would know then whether he had a chance of being accepted. In the meantime, he would watch. And wait.

Arthur had been quiet all day, Clare rather suspected he was more worried about Ivo than he was prepared to admit. The infirmarian had given her various herbs and spices, and the day passed with her sitting by the fire in the main chamber of the lodge, brewing up various remedies. Arthur sat by the door, sharpening his sword. Clare found the rhythmic rasp of whetstone on steel oddly comforting, although from time to time it would pause and she would feel that dark gaze on her. She tried not to blush. She tried not to look at him or worry about whether her behaviour had shocked him. She concentrated on Ivo, who needed her help.

Last night, Arthur had taught her what it meant to give and take pleasure. She was only too aware of how responsible he'd been. He could have taken her virginity, but he hadn't. He'd been careful not to give her a child. Clare recalled the moment when she had held him in her arms and he had reached his pleasure. It was so intimate. Just thinking about it made her warm—she couldn't help wondering what it would be like to know him fully. She couldn't help wishing. And she couldn't help but feel just a little jealous of the girl at the Black Boar...

'Try this, Ivo,' she said, putting her arm about the boy's shoulder so he could drink.

Ivo eyed the cup suspiciously. 'What is it?'

'Elderflowers and honey.'

Grimacing, Ivo tried it. It didn't seem to do much good. He coughed and wheezed and sank back against the pillows.

Arthur came over and threw some logs on the fire, making it sputter. 'I'm going to see to the horses,' he said. 'Then I'll ask the monks if they have any wine to spare.'

Whilst he was gone, Clare tried another brew out on Ivo.

Ivo looked blearily at it and moaned.

'You'll like this,' she said, brightly. 'It's elder-flowers with ginger, cloves and cinnamon.'

'No honey?'

'I'll put honey in, if you like.'

Arthur returned in time to see Ivo set that cup aside.

'We can try him on this,' he said, waving a wine flask in front of her. 'If we add some of those spices and mull it, it will at least warm him. It might clear his head, too.'

Evening came. The novice had been to tidy away their supper and Clare was upstairs in the dormitory staring through the lamplight at the pallets lying side by side by the chimney flue. She bit her finger. Arthur would be up soon—should she pull the pallets apart, or leave them where they were?

The click of the latch and a rush of air announced him.

'Clare.'

Taking her by the shoulders, he turned her to face him.

'Arthur, the pall—'

Warm lips covered hers and all doubt was gone. She wound her arm about his neck and held him to her. His dark, earthy scent wound through her senses and the kiss went deeper. He made that noise—the one that meant pleasure—and she felt herself melt.

She pulled back. 'How do you do that?'

He nibbled her ear. 'Do what?'

A large hand covered her breast and tingles ran all the way to her womb. She closed her eyes, and swallowed. 'That sound you make, it weakens me.'

A dark eyebrow lifted. 'Weakens you?'

'My knees…'

He looked past her at the pallets, a grin lifting the edge of his mouth. 'You're tired. Worn out looking after Ivo. You need to lie down.'

She shook her head at him and smiled back. His eyes gleamed with intent and he nudged her over to the chimney flue.

'And I…' he kissed her nose '…need more of your kisses. I've been needing them all day.'

Before she knew it, they were side by side on the pallets and Arthur's hands were covering her breasts, shaping them through the fabric of her gown. Her nipples tightened.

'I think we both might need a little more of that pleasuring,' he said, watching for her reply.

Boldly, she reached for the hem of his tunic, sliding her hand downwards so she could feel him in return. Testing. He made that little sound again and pushed himself into her hand. He was hard and large, begging to be free of his braies.

'Pleasuring,' she murmured. 'Mmm.'

He tugged at her gown and peeled it up, and she dragged his tunic and shirt over his head. The silver unicorn swung on its chain as he leaned over her. It flashed in the lamplight.

Arthur kissed her mouth. Her cheeks. He wrapped a strand of hair round his fist and kissed that. When he returned to her mouth, she gripped his shoulders, enjoying the play of their tongues. He toyed with her breasts and blew on them. When he kissed her nipples, pulling on them, sucking, she thought she might dissolve with desire. She moaned and wriggled, part-delight, part-frustration. Arthur's hand trailed on, leaving fire in its wake.

'Open for me, *ma mie.*' He pushed at her thighs and slid his finger into her curls.

And then she was groaning as badly as he, the dormitory filled with pants and sighs.

She closed her fingers around him and let herself be tutored by the small noises. There was a sigh that told her she had the rhythm just right. There was one that begged for more speed and another for less. Another for firmer. Up. Down. There was, it seemed, a moan for each subtle movement and she was learning its language.

Only with this man, she thought. She could only do this with Arthur.

His sighs, and hers, were coming faster.

Arthur shifted. He was covering her, lying between her legs, and it felt wonderful. They were both pleasuring each other and they were surely almost there. Almost…

She stopped breathing, her womb seemed to tighten, and the moment was upon her. That sense of deep pleasure swallowed her. She was lost, she was found. *'Arthur!'* She pulled her hand out from between them. 'I want you. *Please.*' Only this man could have this effect on her, and she wanted to know him fully. *This might be our only chance.*

His breath fluttered. He eased back and those dark eyes ran over her face. 'I want you, but…' Shaking his head, he rested his forehead against hers.

'There are ways to be careful—you know them?'

The dark eyes glittered. 'I know them. You're certain?'

For an answer, she tugged at his hips.

He groaned and pushed against her. 'Clare. Irresistible Clare.' He pushed again. He pushed inside her.

The pain was a shock. Sharp. She had known what to expect, she had been a virgin and everyone knew that the first time one lay with a man was likely to be painful. Nevertheless, her eyes stung. She felt as though she was being torn apart. Biting her lip, she hid her face in Arthur's neck.

Rather this man than any other. And he had given her pleasure. It was just that, coming so swiftly after the pleasure, the pain had caught her unawares, she hadn't been braced for the contrast between the bliss and the pain.

Pain was to be expected.

Arthur didn't seem to have noticed her discomfort, he was moving over her with slow deliberation.

'That feels…perfect,' he muttered.

'I'm glad.' And she was glad. Now the initial shock was past, the tightness was easing. When she had her expression in control once more, she looked up at him. His eyes were closed, his face was dark, intent. She couldn't blame him for the pain, she hadn't told him she had been a virgin, and he had mentioned more than once his belief that she and Geoffrey had been lovers.

Arthur muttered again. Something about being careful, that he wouldn't leave her with a child, but all she could think was that the feeling of tightness was easing with his every stroke.

'So good, *ma mie*,' he said.

She touched his cheekbone and ran her fingertip round his ear. He turned his head and caught her finger in his mouth.

'Clare. You feel…' she felt his groan in her belly '…so very good.'

Inner muscles clenched as she watched him. She was conscious of a sense of discomfort. Not physical discomfort—that had gone. It was—she struggled to identify it—it was entirely different to physical pain.

Was it the pain of wanting something that was not hers? If so, it should be easy to ignore. Over the years she had had enough practice at ignoring her wants. Was it yearning? The answer lay out of reach. There was only this man moving above her. Wanting her. Enjoying her. His face was rapt and it wasn't because she was a slave who he thought was his for the taking. Arthur wanted her for herself.

'Clare.' His breath was coming fast, his musky scent surrounded her.

'Mon Dieu!' His groan was tortured. He withdrew from her body, spilling his seed not in her, but in his tunic. The sight of his face, torn between rapture and agony, twisted her heart.

He collapsed against her. 'Sorry, Clare,' he mumbled against her neck. 'That was too quick.'

She kissed a broad shoulder, enjoying his scent. 'I had my pleasure.'

'I know, but…' he shifted his head and she saw his mouth curve into a warm smile '…I meant for you to have it again. No matter, there is always later.'

His head fell back against her breast and his breathing began to steady.

'Later,' Clare murmured. 'That sounds interesting.'

She wove her fingers through his hair, and her

heart squeezed. She had no regrets. Tonight, Arthur had wanted her as she wanted him. With luck, he would be hers for the rest of the journey. Although…thinking about the other places they would be staying, none would be as convenient as this one. Ivo by the fire in the chamber below; the warmth of their beds by the chimney; the lack of other travellers…

'Arthur?'

'Mmm?'

She kissed his cheek. 'You do realise that Ivo might not be well enough to travel for some days?'

The mattress creaked as he leaned up on one elbow. 'Oh?'

'We might have to stay at St Peter's for a while.'

He tipped his head on one side. A wicked, toe-curling smile told her that he'd understood what she was saying. 'Is that so?'

She fixed her eyes on the silver unicorn and nodded. 'Yes, before we resume our journey, we really ought to make sure Ivo doesn't have the lung fever.'

Arthur awoke at daybreak with a smile on his face. His arms were full of warm, sleeping woman and bright hair, fragrant with lavender, cloaked his chest. In complete contrast, the air in the lodge dormitory was frigid. His breath puffed out like white smoke. Reaching out, he laid a hand on the chimney breast. It was stone-cold. The fire below had gone out.

Easing away from Clare, he reached for his pack and found his warmest tunic. The one he had worn yesterday—he felt his face soften as he glanced at her—would have to be washed. He hadn't planned to join with her, but her request had caught him off guard. His body had been in charge and he'd been inside her before he could stop himself. As he picked up his tunic and screwed it into a bundle for Ivo to deal with when he was recovered, a mark in the fabric caught his eye. It was faintly pink.

Blood?

He stared blankly at it. Then his stomach dropped away and he shifted his gaze back to the sleeping girl. Once again, she had kept things from him. Self-loathing burned in his gut. She had been innocent. What had he done?

'Clare? *Clare!*'

She murmured and flung out an arm. 'Mmm?' She opened her eyes and clutched the blanket to her breast. 'Holy Mother, are the monks upon us?'

'No, it's not the monks.' Tunic in hand, he dropped to his knees by the pallet. 'You didn't tell me. Why in hell didn't you tell me?'

She yawned and adjusted the blankets. 'Tell you what?'

Her voice was husky, and even though Arthur was hurt—no, not hurt, *angry*—it made him want to kiss her. It made him want to climb back under that blanket with her and continue where they had left off last night. But Clare was still more than half-asleep and it was wounding to discover that just when he was beginning to think she was learning to like him, he should find something else that she had not told him.

'You should have told me.'

She looked sleepily at him. 'Told you what?'

'Look.' He shook out his tunic and pointed at the stain. 'Virgin blood.'

Hot colour rushed into her cheeks and her eyes searched his. 'It makes a difference?'

'Of course it makes a difference! I should have known. I should not have taken you. I might have noticed, except all I could think was that I must remember to withdraw so that you would not get with child. I should not have taken you.' Tossing the tunic aside, he shoved back his hair. 'I must have hurt you.'

A small hand emerged from under the blanket and rested soothingly on his arm. 'The pain was nothing, it didn't last. You didn't hurt me. Arthur, you have to know that.'

He hesitated, studying her. Both her tone and expression were earnest, but he hated that she hadn't told him. 'I might have hurt you.'

'You didn't.' She smiled and gently touched his cheek. 'Arthur, you know we…we…' her flush deepened '…you joined with me several times last night and each time we both found pleasure.'

'I shall have to speak to Count Myrrdin when we reach Fontaine.'

Her eyes widened. 'You will tell him?' She shook her head and her hair went flying. 'Arthur, please don't.'

'Why not? I want to marry you. I told you as much when we arrived here. Lord, Clare, I thought you were experienced, but you weren't.' He glanced at the tunic. 'I've had your maidenhead and I am honour-bound to speak to your father. Clare, I have to offer for you.'

Arthur leaned back on his haunches, and watched her like a hawk, alert for the slightest change of expression. He wasn't sure what he was looking for. She was a surprising and unusual woman. He certainly wasn't expecting her to snatch her hand from him as though he had scorched her.

Her eyebrows snapped together. *'No.'*

'No?' Her vehemence was galling. If Clare had been brought up as a noblewoman, her response would have been understandable. But she hadn't been bred to look down on ordinary folk. She had lived in a foreign land, where God only knew what her life had been like, but it hadn't been a life of luxury. Like him, she was illegitimate. And it wasn't as though he were a peasant, he had clawed his way up to knighthood.

I am a knight. Illegitimate, yes, but I am her equal.

'Whatever happens at Fontaine, I don't want you to speak to Count Myrrdin.'

Arthur clenched his jaw. 'I am sorry if it displeases you, Clare, but I will speak to him. I have dishonoured you and—'

A sharp laugh cut him off. 'You have dishonoured me? That's ridiculous! You did me great honour, if you could but see it. Arthur, I wanted you. You wanted me.'

'It's not that simple…'

She sighed and her breasts lifted, Arthur kept his gaze on her face.

'Arthur, this is exactly what I was afraid of. You feel beholden.' Her mouth firmed. 'There is no need, none whatsoever, to speak to Count Myrrdin. Besides, I would never accept you.'

'Never?' Arthur pushed to his feet. He had never felt so confused in his life. 'You like me.' It wasn't a question nor was it arrogance. He knew Clare liked him. In truth, he hoped she felt more than that. He certainly felt more for her. He wasn't sure exactly what it was he felt—conflicted certainly—his insides had twisted into a thousand tangles. He looked bleakly at her—eyes, hair, mouth…

They were arguing and he still wanted her. He wanted to join with her again and he wanted to marry her. He certainly didn't want her to marry anyone else. 'You never joined with Geoffrey, you gave me your maidenhead, that must count for something.'

'It does. Arthur, of course I like you,' she said, eyes soft.

'Why not marry me? If you don't, the chances are that Count Myrrdin will find you another husband and you might not warm to him.'

'Since we don't know what Count Myrrdin will say when he meets me, this whole conversation is irrelevant. And I might add that I find the idea of marriage abhorrent.'

He felt as though she had slapped him in the face. 'Abhorrent?'

Her eyes drifted past him. She was staring at the window slit. 'Marriage is a form of slavery.'

'Slavery?' Arthur was going to say more, but when he saw how her hands were twisting together on top of the blanket, he paused. He could see the whites of her knuckles. Slavery. His eyes narrowed and before he knew it he was back at the pallet, kneeling at her side. He covered her hands with his and, when those intriguing eyes looked his way, he smiled. 'Never mind. Clare, I don't wish to quarrel.'

She returned his smile, but it seemed to him that there was sadness behind it. 'Nor do I. Arthur, please don't feel beholden. I really don't want you to feel beholden.'

'Very well, I won't.' He grinned and bent to

kiss her. The eagerness of her response, the way she gripped his shoulders and kissed him back, the way her tongue slid along his, loosed some of the knots. Unfortunately, as the scent of lavender began winding through his senses and the blanket fell from her breasts, the harder it was to remember what he'd been about to say.

He pulled back and stared at her. What was it about this girl? One kiss and he was utterly dazed. Gabrielle, for all her expertise, hadn't half her power. He cleared his throat. 'I give you fair warning, I shall spend the rest of the journey trying to bring you round to my way of thinking.'

She laughed, and this time there was warmth in the sound. 'That sounds intriguing, but I give you fair warning—I shan't be swayed. Marriage isn't for me.'

Dropping a last kiss on her mouth, refusing the urge to linger, he forced himself to his feet. 'In the meantime, I'm going to see how Ivo is faring.'

'I'll follow shortly.'

Chapter Nine

They remained at St Peter's for four more days, and for three of them it snowed. The sky was the colour of pewter and snow blew into the monastery cloisters. The monks shovelled it out again, but no sooner had they done so than the wind blew it back. The fish pond froze.

Over the four days, Ivo regained his strength. Fortunately, it was soon clear that he didn't have the lung fever, he had merely caught a bad chill.

Since snow made the roads impassable, Arthur and Clare had the lodge dormitory wholly to themselves. Clare was determined not to argue. She wanted to make the most of her time with Arthur. She wouldn't marry him, she wouldn't marry anyone. If anyone tried to force her into it, she would run away. She'd run before, she could

do so again. At a pinch, she could always take
refuge in a convent.

'No, no, Ivo,' Arthur said each night as Ivo
rather croakily enquired if he should join them
upstairs. 'You must rest where it's warmest. By
the fire.'

On those four nights Arthur had laid siege to
Clare's senses.

'If the good brothers knew what we were
doing, they would be horrified,' Clare said on
the third night. She and Arthur had retired far
earlier than necessary. 'It's not dark yet!'

'And we are not married,' Arthur said, with
a sly grin.

She pulled back, frowning. 'Arthur, I am warning you...there must be no mention of marriage.'
However much she liked this man, she could
never forget her mistress, beaten almost daily
by her beast of a husband. A wife was subject to
the authority of her husband. Never again would
Clare be subject to anyone.

'We'll see.' Arthur bent assiduously over the
lacings of her gown and drew it over her head. 'I
shall win you yet.'

Clare was tempted to agree as she lifted his
tunic over his head and placed her hands on the
warmth of his magnificent chest. Leaning forwards, she kissed the short curls at the centre and
couldn't resist running her nose gently against
them. Arthur moaned. She loved the shape of

him, his chest especially. She could worship his chest. Those wide shoulders, the way that toned, muscled torso tapered down to that slim waist.

On the fourth night in the monastery, Clare came to the conclusion that she had been wrong about Arthur's chest. It was his buttocks she loved most. She loved to slide her hands down the curve of them whilst they were making love. She relished their strength as he moved over her, over her and in her. They, too, tempted her to change her mind...

On the fifth night, she was seduced by his eyes. The way they darkened almost to black as, curious as to how he would react, she had skipped laughingly out of his reach and lingered over undressing. She loved the intensity of his focus as a large hand reached out and pulled her impatiently to him. She loved the way his gaze never left her, whatever she did. She loved the way those thick eyelashes lowered and the way he groaned when she reached for him.

'Arthur, Arthur,' she murmured.

'Ma mie.'

The one thing she did not love was the abrupt way he pulled out of her each time he reached his pleasure. She tried to tell herself it was foolish thinking like that, but it didn't seem to help. She watched his face as he did it and she could see it pained him.

As he had promised, Arthur was taking care

not to give her a child. Neither of them wanted one. Yet each time he withdrew, Clare flinched and guilt ate away at her. She could tell he didn't like having to pull out of her like that. Arthur was giving her more pleasure than she was giving him.

It didn't seem right.

On the morning after the thaw, Ivo had insisted he was well enough for them to continue their journey.

They stayed at inns, at manors and castles, but the opportunity for intimacy with Arthur was over. Clare found herself regretting their departure from the monastery more than she had expected. As their journey progressed, a heavy weight seemed to take the place of her heart. It got heavier by the day.

Arthur was keeping his distance and it felt wrong. It made her miserable. She found herself glancing sidelong at him as they rode. He rarely returned her glance and, whilst she knew that was only sensible, that he was trying to protect her reputation, it cut her to the quick. It seemed that since they had left St Peter's, Arthur had forgotten he had ever wanted her. From his manner, no one would guess they had been lovers. Did Ivo suspect? She had no idea.

Arthur seemed to have no difficulties keeping her at arm's length. Indeed, he went out of his way to make it plain that his desire for her had vanished along with the snow.

He was polite. '*Ma demoiselle*, are you able to ride a little further today?'

'I think so.'

He was heart-wrenchingly formal. '*Ma demoiselle*, are you warm enough?'

'Yes, thank you.'

They entered Brittany and the road snaked through a great forest. Leafless branches dripped with moisture. Robins and blackbirds pecked about in dead leaves. Once, a distant howl had the hairs rising on the back of her neck.

Her eyes went wide. 'Is that a wolf?'

Arthur nodded, his eyes firmly fastened on the road ahead. 'Never fear, wolves won't approach in daylight, and when the light fades we shall have reached our lodgings. *Ma demoiselle*, in the morning we will reach the edge of Count Myrrdin's estate. You will be glad to hear that by nightfall tomorrow you will be at Fontaine Castle.'

Clare stared at his profile, absently rubbing her breastbone. He spoke so coolly. Had she imagined the heat in his eyes? There was none there now— he wouldn't even look at her. Had she imagined his lips softening as he had watched her dancing about the dormitory? It seemed almost as though she had dreamed their time together.

Her eyes stung. He had satisfied his lusts and

she was obviously to be forgotten. That talk about wishing to marry her—it must have been part of his seduction. She'd been a fool to think he cared.

Blinking rapidly, Clare stiffened her spine and told herself she should be pleased. If Arthur wanted to forget their liaison, that was fine by her. She'd always hated the thought of marriage, in any case. She found herself following his gaze and smiled sadly at the horizon.

It had flattered her to think that this great knight had wanted her. It had flattered her to think that he would ask for her hand, even though she had vowed never to marry.

She was doubly a fool. Her heart felt like lead because the knight she had refused was no longer interested in her. Really she should be rejoicing. If Arthur no longer desired her, he would not be soliciting her father for her hand. There would be no embarrassing revelations at Fontaine.

Good. *Good.*

She would feel better after she had met Count Myrrdin. She could hardly feel worse than she did now.

Arthur couldn't wait to reach Fontaine. Clare had refused him, she wouldn't even let him mention marriage. He watched her out of the corner of his eye—his thoughts were going round in circles. Riding at his side was the most responsive woman in the world and she wouldn't discuss marriage.

Why? Was it his lack of lands? Was she hoping that Count Myrrdin might find her a nobleman? Someone to erase the shame of her illegitimacy?

He swore under his breath. What they had together was so rare. She'd been innocent, so she couldn't know. But she'd felt perfect—the warmth of her mouth, the way her muscles tightened about him, the scent of her arousal. Stupid woman.

Mon Dieu, when he'd left Troyes he'd known that the journey would be a trial, but he'd been worrying about the state of the roads. He'd never realised this elfin girl would be testing him beyond his endurance. *She will change her mind about marrying me. She must.*

When he got to Fontaine, he would speak to Count Myrrdin. In the meantime, he would treat her with the greatest respect. It went against every instinct to hold himself back from her, but he could do it. No one must guess what had passed between them.

It was killing him, though. Not being able to reach out and take her hand; not being able to smile at her. But worst of all was not knowing whether she would refuse him again. The uncertainty was unbearable.

Why won't she have me? Why?

The road lifted and Clare shivered as the Brocéliande closed in on them. Gnarled and twisted oaks stood over the sleeping forest like sentinels. Moss clung to the fissured bark. Dead creeper hung like netting from leafless branches. In spring, when the wood burst into a froth of green, the scratchy, spiky lines of tree and branch would be softened. In winter the Brocéliande had beauty, but it was spare and stark.

As they rode, the land dropped away on one side, and Clare found herself with a bird's-eye view over mile after mile of woodland. There were beech trees and birch trees and coppiced hazels. Holly bushes. The earth was carpeted in fallen leaves—russet, ochre, gold…

Streams rushed in and out, appearing and disappearing without warning. The bubbling water sounded like music. Here, a fountain frothed into a stone basin in a torrent of white water. There, a woodland grove looked as though it had been deserted since time began. Other than the streams, the forest was wrapped in silence. Leaf mast deadened the horses' hoofbeats, and the birds were silent. If someone had told her that the forest of the Brocéliande lay under an enchantment, she would be tempted to believe it.

Fontaine came upon them as suddenly as the streams.

Clare was peering down the hillside, through a black tangle of interwoven branches, when she glimpsed a crenellated wall. Solid. Impregnable. Like the forest, it looked as though it had been there since the dawn of time.

She reined in. 'Fontaine Castle?'

Arthur pulled up beside her and murmured assent. He didn't look at her.

A grey tower pushed up through the trees. When Clare twisted in the saddle, she glimpsed another. And another. Three towers in all and a clutch of other buildings she couldn't quite make out.

A cold sweat broke out on her brow. Fontaine.

'Arthur?' *Please look at me.* 'Arthur?'

Finally, those dark eyes met hers.

'Count Myrrdin might be away,' she said, fumbling nervously with the reins.

Arthur had told her that as Fontaine was but one of Count Myrrdin's holdings, he might not be in residence. Arthur had explained that the young Duchess of Brittany needed good counsel—the Count might be attending Duchess Constance...

'The Lord of Fontaine will be here, never fear. I believe I mentioned that he has become reclusive of late.'

I believe I mentioned... Arthur's tone was chillingly formal. It crossed her mind that he might almost be chastising her for not remembering what he had said.

Clare clenched her teeth, checked that her veil was in place—it wouldn't do to disgrace Count Myrrdin by appearing at his gate dressed like a pedlar—and kicked Swift into a trot. She didn't look Arthur's way again. She didn't need anyone's help, she never had.

Sweat prickled at the back of her neck—she was about to greet the man Arthur swore was her father. She had no high expectations of this meeting. Arthur could be wrong. And even if he were not, the men in her life had either been tyrants like Sandro and his father, or misguided like Geoffrey. Even Arthur, who had said that she might count herself as his friend, was proving to be a disappointment.

Arthur had professed friendship to encourage her to bed him. There was no other explanation. She didn't and wouldn't regret bedding him, it was the loss of his friendship that she regretted— that, and the fact that he had thought to manipulate her by offering it.

The trees fell back as they approached the castle walls and a gatehouse loomed over them. Clare pushed her misgivings to the side and clattered over the drawbridge with her nose in the air.

As Clare rode into the bailey, her blue veil flew out behind her like a knight's pennon.

Arthur knew she was nervous and wished he could help her, but it wasn't his place. It would be best for both Clare and Count Myrrdin if he simply introduced them and stood back. They needed a chance to get to know each other. When that was done, whatever the outcome, Arthur would offer for her.

He was ruefully aware that trust between Clare and the Lord of Fontaine wasn't likely to develop overnight. Which meant that he might not be returning to Troyes for a week or so. It was strange to realise that when he had agreed to be Clare's escort all he had been thinking about was how soon he might return. Much of that urgency had gone. There was nothing to be gained by him speaking up too soon. Count Myrrdin might take against him. He might suspect that Clare and he had between them hatched up some kind of conspiracy to worm their way into his favour.

No, harsh though it seemed—Arthur hadn't missed the dark looks flung his way since they had left St Peter's—Clare must establish a bond with Count Myrrdin before he asked for her hand.

After that, however…

Arthur frowned at the set of Clare's shoulders as she drew rein in the courtyard. She wasn't an easy woman and he wasn't certain she would accept him even if he had Count Myrrdin's blessing. In truth, her rejection at the monastery, particularly after they had given each other such pleasure, had been galling. She baffled him. Surely marriage to him was preferable to marriage with a complete stranger? *We are equals and there is affection between us.*

He would give her time. Time to become more receptive to his offer. With luck she would be pleased to return to Troyes as his wife—she did have friends there.

Arthur thought of Raphael of Reims, standing in for him as Count Henry's Captain. He grimaced. He might not be in a tearing hurry to get back, none the less, he would rather get back sooner than later. It wouldn't do to allow Raphael to get too settled.

Clare was acting as though he had disappointed her. Surely that was promising? If she was disappointed by his seeming neglect, that must mean she had feelings for him. He certainly had feelings for her. He would never forget those nights in St Peter's. Arthur smiled as he watched her dismount and hand her reins to an ageing groom. She looked very much the lady. She was a fast learner. In everything.

Whatever happened here, that would stand her in good stead.

The groom's cheeks were as deeply fissured as the bark of the oaks they had passed on their way. Clare watched his jaw drop when he noticed her eyes. As she turned to make her way up some steps to a studded oak door, the groom led Swift away. Behind her, she heard voices.

'André, you won't believe what I've just seen. A woman's arrived, she has Count Myrrdin's eyes! And her hair—her hair…'

Clare didn't catch the rest. Heart in her mouth, she allowed herself to be shown into the hall.

Dimly she heard Arthur enquire after Count Myrrdin. Her cloak was removed and she was ushered into a side chamber where water was poured into a basin.

'To refresh yourself, *ma dame*,' the girl said, darting little glances at her eyes. 'Before you speak with Count Myrrdin.'

'My thanks.'

When Clare returned to the hall, several women—their simple dress proclaimed them to be servants—had appeared as if from nowhere. They all seemed to find reason to walk close by and they all happened to glance at her eyes. Her hair.

What was wrong with her hair? She resisted the urge to straighten her veil and was shown to a seat by the top table. With her nails digging into her palms, she lowered her gaze and focused on the rushes. She was vaguely aware of Arthur speaking to a man who looked to be one of her father's household knights.

Arthur and the knight left the hall. A door slammed.

Several breaths went by. She peeped up. A couple of men-at-arms had joined the maidservants. Everyone was looking at her. She stiffened her shoulders. *It is not my fault if I am baseborn. It was not my sin.*

The door Arthur had vanished through opened.

A young woman emerged and came slowly towards her. She must be of some importance, for she was richly dressed in a crimson gown and her veil was secured by a silver circlet that had been fashioned to look like rope. The maidservants dropped into quick curtsies as she passed.

Arthur's voice floated through the open doorway, deep and familiar. 'My lord, this is a delicate business and I feel a private conference would be best. My lord—'

'Enough! The wench cannot be mine.'

Clare's stomach lurched. That must be the Lord of Fontaine.

'Count Myrrdin…' Arthur again '…if you would but see her—'

'Sir, you insult me. I have *no* illegitimate children.'

Clare strained to hear more, but the lady in the crimson gown and silver circlet had stopped directly in front of her, frowning. She had grey eyes and hair that was as black as night. 'What is your name?' she asked.

Clare stood up, stomach churning. 'Clare.'

'Clare.' The girl's voice was as soft and clear as a bell. 'I am Countess Francesca.'

'My lady, it is a pleasure to meet you,' Clare said, curtsying. Her mind raced. This was her half-sister, the Comtesse des Iles, and the frown didn't bode well. Was she going to take against her? Did she resent the appearance of an illegitimate half-sister? Clare's misgivings grew as the Countess studied her, lips thinning. 'My lady?'

'Your hair is red,' the Countess said.

What was it about her hair? Clare had become used to the way everyone invariably remarked on her eyes. But her hair? She shrugged and looked over her shoulder at the doorway. To be sure, it would not be pleasant if Countess Francesca took against her, but far more to the point was how Count Myrrdin was reacting.

I will not stay where I am not welcome. What's happening out there?

It was beginning to look as though Arthur might have made an error about her parentage. It certainly sounded as though the Lord of Fontaine had taken great offence. It was natural, she supposed, that the Count should be angry. If she was not his child, he would be offended, and if she was—well, few men liked their sins being paraded before them.

The door flew open and hit the wall with a crack. A man surged through it. Count Myrrdin. He was tall and gaunt and was wearing a long cream tunic, tightly belted at the waist. A band of green swirls ran along the hem. The way the tunic hung off the Count's frame suggested that he had once been a heavier man. He had wiry white hair and a beard that reached halfway down his chest.

Throat dry, Clare dropped into a deep curtsy.

She rose to find herself blinking up at mismatched eyes that were exactly like hers.

'One grey, one green,' she murmured.

Oddly, Count Myrrdin wasn't looking at her eyes. Like his daughter, Countess Francesca, he had fixed on her hair. A gnarled hand reached out—it was shaking—and pushed her veil aside. Catching a coppery strand on his finger, he hooked it out and rubbed it between his fingers. He lifted the strand to his nose, and Clare's stomach cramped.

The Count went as white as his hair. *'Mon Dieu,'* he muttered, swallowing hard. *'Mon Dieu.'*

Hand on his heart, Count Myrrdin flopped on to a bench.

Tears welled in the Countess's eyes. Stumbling back, she picked up her skirts and ran from the hall.

'My lord?' Arthur stepped forwards. 'You are well? Do you need assistance?'

Count Myrrdin's eyes bored into Clare. 'Your name, girl?'

'My lord…' biting her lip, Clare gestured after the Comtesse des Iles '…your daughter is distressed.'

'I'll deal with Francesca later. I take it you have a name?'

'I am called Clare, my lord.'

The mismatched eyes sharpened. 'You were christened Clare?'

'I…I do not know if I was christened, sir. Clare is the name I chose.'

A white eyebrow lifted. 'You chose your own name?'

'Yes, my lord. I…I liked it,' Clare stammered to a halt. She could say no more without revealing that she had chosen the name herself when she had fled Apulia.

'You chose it because you liked it.'

'Yes, my lord.'

The colour came back into Count Myrrdin's cheeks. With a decisive nod, he looked Arthur's way and pushed to his feet. 'Sir Arthur, I apologise for not believing you. You warned me that this is a matter of great delicacy. In truth, you have understated the gravity of it. Follow me to the solar, both of you.'

Count Myrrdin led them into the solar and went to stand with his back to the fire. He waved at Arthur. 'If you please, sir, the door…'

Arthur shut the door.

The solar was large. A semicircle of cushions lay along the window seat of a tall, traceried window. Glass in the upper lights was coloured. Green-and-gold splashes fell across the rush-strewn floor. There was a polished table, a couple of benches, a wall cupboard—Clare had no time to see more.

'I have no illegitimate children,' Count Myrrdin said.

Arthur shifted. 'Few men could be certain of that, my lord.'

'I am, I was faithful to Mathilde.' Count Myrrdin tipped his head to one side, eyeing Clare with such intensity that she felt as though she were being flayed alive. 'I will speak to you in a moment, my dear. First, I have questions for Sir Arthur. Where did you find her?'

'In Troyes, my lord. I saw her at a joust and was immediately struck by her eyes and their re-semblance to yours.'

'I was unaware that we had met, sir.'

'We haven't. You came to Troyes when I was a boy. I saw you talking to Count Henry and I no-ticed your eyes. My lord, everyone was remark-ing on them.'

Count Myrrdin lifted a brow at Clare. 'It's the strangers who stare the most, don't you find?'

The question, and the gentle way in which it was phrased, had something inside Clare feeling as though it had snapped. She swallowed. 'Yes, my lord, they do.'

'Papa, you may call me Papa.'

Arthur felt his throat tighten. This was it then, his mission was accomplished. The official part, at least. Whatever Count Myrrdin might say about being faithful to his wife, he was obvi-ously prepared to accept Clare as his daughter.

'Come here, my dear.'

Count Myrrdin led Clare to the fire. When for

the second time he lifted a coppery strand of hair and brought it to his nose, Arthur's skin chilled. *What is going on?*

'Forgive me, my dear—' The Count's voice cracked. He turned away, fists clenched at his side. When he turned back, his eyes were glassy. He tipped up Clare's chin and slowly, thoroughly, scoured her features. 'My daughter,' he murmured, with much clearing of his throat. 'At last you have come home.'

At last?

Wrapping his arm about her shoulders, Count Myrrdin's face relaxed into a smile. 'My daughter.' He hugged her. 'I searched and searched, but never found you.'

Count Myrrdin kept his arm about her. It was plain he was reluctant to take his eyes from her. He kept fingering her hair. Shaking his head. 'You are made in her image.'

The chill deepened, Arthur recognised it as foreboding and tried to dismiss it. Count Myrrdin was getting on in years, likely he found it hard to recall the sins of his youth. None the less, it was a relief to know that Clare had found her place.

Arthur caught Clare's eyes. 'I told you,' he murmured. 'I told you, there would be no doubt. You are his love child. You are safe now.'

Snowy eyebrows snapped together—despite his advanced age, there was nothing wrong with Count Myrrdin's hearing.

'My love child? You are mistaken, sir, Clare is the image of my Mathilde. She is my daughter, my *legitimate* daughter.'

Arthur felt himself go stock-still. 'Clare is the image of Countess Mathilde?' His voice sounded as though it belonged to someone else.

'What's the matter with you, boy? I told you I have never been unfaithful to Mathilde.'

Clare's mouth fell open. 'My hair,' she muttered, twining a strand round her fingers. 'In the hall, everyone was looking at my hair as much as my eyes. I must have my mother's hair.'

'You do indeed. You have also inherited her delicate features.' Briefly, the Count tore his gaze from his new-found daughter. 'Sir Arthur, you weren't to know, but if you'd seen my Mathilde, you would be in no doubt.' His eyes lost focus as he gazed down the years and his expression softened. And then he was staring dotingly at Clare again.

Arthur felt as though he had been kicked in the guts. His mind was a shambles.

Clare's legitimate? I've taken her maidenhead and she is heiress to a county. If only I'd known. If Clare had met Count Henry, it's possible he would have realised, but she left Troyes without meeting him.

His throat was tight. He cleared it. 'My lord, did Countess Mathilde ever meet Count Henry?'

'They met in Paris, shortly after our wedding. Why?'

Arthur looked bleakly at Clare. 'I am sorry you never met Count Henry, he would have recognised your true status immediately, my lady.'

'My lady,' Clare echoed, in a dazed tone. She gripped her father's sleeve. 'My lord—'

Count Myrrdin made an impatient sound. 'Papa. I am your father and you must address me as such.'

'Papa, how can you be sure?' Clare's voice was little more than a whisper. 'I don't even know when I was born.'

'No matter, I know exactly how old you are, Mathilde only birthed one child. You are eighteen years of age.'

Clare gasped then took a huge breath. 'I am legitimate.'

'Yes, my dear, you are.' Count Myrrdin stroked her cheek. 'Sir Arthur, I grant you Clare has my eyes, but these are Mathilde's features. This is her hair, this is her build. Everything save for the eyes is Mathilde.' His chest heaved. 'Clare is Mathilde reborn. If it weren't for my eyes, Clare is Mathilde come back to life.' He gave her a possessive hug. 'Welcome home, my dear. Welcome to Fontaine.'

Arthur felt hollow, but now he understood why so many people had been staring at her as she'd ridden into the bailey. They had been too far away to mark her eyes—it was the resemblance to Countess Mathilde that had caught their notice. Much as he was pleased by Clare's good fortune, he didn't want her to be the Fontaine heiress. The thought shamed him, but it didn't leave him.

'How is this possible, my lord? How does one *lose* a daughter?'

'That, Sir Arthur, is the burning question. I shall attempt to answer it as speedily as possible.' Count Myrrdin turned back to Clare. 'You are happy to continue being known as Clare, my dear?'

Clare swallowed. 'Yes, my lord.'

'Very well, henceforth you shall be known as Lady Clare de Fontaine, although it's possible you were christened Francesca, shortly after your birth.'

Clare's lips were slightly parted as she listened to her father. Her eyes bright, she was drinking this in. Her brow was clear and her expression was filled with hope and not a little wonder. Already she was changing. She was, Arthur gritted his teeth, moving further and further out of his reach. Finding her father had been one thing, but it was becoming clear that not only had she been born in wedlock, but that her parents had loved each other very much...

Mon Dieu. He was looking at Lady Clare de Fontaine. This changed everything.

The Count's eyes were sad as he continued, 'I

am ashamed to say I cannot recall exactly what happened after your birth. The only thing I remember from that time is that my Mathilde died.'

Clare laid a hand on her father's sleeve. 'She died in childbed?'

A brusque nod answered her. 'I was stumbling about, blind with grief, and when someone thought to snap me out of it, they brought me a baby who had been christened Francesca. Mathilde had always liked that name.' Count Myrrdin covered Clare's hand with his. 'Back then I never thought to question that the child was my daughter. Why should I? I was mourning Mathilde. It was weeks before I truly looked at Francesca and it was some years before I began to suspect that she was not truly my daughter.'

'*Countess Francesca!*' Clare put her hand to her mouth. 'Holy Mother, do you think she knew?'

The Count shook his head. 'No. *No.* Francesca was presented to me as a babe-in-arms, she is innocent of any deceit.'

'My lord…Papa, I think she has realised now. Did you see how she ran from the hall?'

The white head shook. 'Can't say that I did.'

'Papa, I thought your dau—I thought Countess Francesca didn't wish to acknowledge me, but I was wrong. She's distraught—someone should go after her.'

She stepped towards the door, but the Count

stayed her with his hand. 'We do nothing rash.'
He looked to Arthur. 'Sir, I may rely on your
discretion?'

'Of course, my lord.' Arthur frowned. 'Are you
certain Countess Francesca is innocent in this?'

'I am. I've watched her grow up. She's a sweet
girl—I've learned to love her.' He smiled at Clare.
'Francesca might not be my daughter in blood—
please don't misunderstand me, my dear—but I
feel it's fair to say that she has become my daughter by adoption. Your arrival here will have turned
her world upside down. She has certain expectations and I would like to minimise her distress. I
shall not abandon her, of course.'

'I understand,' Arthur said.

'And you, my dear, do you understand?'

'I understand, Papa.' A tear formed on Clare's
eyelashes, and she cleared her throat. 'You are not
abandoning her.'

'How could I? Such a sweet child.' Count
Myrrdin sighed. 'Over the years, it dawned on
me that she might not be mine. I couldn't see
anything of Mathilde in her. Or of myself for that
matter. It's hard to be sure of these things when
children are small, but as Francesca grew...' he
shrugged '...by the time I was certain it was too
late, for I loved her. I made enquiries at the village, discreet enquiries, in case Francesca should
come to hear, but if anyone knew anything, they
kept quiet. There was no trace of you and all I

had was a gut full of suspicions that could never be proved.'

Clare is legitimate.

Arthur's fist clenched. He couldn't offer for her, not the legitimate daughter of a count. A dazzling political alliance would be open to her—he couldn't stand in her way. He was dimly aware of Count Myrrdin asking her how she was brought up, but he barely heard him, he was staring at Clare's mouth.

I will never kiss her again.

Chapter Ten

'You had no family?' The Count looked appalled. Whatever Clare had said to him had shocked him. 'Clare, you must have had a family—how did you survive?'

Arthur longed to know what was going through her mind. *Lady Clare*. Lord, if he was having difficulty accepting that she was Count Myrrdin's legitimate daughter, it was unimaginable what it must be like for her. She must feel completely adrift. He held his breath as he waited for her answer. He had been trying to get her to open up to him for weeks, maybe the Count would have more success.

'My l—Papa, I am sorry, but I don't wish to talk about it.'

'You fear chastisement,' the Count said gently.

'You need not. Like Francesca, you were an innocent.'

'Papa, didn't you say that Francesca was presented to you as a baby?'

'That is so.' The skin around Count Myrrdin's mismatched eyes crinkled as he gave a lopsided smile. 'Believe me, I have invented dozens of theories over the years. All of which are plausible, but so far none have been proven. The exchange could have taken place at any time in your first few months. Eighteen years ago, I was out of my mind with grief. If you had been stolen, the nurse might well have feared punishment. She might have found another baby and put her in your place.'

'Papa, where's the nurse today?'

Count Myrrdin lifted his hand from Clare's long enough to rub the bridge of his nose. 'She died many years ago.' He sighed. 'We may never know the full truth—what is important to me is that you have come home.'

Arthur caught the Count's gaze. 'My lord, over time you may yet learn why Clare was taken. By now everyone in the castle will know of Clare's— of *Lady* Clare's—homecoming. Word will have surely spread to the village. If anyone in Fontaine has been lying low in the hope that this secret never comes to light, they will realise that everything has changed. You may yet learn what happened.' Two pairs of mismatched eyes looked

at him. 'Count Myrrdin, I should like to make enquiries on Lady Clare's behalf.'

The moment the words left his lips, Arthur
wished he could call them back. What was he saying? There was no point him remaining in Fontaine any longer than he had to. Since he couldn't
offer for her, he ought to get back to his captaincy
in Champagne. He should be watching his back
there. Sir Raphael was all too eager to step into
his shoes…

Thankfully, Count Myrrdin made a negative
gesture. 'There will be no enquiries, not until
I have arranged matters satisfactorily with my
daughter—my other daughter—Francesca.'

'Very good, sir.'

'Now, my dear…' the Count drew Clare to the
window seat '…I should like to learn all about
you. Where have you been? Why has it taken you
so many years to find your way home?'

Clare shifted. 'I…I grew up in Apulia, Papa.'

'Apulia? What the devil were you doing in
Apulia?'

Clare spread her hands and Arthur held himself very still. These were the very questions he
wanted answering and thus far she had avoided
every one.

'I have no memory of Brittany, Papa. The
Duchy was new to me when I rode in with Arth—
Sir Arthur.'

Count Myrddin's eyes narrowed. 'What is your earliest memory? What happened in Apulia?'

'I...'

Clare's gaze drifted sideways. She looked so miserable that even though Arthur wanted her answer, he found himself racking his brains for a way to deflect the Count's questions. She beat him to it.

'Papa, tell me. What's to be done about Countess Francesca?'

'Francesca.' Grimacing, the Count ran his hand round the back of his neck. 'That is a pretty mess and no mistake. As you doubtless know, Francesca is married to Tristan le Beau, Comte des Iles. They both believe her to be my heiress and, until today, so she was. She will have to be tactfully handled. As will Count Tristan.' Sighing, Count Myrrdin took Clare by the shoulders and looked deep into her eyes. 'Rest assured, my dear, you will be fully acknowledged.'

Clare's eyes searched his. 'I am happy to wait, Papa. This is all very...sudden.'

Arthur found his stomach clenching on Clare's behalf. He could read her thoughts as though she had spoken aloud—she feared her father would change his mind. And then it seemed that Arthur wasn't the only one who could read her, for Count Myrrdin smiled and shook his head at her.

'Clare, my blood flows in your veins, *you* are my rightful daughter. You will be acknowledged and you will be restored to your rightful place. But we must tread delicately. I shall have to consider what best to do. Francesca will have a dowry, of course, but both she and Count Tristan have had certain…expectations. The Comte des Iles has been steward of Fontaine for the past two years, preparing for the time when he takes the reins.'

Clare bit her lip. 'I will meet him today?'

'Not today, he's away in Rennes on the Duchess's business.'

Clare let her breath out on a sigh. 'Papa, Countess Francesca did look distressed when she ran outside…'

'I shall speak to her later. She won't have gone far.'

As he watched Clare with her father, Arthur realised he should take his leave. They needed time to get to know each other. And he needed time to think. Clare was heiress to a county. Reference to the complications that her appearance had caused was a stark reminder that he could no longer offer for her. Lady Clare de Fontaine would be expected to make a political marriage— Fontaine was an important Breton holding. The man who married her would need the agreement and blessing of the Duchess and her chief adviser, Roland of Dinan. And then there was the King of England, who was overlord of Brittany. The King of France would also have to be notified…

Count Myrrdin would never permit a mere knight to marry his daughter. Lady Clare de Fontaine was beyond his reach.

Arthur's next thought had him staring blindly at the green-and-yellow glass in the window. *Clare's husband will expect her to be a maid when she goes to her marriage bed...*

'Excuse me, my lord,' he said. 'I shall leave you to get to know each other.'

He really needed to think.

The rest of the afternoon passed as if in a dream. Clare felt dizzy with her good fortune. It couldn't last—surely she would awaken and her old life would rush back at her?

But, no. Here was her father—a father who was giving every sign of being the sort of father she had given up hope existed. And with Arthur's help she had found him. Count Myrrdin seemed to be loving. Kind.

However, she soon noticed that Count Myrrdin was slightly eccentric. From time to time, he was in the habit of falling silent and gazing off into the distance. Clare could deal with a little eccentricity, though—she could deal with anything. For today she had learned that, contrary to her long-held beliefs, she had not come unwanted into the world. She had not been abandoned by parents careless of how their daughter would make her way through life. *I am no longer alone.*

Despite her father's dreaminess, his concern for her seemed genuine. She and Count Myrrdin didn't know each other yet, but the future was rich with possibility. And responsibility. She wanted to pinch herself. *I am no longer alone.*

There were problems, naturally. The most obvious being Countess Francesca...

'Papa?'

'Hmm?'

'I should like to think of Countess Francesca as my sister. Do you think she will be agreeable if I address her as such?'

Count Myrrdin smiled and patted her hand. 'I hope so. I will seek her out shortly and talk to her.' His expression clouded. 'Clare, I gave her a manor as part of her dowry, I should like her to keep it.'

'Of course she must keep it!'

Count Myrrdin's gaze sharpened. 'I should warn you, the manor at St Méen is traditionally held by the Counts of Fontaine. By rights it should devolve to you upon your marriage.'

Clare shook her head. 'You gave it to Countess Francesca, you can't take it away again.'

'That is generous. Perhaps you should wait until you see it.'

'I won't change my mind. The Countess must keep her manor.'

Count Myrrdin nodded. He gazed into the fire, and the lines on his face deepened. 'It's

Francesca's husband rather than Francesca who's likely to present the greatest challenge. Count Tristan is ambitious, but whilst he is fond of her, there's no doubt that he married her for her inheritance. An inheritance that is no longer hers.'

Clare didn't know what to say. 'I feel dreadful about this.'

Count Myrrdin stroked his beard, the movement jerky and abstracted. 'Thankfully, affection seems to be growing between them. Certainly it is on Francesca's part. I am hopeful that her husband has had time to grow fond of her, because if he has not...'

'How long have they been married?'

'Two years. They wed when Francesca was sixteen.'

'Do they have children?' Clare held her breath while she waited for the answer. She hated to think that she might be the cause of a family breaking apart.

'Not as yet.'

'You fear that Count Tristan might seek an annulment?'

'He might.' Her father heaved a sigh. 'If you had come home at the beginning of their marriage, it's my belief he would have done. As I say, he is ambitious. Proud. I shall send an envoy to Rennes to explain what has happened.'

'The Count leaves Fontaine often?'

'He acts as my steward most of the time, but

he has his own lands to administer. He also keeps a watchful eye on what's happening abroad. He's an excellent steward. He soon learned his way about Fontaine.'

'It must have helped him to think that he would one day rule over it.' She bit her lip, there was so much to think about.

'What's the matter?'

'Papa, it's distressing to realise that my good fortune comes at so great a cost and it grieves me that the Count and Countess des Iles are the ones who'll be paying the price.'

Count Myrrdin's face went hard. 'Never say that. *Never.* My dear, *you* are my true-born daughter. Nothing can alter that. I won't abandon Francesca, but of the two of you, you are legitimate. Much as I love Francesca, nothing alters the fact that you and I are flesh and blood. Understand me?'

'Yes, Papa.'

Count Myrrdin gave a little grunt. 'Enough of this, where were we?'

'You were saying that Count Tristan is an excellent steward.'

'Ah, yes. My dear, Francesca and her husband will not be impoverished—as I say, Count Tristan has lands. It has suited him recently to focus on Brittany, which is why from time to time he joins Duchess Constance's entourage at Rennes.'

Clare stared at her father, doubts coiled inside

her like snakes. Count Tristan didn't sound like a man who would relinquish Fontaine without a fight.

Hands on his thighs, Count Myrrdin pushed to his feet. 'Our Duchess is a child and the English king bears watching. King Henry puts his interests before ours, every time. I will explain at length later. There will be much to learn. In the meantime, it would give me pleasure to show you round the castle.'

'And Countess Francesca? We will speak to her?'

That vague look returned. 'Yes, yes, naturally we shall speak to her. Now…' Count Myrrdin offered her his arm '…if you would be pleased to accompany me, my dear, there are people you must meet.'

For the next couple of hours, Count Myrrdin was as good as his word, but they didn't see Countess Francesca. Or Arthur for that matter.

Clare's head was whirling. She was longing to talk to Arthur. What would he think of her rise in status? She was not illegitimate as they had thought, she was legitimate. A lady! How was she going to cope? Arthur had himself come up through the ranks, he would surely have advice.

She entered the great hall on her father's arm. Some young women were setting out a cloth on the long table, preparing for supper. Neither Countess Francesca nor Arthur were in sight.

Count Myrrdin beckoned one of the women over. 'Enora, if you please…?'

Enora bobbed into a curtsy. 'My lord?'

'Clare, this is Enora. Enora, this is my daughter, my *true-born* daughter, Lady Clare de Fontaine.'

Enora curtsied at Clare and the whispers raced round the hall.

'Lady Clare de Fontaine.'

'Did he say de Fontaine?'

'She's his daughter?'

'He said true-born. Legitimate.'

And, inevitably, 'What about Countess Francesca?'

Enora's dark eyes met Clare's. 'My lady,' she murmured.

Count Myrrdin cleared his throat. 'Enora, do you care to try your hand at new skills?'

Enora's eyes widened. 'What sort of skills, my lord?'

'Many years ago, your mother was my wife's maid. Do you think you could assist my daughter in the same way?'

'Oh, my lord…' Enora clasped her hands together and gave a wide smile '…I would *love* to be Lady Clare's maid.'

Count Myrrdin turned back to Clare. 'Well, Daughter, will you take Enora as your maid?'

Clare saw Arthur next at supper, but she couldn't catch his eye. She had been seated on the dais next to her father and Arthur was at the far end of one of the trestles, with the men from the guardhouse. He looked at home with the soldiers, she thought, as she watched him laughing at some witticism of her father's Captain.

Briefly, that dark head turned her way—at least she thought it did, but she must have been mistaken, for he immediately hunched his shoulder and leaned his elbow on the trestle in such a way that his gaze fell elsewhere. Her heart ached. Arthur was avoiding her. Truth be told, he was acting as though he barely knew her. It seemed impossible. Was this the same man who had made love to her so tenderly?

He offered me marriage—won't he look my way?

As she glanced again at his averted head, the answer hit her like a blow to the belly. Arthur was concerned for her reputation—he was trying to protect her. He'd been holding himself aloof since they'd left St Peter's and that had been before he'd known she was legitimate. He would be doubly careful now.

I am Lady Clare de Fontaine, the legitimate daughter of a count.

She stiffened her spine. Life was changing beyond all recognition. There were bound to be difficulties, but this—Arthur's distance— was especially hard to swallow. She must face it though—the world would have certain expectations about how she ought to behave. There would be rules and she must learn them if she was to thrive here.

Her chest still ached and she groped for her goblet. Surely it shouldn't hurt so much? Arthur was concerned for her reputation, that was why he was keeping his distance. He would surely be more open with her in private. Her heart lifted—yes, if they met in private, he wouldn't refuse to speak to her. In private, everything might be easy between them, as it had been in at St Peter's. She must see him on his own, as soon as possible.

She stared blindly into her wine. *I am a lady.* It was hard to absorb. There was one sense in which her title was surely meaningless, a sense in which, although she had found her family, she was still alone.

Sandro. The charges laid against me in Apulia.

Those charges had not gone away. She'd learned she was a count's daughter, yet she felt no more able to discuss them today than she had yesterday. Arthur was the only person in whom she would consider confiding, but his position as Captain of the Guardian Knights made that impossible. No, as far as the accusations levelled against her, her change in status meant nothing. But these thoughts were too bleak for today. She had found her father! She had a family...

Resolutely, she steered her mind in another direction. Where was Countess Francesca? She must speak to her. All afternoon, she had been watching out for her.

Her father touched her arm. He was holding out an eating knife with an elaborately tooled blue sheath. 'Daughter, I should like you to accept this.'

She took the knife. The handle was ivory and a Celtic pattern swirled on its surface. The blade gleamed razor-sharp in the candlelight—with its blue sheath and carved handle, it was fit for a princess. 'Thank you, Papa, it's beautiful.'

'You will share a trencher with me.'

Clare swallowed. Everyone was staring at her and she wasn't used to it. Slaves were invisible, ladies were not. What did she know about how a lady was meant to behave? Sitting on the high dais next to her father was beyond her wildest dreams. Yet here she was. After a heart-stopping moment when her mind went blank, it came to her that she was not entirely ignorant. Her father was doing her much honour by sharing his trencher with her. And as an overt signal to his retainers that he had acknowledged her as his heiress, it was a master stroke.

'Thank you, Papa. Is Countess Francesca not eating with us?'

Count Myrrdin beckoned for a manservant. 'Dréo, have you seen Francesca?'

'No, my lord.'

'Send to her chamber, will you? I would like her to join us.'

The servant bowed. Dréo was soon back, returning as Clare was trying not to look down the trestle towards where that broad back and dark head were turned so firmly against her.

Her father was offering her venison. 'From our own chase, my dear,' the Count said. 'Do try some.'

'My lord?' Dréo bowed. When he stared blank-faced at the tablecloth, Clare braced herself—she knew exactly what he was going to say. 'My lord, Countess Francesca is no longer at Fontaine.'

Count Myrrdin's fingers stilled on the venison. 'Don't be a fool, man, of course she's at Fontaine.'

'No, my lord. I've spoken to Sergeant Léry. The Countess rode out this afternoon.'

'What?' Count Myrrdin made an impatient noise. 'What do you say?'

Dréo's gaze flickered briefly to Clare. 'It was shortly after Lady Clare rode in.'

'Hell and damnation.' Count Myrrdin's knife clattered to the table. 'I thought Francesca had more sense than that. I take it she took an escort?'

'Yes, my lord, two grooms. Her maid went, too.'

Count Myrrdin squinted at a darkened window. 'The light's gone, it's too late to go after her. Did she say where she went?'

'Yes, my lord. She told Sergeant Léry she was going to the manor at St Méen.'

'Why in hell didn't the sergeant mention this earlier?'

Dréo kept his eyes firmly on Count Myrrdin's trencher. 'The Countess asked the sergeant not to mention her departure until you were about to retire.'

'I see. Thank you, Dréo, that is all.'

Clare waited, half-expecting that her father would summon a guard and order him to follow Countess Francesca, but he did no such thing. Instead he fell into an abstraction, staring moodily at a pattern in the weave of the cloth and absently picking meat from their trencher.

'Papa?'

There was no response, not from her father. However, one of the household knights, Sir Brian, looked across. 'My lady, if I may offer some advice?'

'Please do.'

'Best leave your father be for tonight,' the knight said, quietly. 'Count Myrrdin is not as young as he was and your arrival is bound to have kicked up the dust.'

'He is unwell?' Clare shot her father an anxious look. She had only just found him, she didn't want to lose him again.

'No, no,' Sir Brian hastened to assure her. 'It is just that he has these…spells from time to time.'

'Odd silences? Moments of dreaminess?'

'Yes, my lady, just so. He will be himself again shortly. My advice is to say nothing too taxing until tomorrow.'

Clare nodded and speared herself a piece of venison. She chewed thoughtfully. What should she do about Countess Francesca? The poor woman must be in some distress to have ridden out of Fontaine so abruptly. Her father should have realised, he should have sought Francesca out, if only to relieve the poor girl's mind.

Was it possible that her father's so-called 'spells' masked a deep malaise? Clare hoped she was wrong, but given he professed real feelings for the Countess, he really should have made some attempt to talk to her this afternoon. Surely a few words of reassurance wouldn't have been too taxing? Something was wrong, very wrong.

'Sir Brian?'

'My lady?'

Count Myrrdin looked as though he was in another world. He was tracing arabesques in the damask tablecloth with the hilt of his knife. Clare didn't want to risk upsetting him by mentioning Countess Francesca, but she couldn't bear it if the Countess felt she had been driven from her home. Since Count Myrrdin was obviously less capable than he had first appeared, it was up to her to try to help. She must speak to her adopted sister. Soon.

The Countess must be made to see that Count Myrrdin loved her and that she would always be welcome at Fontaine.

She lowered her voice. 'How far is it to the manor at St Méen, sir?'

'About twelve miles, my lady,' Sir Brian said, reaching for the bread.

'So it would take two or three hours to reach it?'

'On horseback? Yes, my lady, that would be about right.'

Her shoulders drooped. 'Then it's too late to send someone after her this evening.'

Sir Brian set the bread aside. 'I should think so. Particularly with the snow.'

'It's snowing?'

'Yes, my lady, it started as night fell.'

Clare had been given a bedchamber in one of the towers and a whole bed to herself. It was odd to wake alone next morning. She yawned and stretched, luxuriating in the feel of the clean linen sheets, of the softness of a mattress filled entirely with down…

Her father might have failed to reassure his adopted daughter of her continuing welcome at Fontaine, but not only had he given Clare a personal maid, he had also insisted that a host of gowns be made for her. When Clare had explained that she already had several new gowns, Count Myrrdin had brushed that aside. Enora had been taken with her into a chamber where the walls were lined with brightly painted clothes-chests. A gown in topaz-coloured silk had been found in one of them. It fitted her exactly. Clare was shown some green brocade from Thessaly and several lengths of English worsted even finer than the wool she had bought at Arthur's behest.

'This green looks warm,' she had said.

'Have it,' Count Myrrdin had said. 'It will make a good cloak.'

'I already have a cloak.'

'You will need more than one.' Count Myrrdin had looked at Enora. 'I want nothing but the best for my daughter. Make her whatever she likes.'

'Yes, my lord.'

With that, Count Myrrdin had swept out, white tunic trailing after him. 'I shall see you in the hall later, my dear.'

'Yes, Papa.'

Yesterday, Clare had been so overwhelmed she hadn't given enough thought to her father's strange moments of distraction. This morning, however, she lay in bed, thinking. Remembering Sir Brian's warning: *...your arrival is bound to have kicked up the dust...he has these...spells...*

It would seem that whilst her father appeared physically fit, that same might not be said of his mind.

She must speak to Countess Francesca. She would know what to do.

She flung back the bedcovers, snatched up a shawl and padded to the lancet. Her breath misted the air. She tugged open the shutter, wiped frost flowers from the glass with her fist and peered out.

The sky was murky and the light poor. Snow-flakes were falling in thick flurries and every-thing was white—the castle walls, the bailey, even the water in the troughs. Unfamiliar as she was with Fontaine, the snow-bleached land-scape looked entirely alien. Tree branches were fat with snow and she could no longer see the road through the forest.

A blur of green caught her eyes. A hooded man—it was Arthur, she knew that cloak—was crossing the bailey. She watched him go into the stables, then quickly turned to dress herself. If she hurried, she might catch him. She wanted to talk with him—she would welcome his advice regarding her new role in life—and the stables might be just the place. With only the stable boys and horses to hear them, Arthur would surely lose his new-found formality.

She would start by asking him to escort her to St Méen to see Countess Francesca.

Chapter Eleven

'Arthur? Sir Arthur?' Clare stepped out of a biting wind and into the relative warmth of the stable. Steel was in the end stall and she could hear the quiet murmur of conversation—Arthur was talking to one of the grooms.

Surprised brown eyes turned her way. 'Lady Clare?'

Hugging her cloak to her, Clare went towards him. 'Good morning, sir. I've come to ask a favour of you.'

'My lady?'

My lady. Clare felt a chill that had nothing to do with winter. 'Arthur, I'd like to ride to a nearby manor and I need an escort. Would you accompany me?'

Arthur drew his head back, frowning. 'How near is this manor?'

'I'm told it's a couple of hours away.'

The dark head shook. 'I don't think you should be riding in this weather, my lady. Not even for half an hour. I am sure Count Myrrdin's men will agree with me.' Arthur nodded a dismissal at the groom. 'Thank you, Marc, that will be all.'

'Please, Arthur, I wouldn't ask if it wasn't important.'

He folded his arms across his chest. 'I fail to see what could be so important that you would risk riding off into the teeth of a snowstorm—'

'Countess Francesca left Fontaine shortly after we arrived. I need to speak to her.'

Arthur propped a broad shoulder against the end wall. 'She's upset and you want to make amends.'

Clare took a step nearer, looking earnestly up at him. 'Arthur, you must see it's important.' She hesitated, unwilling to say anything that might show her father in a poor light. 'I want her to understand that I didn't intend that she should be…'

'Disinherited?'

Briefly, she closed her eyes. 'Put like that, it sounds terrible.'

He shrugged. 'Well, whether or not it's what you intended, that is the result. She's not likely to be dancing with joy.'

Clare glared at him. 'You make it sound as though I planned to take her place all along and you know that's not true. Whose fault is it I came?' She poked a finger at him. 'If you hadn't gone to Count Henry, I'd not be here at all.'

His face hardened. 'You regret coming?'

'Of course not, I'm thrilled to meet my father.' She sighed. 'I'm sorry, Arthur, I'm pleased to be here and I have no business blaming you. It's just that I never dreamed that my life could be so transformed. Arthur, I'm legitimate!'

His mouth twisted. 'Makes quite a difference, doesn't it?'

'It makes no difference to who I am, as you of all people will appreciate. But I certainly didn't expect it. And you have to admit it makes difficulties—Countess Francesca is but one. If my father holds true to his word, I am his heiress. Arthur...' she smiled '...you're wearing your stony look and I wish you wouldn't. I need your counsel. I have no experience at playing the lady. I would like to ask, to beg, if need be, that you delay your return to Champagne.'

'My lady, it's my intention to leave as soon as the storm clears.'

Outside, the sound of shovels scraping against stone spoke of the battle the grooms were waging to keep the bailey clear of snow.

'That may not be for some days. Arthur, please stay. At least for a little while. I need your counsel.'

'Your father will tell you everything you need to know.'

'I wish I could be sure of that,' Clare murmured. 'There are times when my father is somewhat…vague.'

'There's bound to be a steward here, you can ask him.'

She put her hand on his forearm. He seemed intent on keeping a wall between them, yet surely it was unnecessary—the groom had gone, they were the only people here. 'Arthur, don't you remember? Countess Francesca's husband is steward of Fontaine.'

'Ouch.'

'I am sure Count Tristan is honourable, my father wouldn't have chosen him to marry Francesca otherwise, but I doubt very much that he will take kindly to having to explain the management of this estate to the woman who is snatching it from his grasp. Arthur, I really need your help. You will understand the challenges ahead of me.'

'Will I?'

'Don't be obtuse. Arthur, I'm not blind to your achievements. You were not born to knighthood—you have risen through the ranks the hard way. You must be able to help me.' She frowned, as a hazy memory snapped into focus. 'You were Count Lucien's steward, were you not?'

He gave a brusque nod. 'I was steward at Ravenshold before I joined the Guardians.'

She smiled brightly. 'There you are then, you are just the man I need.'

'Clare…*Lady* Clare, I have to return to Troyes.'

'Why?'

Clare's question knocked Arthur back and it was a moment before he found a response.

Because, my innocent, you have moved beyond my reach. You are an heiress, and I cannot bear to sit in your father's hall, watching you from afar. I ache to hold you, to feel the warmth of your skin next to mine. I want to learn every inch of your body. I want the scent of lavender to be more than mere memory; I want it winding through my senses at every dusk and dawn. I want to kiss that curving mouth, to…

'Cl…my lady, you know I am sworn to Count Henry. I must return to Troyes.'

'But, Arthur—'

'I have given my word, on sacred oath. I am Captain of the Guardians.'

'You were sworn to Count Lucien, yet you serve Count Henry. Couldn't you swear to my fath—?'

'No!' Arthur softened his voice and laid his hand on her kidskin glove. 'Clare, you must see I have to return.'

Mismatched eyes gazed up at him. She drew in a deep breath. 'I understand. Your commitments in Troyes are important.' Her gaze sharpened. 'I think there is more to it than that.'

'More?'

Her shoulders lifted. 'It is merely an impression.

You were most reluctant to leave Troyes. Something pulls you back, something you feel you must face.'

Arthur stared. 'How on earth do you know that?'

She smiled. 'What is it, Arthur? Tell me.'

'It... I...' Inexplicably, her insight made him want to pull her into his arms and kiss her senseless. 'It concerns my humble birth. You put your finger on the nub of it when you said I was not born to my position. Unfortunately, Troyes is full of knights who were.'

Clare made an impatient sound. 'Noble knights with legitimacy on their side are ten a penny, I expect.'

The scorn in her voice made him smile. It was almost as though she could see no difference between him and a knight born into the nobility. She would soon learn. It was early days for her at Fontaine, but it was likely Count Myrrdin would find a well-bred knight for her to take to husband. Or maybe a count. The Lord of Fontaine had found a count for the girl he had brought up as his, and he would hardly do otherwise with the daughter who was his true flesh and blood.

Arthur didn't want to be around to watch *that*.

'As you say, they are ten a penny. And Count Henry has chosen one, Sir Raphael de Reims, to act as Captain of the Guardians whilst I am away.'

'You fear he will supplant you.' It was not a question.

'I need to watch my back.' Arthur stared at the

wall behind her. 'I am concerned lest Count Henry should decide that Sir Raphael is the better man.'

'He won't do that.'

Her calm certainty stole the words from his lips and he stared at her as, with a shy, tantalising smile, she turned away.

Instinctively, he put out a hand to draw her back. 'I shall stay for a few days, my lady, if that is of use.' He shrugged. 'The snow. And Ivo—he's too valuable to risk with the lung fever.'

She gave him a warm look, a look that made Arthur forget they were standing in an icy stable with their breath forming clouds about them. 'Arthur, you can't fool me, you are fond of that boy.'

'That I am.' Realising he had retained her hand, he released it and shoved back his hair. 'My lady, if it pleases you, when the weather eases I will escort you to this manor. But after that, I will return to Troyes.'

Leaning forwards, she went up on her toes and pressed a kiss to his cheek. Heat shivered through him.

'Thank you, Arthur, you are a true friend. I know my father would grant me another escort, but I so much prefer it to be you. Everyone... *everything* here is so strange.'

Arthur cleared his throat and tried not to look at her mouth. He couldn't stop thinking about the sort of deep, drugging kiss he really wanted. 'It will take some getting used to, I am sure.'

'That is an understatement.'

Arthur swallowed. That small kiss had been a revelation. It had been offered in a casual manner and had felt like a kiss of genuine affection, but he had no real idea what she was thinking. She was smiling that innocent smile at him—apparently completely unaware that he burned for an altogether different sort of kiss. A real one. He wanted to kiss her in the way he had kissed her in the dormitory at the monastery. As a lover. Which reminded him...there was something he must have out with her and it was likely to prove awkward.

I took her innocence. She must not suffer for it.

'My lady?'

Some of the light went out of her expression. 'I prefer it when you call me Clare.'

'My lady,' he repeated, firmly. 'I have been thinking about what happened between us at the monastery and have come to a decision. I must tell your father.'

Her breath caught. Small fingers reached for his tunic. 'Not about what we...that you and I... Arthur, *no*! You cannot be serious.'

'I am. Clare, you must see that I...that we... It shouldn't have happened. Your father is bound to find a husband for you and when he does... Clare, you should go to him chaste.'

Her chin jutted out. 'Arthur, I explained, I have no wish to marry, so it's irrelevant.'

He shook his head. 'Clare, as heiress of Fontaine, you must marry. Your father will insist upon it.'

'Father will do as I say.' She spoke forcefully, but Arthur could see she was trying to convince herself.

He squeezed her arm. 'You might persuade your father round to your way of thinking, but believe me, you won't persuade the English king.'

'King Henry?' She blinked. 'What has my marriage to do with King Henry?'

He took a deep breath. She really was such an innocent. 'Brittany is a Duchy and King Henry is overlord. He will not permit a large county in Brittany to be left in the hands of a woman.'

'You would put me in bondage?'

His eyebrows shot up. 'In bondage? I merely state the obvious. Fontaine is a rich county, it needs a strong hand on the reins.'

'I've already told you, I've no wish to marry.'

'Clare, it's inevitable.'

'Arthur, I will never marry. Not you, not anyone.' With an angry flurry of skirts and a swirl of her cloak, she stalked from the stable.

Arthur's finger lifted to his cheek, where her kiss burned on his skin.

Following their meeting in the stables, Clare didn't speak to Arthur for almost a week and, with little to occupy him until the roads were clear, her parting shot rang in his mind. *I will never marry.*

More snow fell. The roads were choked with it, and they were cut off from the outside world. The forest of Brocéliande was a dazzling white. Sounds were muted. Icicles ringed the castle battlements—a glittering garland that sparkled in the sun. One day it began to thaw and the soft drip of icicles was everywhere. Dark puddles formed in the shadows under the walls. Then it snowed again and another garland of ice ran around the castle walls.

I will never marry.

Oddly, Clare's vehemence had lifted a weight from Arthur's mind. At the monastery, she had rejected his offer of marriage with such speed, it had felt like a slap in the face. The sting of her rejection had lingered and Arthur had felt insulted. Hurt. Befuddled by a powerful mixture of desire and need, he hadn't been thinking straight.

But supposing Clare's objection hadn't been to him personally, but to the sacrament of marriage?

I will never marry. She spoke with such conviction. Why? It was almost as though she was afraid of marriage, but how could that be? Most women longed for it. They spent their days hinting, begging or cajoling men into it. Even Gabrielle, who made no bones about how she made her living, had dropped so many hints Arthur's way that he had been forced to warn her that if the hints continued, he would seek his pleasure elsewhere.

Clare's antipathy to marriage was rare, but not, in his experience, unique. His mother's face rose up in his mind. Like Clare, his mother's fear of marriage had been strong, yet she'd been blissfully content living in sin with his father.

Arthur had been a boy when his mother died. He'd often wondered about his parents' unsanctioned relationship. When he'd questioned them, they'd refused to explain, but Arthur had overheard them talking from time to time, and he'd been able to piece together enough to realise that his mother must have been already married when she'd met his father.

Her husband had mistreated her and, when Arthur's father had offered her sanctuary, she had been quick to move to the house by the forge. His parents had been happy despite their illicit relationship and despite the taunting of some of the townsfolk. They'd called her a slut. A whore. His mother had been deaf to the insults, insults which had stopped only when Miles won the approval of Count Henry and was given his spurs.

His mother had avoided remarriage because of her husband's violence. What had given Clare her loathing of marriage?

While Arthur waited for the road back to Champagne to emerge from beneath its covering of snow and ice, he vowed to find out. It didn't prove easy. As one wintry day followed another, it became obvious that Clare was so angered by his remarks concerning marriage that she was avoiding him. He began to think that he had dreamed she had asked him to escort her to St Méen.

One evening he saw her warming her hands by the fire in the hall, her maid at her side. She left the hall as he entered.

Coincidence? Possibly.

The next day, he tried a more direct approach, going up to her in the bailey. She spoke to him but briefly.

'Excuse me, sir, I must speak to the cook.' With that, she slipped into the bakehouse, leaving him staring at the door.

Another coincidence? Not likely.

When Arthur next saw her, she was standing by the drawbridge, talking to Sergeant Léry. He simply raised an eyebrow at her and he knew she had seen him because she stuck her nose in the air. She made no move to join him.

Another time he was leaving the stables, when a movement up on the wall-walk caught his eye, the flutter of a green veil. Clare was promenading along the battlements on her father's arm. Given she wouldn't speak to him, it was obvious she had changed her mind about accepting his escort when she went to St Méen. His mention of marriage had scared her off.

She fears marriage. Why? It's not the act of

*love that she fears, she was eager enough to bed
with me. What is she afraid of?*

Arthur had been half-hoping she had forgotten
his impulsive offer of marriage. It hadn't seemed
impulsive at the time, it had seemed a perfectly
logical solution to many dilemmas, not least of
which was that he liked the woman and hadn't
wanted to part from her. But that had been before
he had known the truth of her birth.

Like it or not, Clare would have to marry.
Count Myrrdin had acknowledged her, so her
marriage would be dynastic. The King of England would approve it and it would be accompanied by much fanfare.

What would her husband do when he realised
she was not a virgin? Clare wouldn't be the first
noblewoman to have lost her innocence before
her marriage, but it could cause problems. Fortunately, her father's estates were extensive and
would likely sweeten the blow to her husband's
pride. None the less, Arthur couldn't shake the
guilt.

Nor could he, as he watched her from afar,
shake his desire for her. A desire which burned
in his veins. Illicit. Dangerous. In one sense, they
remained strangers. In another, he knew her intimate secrets. He'd never forget the warmth of
her slender body as she tucked herself against
him in sleep. He'd never forget the softness of
her hair. He knew the small sounds she made

when the pleasure took her. Her scent—he held in a groan—summers would never be the same, lavender would always remind him of her. As he watched the progress of that green veil as it moved along the wall-walk, he sighed. It seemed that once again, he had misread her. Clare—*Lady* Clare—was adapting to life at Fontaine.

The sooner he was gone, the better he would feel.

Arthur was saddling Steel, preparing to assess the state of the roads, when the light in the stable dimmed. A groom had entered and Clare was standing in the doorway, pulling on her gloves. Arthur held back a frown—was she planning on riding before they knew the highways were clear? She was wearing another cloak, a green one, and her veil matched it. Her veil also—Arthur's frown deepened—hid that glorious red hair.

'Good day, Sir Arthur,' she said, with a polite smile. 'Where's Ivo? Are you leaving without him?'

Buckling Steel's girth, Arthur shook his head. 'Ivo was in the armoury when I last saw him. It didn't snow yesterday and I'm about to see which roads are passable.' His chain mail chinked as he leaned against Steel. A few stalls away a groom was saddling the black pony. 'My lady, you surely weren't planning on riding today?'

Her chin lifted. 'I must speak to the Comtesse des Iles.'

'You're going to St Méen? My lady, I would advise you waited until we have assessed the roads.'

Her foot tapped, her eyes flashed. 'Sir, it's my belief the Countess is distressed. And Papa is missing her. I need to see her sooner rather than later.'

Arthur knew that look. She wasn't going to change her mind. 'I assume you will take an escort?'

She waved at the groom. 'Conan is accompanying me.'

'One groom? No guards?'

She shook her head and the green veil rippled about her.

Arthur's hand tightened round Steel's girth. If an accident befell them, one groom wouldn't be enough. Never mind the ice and snow, there could be outlaws in these woods. 'You need more than a groom.'

'Arth—sir, my father thinks I will be safe.'

'You need a proper guard. My lady, I think I had better accompany you.'

Her brow wrinkled. 'Isn't St Méen out of your way?'

'It's not precisely on my route, but I won't hear of you riding without a decent escort.' Arthur's heart lightened. He hadn't planned to ride in that direction, but the chance to bid her farewell without an audience hanging on his every word was undeniably cheering.

'You're certain? I don't want to delay your return to Champagne.'

'A day won't make much difference.'

Clare stood back as he led Steel into the bailey and they waited by a water trough for the groom to bring out her horse. Arthur studied her. There were faint smudges beneath her eyes—perhaps she wasn't adjusting to life as a lady as easily as he'd thought. The rich clothes suited her, although he wouldn't mind pulling off that veil and running his fingers through her hair. Just once more…just once…

'Yet another cloak?' he said. 'That green looks well on you.'

'Thank you. I have three cloaks now and at least a dozen gowns. And a maid.'

'That is—as it should be.'

She gave him a blank look. 'Is it? Enora's a sweet girl, but I hardly know what to say to her. All this is very strange.'

'You seem to have settled in well.'

Her eyebrows lifted. 'Hardly.'

'Your father will help you accustom yourself to life as a lady.'

She gave him another blank look and shrugged. 'Perhaps, but Papa's vagueness doesn't help.'

'Vagueness?'

'Papa seems to have forgotten I've had no

training in managing servants or in running a household. My accent is foreign—I shall need lessons in speaking properly so everyone will understand me.'

'Your diction has always been perfectly clear to me.'

'Maybe, but I am uncertain how to comport myself in public and—'

She broke off, Conan was leading out the horses. Noticing a pack behind the groom's saddle, Arthur shot her a look.

'Papa insisted Conan brought blankets and food with us.'

'I see Count Myrrdin's vagueness only extends so far,' he murmured, drily.

Clare pursed her lips and shook her head. 'You don't understand,' she said softly, and mounted Swift. 'I don't think Papa is very well. He's not at all well.'

Arthur fell silent. Count Myrrdin looked unusually fit for a man of his years. He'd found her a maid; he'd ordered her an array of gowns a queen would envy. Admittedly it was odd that he was willing to let her ride abroad without a proper escort. Thoughtfully, he clapped on his helmet and kicked Steel's flanks, and they clattered across the icy cobbles and under the portcullis. The groom, muffled in his cloak and hood, brought up the rear.

There'd been scarcely any traffic. The snow

was crisp and fresh and crunched beneath the horses' hoofs. The woods were blindingly bright, and the shadows blue. Before long Clare's eyes were aching. Wooden stakes were driven in at intervals along the margin of the road. Waymarkers. Clare hadn't noticed them on her arrival and today they were hardly necessary, but she could see that, if the snow drifted, they would be invaluable.

Arthur's saddle creaked as he turned to her. 'How long has Countess Francesca been at St Méen?'

'A little over a week.' Clare sighed. 'Her absence is upsetting Papa. I decided I really must try to bring her back.'

Arthur pushed up his visor. 'She may resent your visit.'

'She may, but I rather think she'll be missing Papa and everyone at Fontaine. Apparently Count Tristan is still at Rennes, so she'll be on her own. She must be miserable.'

'Cl—my lady, you've just found your father, so naturally you can't imagine losing him again, but the Countess has been used to thinking of herself as his daughter. She's likely to be feeling some anger, not only against you, but also against Count Myrrdin.'

'She can't blame Papa—it wasn't his fault someone stole me! Nor was it his fault someone deceived him by putting her in my place.'

'She's bound to be dwelling on it. She'll be wondering if the person responsible is still at Fontaine. She may never want to return.'

'On the other hand, she might want to find her real parents...'

Arthur was quick to shake his head. His helmet flashed in the light. Clare was glad he had lifted his visor; a knight's face was impossible to read with his visor down. And he was more human—more Arthur—with his visor up. She liked looking at him. She'd missed him these past few days. Her throat ached. She'd miss him when he left.

He looked soberly at her. 'My lady, she has been brought up to think of herself as the daughter of a count. The odds are that her real parents will be far less exalted. How well do you think she will relate to someone from the lower orders?'

'Status,' she murmured, frowning at him. 'How it seems to obsess you.'

Arthur narrowed his eyes against the low winter sun. 'Everyone has their place, my lady. Lord, knight, monk, peasant—we must all play our part.'

'And the heavens will fall if someone moves from one level to another?'

He looked at her, wooden-faced. Sensing that he was hiding a profound hurt, she reached a hand towards him. When he made no move to take it, she withdrew it, flushing.

'This has something to do with your brother's death, doesn't it? Arthur, what happened to Miles? How did he die?'

'He died in the lists at Troyes Castle. We were told it was a training session that went wrong. An accident.' His mouth tightened. 'That was one version.'

'There were other versions?'

His shoulders lifted, the gesture was anything but casual. 'Father learned that Miles was cornered by not one, but three knights, each with twice his experience.' He grimaced. 'Apparently, Miles was unhorsed and it came down to hand-to-hand fighting. He didn't stand a chance.'

'And the men who killed him? Was nothing done?'

'I was a boy at the time and Father didn't tell me the whole. I do know that before Miles died he mentioned one of the knights as being particularly resentful of him.'

'Why was that?'

'Miles won his spurs in place of his son.'

'So Miles was cornered by three knights...'

'Three brothers with an impeccable lineage who couldn't stand to see the illegitimate son of an armourer given precedence over their own flesh and blood. They swore it was a training accident.'

'It seems odd that Count Henry did nothing...'

'Count Henry was in Paris. Father went to see him on his return, but it came down to the word of the three knights present at Miles's death against the word of an armourer who was not.' Another shrug. 'You may guess the outcome. Father was told that knights die in training every day and that is certainly true. What could he do?'

Clare sighed. 'Arthur, Miles's death was tragic, but you're letting it rule you. You're assuming all noblemen think in the same way as those who killed him.' Her chest heaved. 'You have ample evidence to the contrary, yet you wilfully ignore it. As I heard it, Count Lucien d'Aveyron took you on as his steward and after that Count Henry of Champagne offered you captaincy of the Guardians. Surely that is proof enough that not all noblemen are cast in the mould of your brother's killers?'

Silence fell. They passed a fallen tree trunk shrouded in white. Animal tracks—a deer, a fox—trailed this way and that. They had proceeded another hundred yards before Arthur spoke again.

'I admit I've been fortunate to find service with open-hearted men. Count Henry and Count Lucien are rare among their peers.'

'I wonder if they are as rare as you make out. Are the barriers between a knight and his lord as high as you seem to think? I am not sure. In truth, I wonder if it isn't you who are putting up the barriers.'

'What do you mean?'

'Seek and ye shall find—you look for barriers and you find them.' Even as she spoke, Clare realised she had hit on the truth—Arthur needed to know the barriers were in place. What she couldn't fathom was why.

Dark eyes flashed. 'I? It is not I who build barriers, my lady. Others do that. Some are born to rule, others must live more humble lives.'

'So these barriers can never be breached? That's nonsense. What about that Norman Duke—what was his name? The one who was a bastard?'

He gave a curt laugh. 'I believe you are referring to Duke William of Normandy.'

'He became King of England—'

'Clare, King William might have been illegitimate, but his father was Duke of Normandy.'

Clare. Her lips curved. He was calling her Clare again. 'William of Normandy's noble blood helped him, is that what you are saying?'

Wide shoulders lifted. 'Your life is changing, is it not? And that is entirely thanks to your birth.'

'And the fact that I am legitimate. I wonder which is the greater barrier to advancement—low birth or illegitimacy?' She looked thoughtfully at him and lowered her voice. 'There's no need to answer that. Arthur, I'm not trying to provoke you. There's something I need to ask and I find myself hesitating because it concerns what I believe to be the most insurmountable barrier of them all. One which you, I believe, have overcome.'

'My lady?'

'It concerns prejudice. Arthur…' Hesitating, she glanced over her shoulder. The groom was trailing them by several yards and, with his hood up, she doubted that he could hear them.

Steel's bit jangled. 'Clare, you should know you may tell me anything.'

Clare.

'I would like to think so.' She gripped the reins. She had already confessed that she was finding it hard to adjust to life as Count Myrrdin's daughter and it had been no lie. None the less, her next confession wasn't going to be easy. 'Rest assured, I shall not ask you to remain at Fontaine, I understand about your commitments in Troyes, but I really would welcome your advice.'

He bowed his head. 'I will do my utmost to help.'

The snow-covered road was sloping down a gentle incline. The trees grew less thickly here. Above the frosted branches, shadowy wisps of smoke were winding into the sky—there were cottages close by.

She cleared her throat. 'This concerns something that happened long ago.'

'After you were taken from Brittany?'

She gave a brief nod. 'I shall tell you my earliest memory.' Smoke was twisting up through the branches. She fixed her gaze on it. 'My earliest memory is of being cared for by a woman in Apulia. Her name was—is—Veronica. The day I realised she was not my mother is engraved in my mind. It was summer. Outside, the bees were murmuring on the terrace. The door was open, sunlight was pouring in, and the floor—it was white marble, streaked with grey—was warm under my toes. Veronica was arranging lilies in a vase on a side table and I was helping her. I was clumsy and water was spilt. She hit me.' Clare fingered her mouth as she remembered the sting of that blow. It had cut her lip. '*"Slave,"* she said. *"Clumsy slave."* She owned me.'

Clare wasn't looking at Arthur as she spoke, but she could tell by the way Steel tossed his head that he had jerked on the reins.

'She *owned* you?'

'Yes.' Clare kept her eyes firmly on a skein of geese straggling through the sky.

'And she hit you?'

'Many times.' A lump formed in her throat. She had to swallow to continue. 'I know Veronica must have hit me before then, because I don't recall being surprised. But that was the first time that I remember, the time that she called me a clumsy slave. I was lucky, I was never whipped—'

Arthur swore. 'Clare, for pity's sake, look at me.'

Bracing herself for she knew not what—scorn?

Pity?—Clare looked. His hand—large and clad in a knight's mail gauntlet—was stretched towards her. The tension ran out of her like water through a sieve. With a sigh, she put her hand in his and felt him give her a comforting squeeze. Her eyes stung and the white forest was lost in a dazzle of tears.

'When we set out from Troyes, I thought I would never speak of this.' She gave a strained laugh.

'I am honoured that you confide in me. I suspected there was more darkness in your past, but this…' he gave a puzzled frown '…why wait until now to tell me?'

She threw another glance behind her.

'Clare, you may speak freely, the groom's not listening, he's too busy wondering how long we will be and whether he'll have to eat a cold supper.'

Chapter Twelve

Arthur could hardly believe his ears. Clare had been enslaved? She had been owned by a woman in Apulia named Veronica? His first instinct was to fire a barrage of questions at her. How long were you a slave? How did you win your freedom? Did you run away? Holding himself in check was hard, but he managed it. This couldn't be easy for her; he mustn't push her.

Her face was pinched with cold and her nose was faintly blue, but it was the tightness about her eyes that concerned him. The strain. *Clare has been carrying this burden alone for too long.*

Her chest heaved. 'Arthur, I really don't want anyone else to learn of this.'

'You may rely on my discretion.'

'Thank you…' She hesitated. 'There are two reasons I am telling you. The first is that I would value your opinion. Do you think my father should be told? He's been asking about my life in Apulia. After we'd left Troyes, I was confident I could keep my past to myself. It seemed to me that what happened to Count Myrrdin's illegitimate daughter was unimportant, but—'

'Unimportant!' Arthur stared at her. 'Clare, no one should be enslaved, whatever their status. I knew such things went on, but I never dreamed I'd actually come face to face with it. You suffered a grave injustice. The slavers—and those who sold you—should pay for their crimes. They must be stopped!'

'It would be good to know that justice had been served, but...' her hood fell back as she shook her head and several bright tendrils of hair escaped '...I really want to leave the past behind me. Yet I find I am an heiress. Should Papa be told?'

'Being a noblewoman certainly puts a different complexion on everything. You have responsibilities.'

She shot him a sharp look. 'Responsibilities? Am I doing wrong by not telling Papa?'

'You fear how he will react.'

Her head dipped, and a burnished curl trembled. 'Yes.'

'Count Myrrdin will be horrified, any father would.' Arthur spoke firmly. 'And it's my belief you should tell him. If slavers were at work in

Fontaine when you were an infant, they could be here now. He needs to know.'

Those unusual eyes searched his. 'Arthur, I am truly worried about Papa. You must have no-ticed—sometimes he falls silent and stares into the distance, and at other times he wanders off the middle of a conversation.'

'I've not heard mention of this from his house-hold knights.'

'You're an outsider—they may be reluctant to speak frankly before you.' Her breast heaved. 'I very much doubt that Papa can cope with any more…surprises.'

Arthur grunted. He hadn't noticed anything amiss with Count Myrrdin, but he was ruefully aware that since arriving in Fontaine, it had been Clare, rather than her father, who had been the focus of his thoughts.

'There's more.' Her breath huffed out in the cold air. 'Papa is clearly anxious about Countess Francesca and I expected him to send after her. They need to speak to each other, yet he does nothing. It's as though he's paralysed—he seems incapable of taking decisive action. It was I who insisted on riding out to St Méen to try to bring her back. Doesn't it strike you as odd that Papa hasn't sent for her?'

'Likely he hoped the Countess would come to her senses. And the roads have been bad.'

Arthur was sure Clare's worry for her father

was groundless. She was a nervous person—and now that she had confessed about her grim past, he understood she had reason to be nervous. Slavery. Lord. What hell to be at someone's beck and call at every hour of every day. The contrast between her past in Apulia and the future opening up in front of her couldn't be more marked. Such a startling rise in status—dizzying...

'Clare, Count Myrrdin doesn't strike me as being overly frail. My recommendation is that you tell him everything as soon as you can.' He cleared his throat. 'You mentioned having *two* reasons for telling me about your past...?'

She bit her lip. 'It's about the slavers. Given you're a Guardian Knight, I dare say I should have told you about this earlier.' She took a huge breath. 'Never mind Fontaine, there are slavers in Troyes.'

Arthur felt his jaw drop. 'Slavers? In Troyes?'

'They're the reason I left. I...I thought I should mention it, as you might like to look into it when you return.'

'I most certainly would, Count Henry will be appalled,' Arthur said. 'It's a pity you said nothing sooner.'

Her eyes lowered. 'I am sorry.'

He sent her an easy smile, to cover the cramping in his belly. She hadn't trusted him. It wasn't surprising given her past, but it was hurtful. He had liked her at first sight and he'd assumed she felt the same. 'You were afraid, I expect. You hadn't known me long. Would you recognise them?'

'I know one of them—my master used to buy his slaves from him—his name is Lorenzo da Verona. In Apulia he is known as the Veronese.' She shook her head, her eyes sad. 'The irony is, I…I went to Troyes because I thought I would be safe. I knew slavery was banned in Champagne and I'd heard about the Guardian Knights. I was certain no slaver would dare set foot anywhere near Troyes and the Guardians.'

For the second time that morning, Arthur found himself struggling to make sense of what Clare was telling him. There were slavers in Troyes. She was saying something about not wanting to leave Nicola and Nell, but that having seen the slaver—the Veronese—she had felt she had no choice. She had feared recapture. And all he could think about was that she had been enslaved and that the slavers must be stopped.

He found himself frowning at her, stomach tight with hurt. 'If only you'd told me, you must know I would have helped.'

She looked away. 'I'm sorry. I would have told you, but I have some pride. If I'd told you, it would have meant confessing that I had been a slave. I was ashamed.'

He studied her profile, eyes lingering on the

curve of her cheek, on the coppery twists of her hair, on the slight pout to her lips.

'Clare, I am honoured that you have managed to put your trust in me,' he said softly. 'And I realise you may find this painful, but before I leave for Troyes, I should like you to tell me as much as you know about Lorenzo da Verona.'

Her eyes went wide. 'I never want to see that man again.'

'That's understandable. But you do realise that if he could be caught, your testimony could be invaluable?'

'My testimony?' Her voice cracked and she lowered her voice. 'What can you mean? I don't want the world to know I was enslaved.'

A muscle jumped in Arthur's jaw. Was he pushing her too far? Or was there more that she was not telling him? He shrugged. 'It may not be necessary. When I reach home, the Veronese is likely to have slipped away, he may never be caught—'

'But if he is, you want me to testify against him? In Count Henry's court?'

'It would help.'

'I couldn't do that,' she said, voice high. 'Arthur, I simply couldn't!'

'Very well,' he said, soothingly. 'No one shall force you into anything.'

'Swear you won't tell anyone…' she threw a

hunted look over her shoulder '…about my life in Apulia?'

'I shan't breathe a word without your permission. As I said, we may never find the man. But before I leave for home, I'd appreciate it if you could furnish me with his description.'

She gave a tight nod and Arthur couldn't press for more. She had already suffered more than most and he had no wish to add to her sufferings.

'My lady?' Behind them, the groom cleared his throat. 'The manor is half a mile hence at the bottom of the hill.'

'Thank you, Conan.' Harness clinked as Clare waved the groom on. 'Would you care to take the lead?'

The manor of St Méen sat in a hollow in the snowy landscape, a square, stone building peeping over an ice-encrusted wall. The moat was white with snow and the gate closed to all comers. A black wolfhound was chained to the wall by the gate. It seemed to be acting as guard, for it sprang up and started to bark.

'I can't see anyone,' Clare said. 'Apart from the dog, it looks deserted.'

'There's smoke over the roof.'

Clare eyed the hound straining at its chain and her brow furrowed. 'Do you think Countess Francesca will refuse to see us?'

Somewhat to Clare's surprise, Conan was able

to open the gate and they rode through it unchallenged. There was just the black wolfhound, barking, barking...

'Where is everyone?' she asked, accepting Arthur's steadying hand to help her dismount. His eyes, as she glanced his way, appeared warm, but as he stepped smartly back with the most formal of bows, Clare decided she must have imagined the warmth. Was he disappointed at her refusal to testify? He must be. Of course, the Veronese might never be caught, but she had disappointed Arthur. It was not a pleasant feeling.

'After you, my lady.'

The Countess wasn't in the hall, though a brisk fire was throwing out welcome heat. Through an open door at the far end, Clare glimpsed a shadowy stairwell.

'Good day!' she called. 'Is anyone about?'

No one answered. St Méen seemed abandoned, although a scattering of chestnut shells on the hearth hinted that someone had been here recently. Stripping off her gloves, Clare moved to the fire and tried again.

'*Holà!* Countess Francesca?' Outside the dog barked, on and on. No one came. 'Someone must be here, there are horses in the stable.' Rubbing her hands together, she exchanged glances with Arthur.

He jerked his head towards the stairwell. 'Shall we?'

The spiralling stairs opened out at the end of a gallery lit only by lancets. Hand on his sword hilt, breath fogging in the cold air, Arthur flung open doors as they walked through the gloom. Storage chamber. Privy. Empty bedchamber. Linen closet…

Solar. Countess Francesca was in the solar, sitting in a cushioned window embrasure with an elderly woman. They were hemming the edges of a large white cloth that was spread over their knees. The fire was low, little more than embers.

The Countess lifted her face towards the door as they entered and Clare realised the sewing was but a pretence. Her adopted sister's nose was red and there were sooty marks beneath her eyes. She looked as though she'd not slept since leaving the castle. The older woman had the air of a trusted retainer. This must be the maid. She, too, had cheeks that were blotched and puffy. They'd been crying.

'Lady Clare.' Countess Francesca's throat worked. 'You've come to gloat. I knew it wouldn't be long. You want me to leave.'

Quickly, Clare stepped forwards. 'Far from it. I've come to ask if you would come home with me. My lady, Count Myrrdin misses you.'

Countess Francesca's mouth thinned. 'Fontaine is not my home, as everyone knows. By birth you—' her voice held authority, but at this point it cracked '—by birth you outrank me. You may call me Francesca.'

'My lady,' Clare said, firmly. Her heart was thudding. She'd been right to insist on coming. This poor woman was in shreds because of her arrival. And she was looking at Clare with utter loathing. Clare stiffened her spine. She had dealt with the indifference of others; she had dealt with cruelty, lust and rage, but never before had she looked anyone in the eye and seen such hatred. It was coming off Countess Francesca in waves. 'My lady, if you would permit, I should like to think of you as my sister. Only if you agree to think of yourself as my sister will I feel comfortable addressing you as Francesca.'

Countess Francesca's gaze swept her from crown to toes. 'You are not my sister. You and I share not one drop of blood. My lady, I—' she lifted her shoulders, eyes cold '—I am the thief at your gate. I am a beggar.'

At her side, Arthur made an impatient movement and, sensing that he was about to intervene, Clare sent him a swift headshake.

'My lady, you are no such thing.' She made her voice warm. 'I believe you were as shocked to learn of my parentage as I was.'

The Countess snorted. 'Shocked—you could put it that way.'

'I really would like to think of you as my sister.'

The Comtesse des Iles stared, her expression no longer cold and proud, but baffled. Baffled and broken.

Clare's heart twisted. She could see she had some convincing to do before the Countess accepted her.

Impulsively, she seated herself on the cushion next to the Countess and touched her hand—it was stone cold. 'My lady, I have something to tell you and it may take some while.' She included the maid in her smile. 'We could go downstairs, the fire is better in the hall. Unless someone could arrange for more wood to be brought up?'

The maid sniffled, surreptitiously wiping her nose with the back of her hand. 'I'll fetch the wood.'

'Thank you, Mari,' the Countess murmured.

Mari gave her mistress a straight look. 'My lady, I reckon you ought to listen to Lady Clare.'

As the maid moved towards the corridor, Arthur cleared his throat. 'I'll get Conan to help you with the firewood.'

'Thank you, sir.'

When Arthur and the maid had gone, Clare leaned back and looked the Countess in the eye. 'I have always wanted a sister.'

'I am not your sister, my lady.'

'Papa loves you.'

'Does he? Then why did he let me go so easily? Why didn't he send someone after me?'

'He...oh, Francesca—you will let me call you that...?'

'As you wish.'

'Francesca, I am so glad that you have agreed to speak to me. I have wanted to talk to you about Papa for days.'

'Oh?'

'He seems to have difficulties and I need to know how you deal with them. Sometimes all is well, but at others, he drifts into another world. You must have noticed.'

Silently, Francesca stared at her, and something in her eyes made Clare realise she had been wrong about Francesca loathing her. It wasn't loathing she was looking at, it was fear. Countess Francesca's angry greeting—*you want me to leave*—echoed in her mind.

The Countess was afraid she had come to claim St Méen for herself. As part of Francesca's dowry, St Méen had been Francesca's gift to her husband; she must dread the thought that she would bring him nothing. Further, it was likely she thought of St Méen as her last, private refuge. She needed reassurance that it was not going to be clawed back as part of the Fontaine estate.

Smiling, Clare made a show of looking about the solar. A silver shield painted with three black cinquefoils hung over the fireplace. The cushions they were sitting on—delicately embroidered silk—were plump and comfortable. Yes, her sister loved this place. It was clear it was full of happy memories.

The door at the bottom of the stairwell banged in the distance and a wall hanging shivered in the draught. Arthur's voice drifted along the corridor. 'Mari, let Conan, that's too heavy for you. You bring the kindling.'

'What a beautiful tapestry that is,' Clare said, studying the wall hanging. Knights and ladies were feasting at a damask-covered table in a woodland setting. A silver border starred with black cinquefoils had been worked along the margins. 'Very sumptuous,' she murmured, lifting an eyebrow at Francesca. 'Silver and black are not the colours of Fontaine.'

'No, those are my husband's colours.'

'Did you work that wall hanging?'

'Mari and I worked it together.'

'It's gorgeous. This solar is a happy place—you love St Méen.'

'This manor is home to me.'

Arthur clattered in with Conan and Mari and Clare lowered her voice. 'Francesca, Father gave this manor to you as part of your dowry. It won't be taken from you, it's yours, for ever.'

Francesca's eyes filled and her throat worked. 'Truly?'

'What kind of sister would I be to rob you of your dowry?'

'Thank you, my lady, but you cannot understand the tradition. For generations, St Méen has been held by the Lords of Fontaine. It was given to me as Pap…Count Myrrdin's heiress, on the understanding that it would eventually pass to my heir—to the next Count of Fontaine. Allow me to keep St Méen, and not only do you rob your children of the manor and its revenues, but you also break with a tradition that goes back generations.'

'Traditions are meant to be broken.' Clare shrugged. 'Particularly this one, which takes no account of present circumstances.'

Eyes bright, a small smile lifted the edges of Francesca's mouth. She wiped away a tear. 'Thank you, my lady. You are grace itself.'

'Nonsense!' Clare held out her hand, and when Francesca took it and returned her clasp, her whole body relaxed. *Thank goodness.* 'Enough of that, I really came because I needed to speak to you about Papa. Later, when our horses have rested, perhaps you might consider coming back to the castle. Papa—'

'He's not seriously ill? He was fine when I left.'

Clare grimaced. 'He doesn't have an illness of the body, but I do fear for him. I suspect what ails him might be to do with his age. It's hard to pin down—sometimes he finds it hard to follow a conversation, at others he's sharp as a needle. When I first arrived, he was very bright. Later that evening though, after we had discovered that you had left the castle, he was completely stricken. I fear he cannot cope with…complexity. And worry makes it worse. He's not been right since you rushed away.'

Francesca stared thoughtfully into the fire. 'I've noticed Papa can be vague, but I put it down to the fact that older people tire more easily.'

'That's certainly part of it. Francesca, he's missing you and it's my belief he needs you. I know it will do him good to see you. Please consider riding back with us. When the horses have rested?'

'Very well.' Francesca smiled. 'I miss Pap— Count Myrrdin, too.'

Clare frowned. 'Papa thinks of you as his daughter, too. You grew up at Fontaine and he loves you. I am sure he will tell you when he sees you.'

'He didn't summon me back to Fontaine and he could have done,' Francesca said, in a sceptical tone.

'My arrival at Fontaine has been a shock to us all, and I suspect Papa finds it more challenging than we realise. He's glad to see me, but—' Arthur was tossing logs on to the fire and the sparks were flying '—his routines have been altered. Nothing is as it was. Francesca, it's as though my arrival has made him lose his way.'

'I'm told you are the image of Countess Mathilde.'

'So everyone says. Francesca, Papa's wandering about in a maze that must seem as though its changing shape with his every step. He's confused by what's happened, as are we all. In Papa's case, the worry is making him ill. We—Papa and I—need you back at the castle. With you at Fontaine, I am convinced he will soon be well. Come back with us. Please?'

Arthur booted a log more firmly into the fire and stared into the embers as Conan went out. Should he wait downstairs? Clare's conversation with her sister was being conducted quietly, but he could hear what they were saying. Clare wasn't telling the Countess anything that she hadn't already told him, but he found her generosity—the easy way she relinquished this manor—staggering. Not to mention galling.

He cleared his throat. 'Ladies, I shall check the horses.'

With a quick bow, he left the solar.

She is giving away a manor. Arthur's fists clenched as he stalked along the shadowy corridor. That one act, done with such negligence, served to emphasise the gulf that had sprung up between them. *She is Lady Clare. Heiress to the County of Fontaine. Whilst I...*

In the stables, the groom had removed the horses' saddles and was brushing Steel down.

'I'll do that,' Arthur said, snatching the brush from the groom.

'Yes, my lord.'

Arthur scowled. 'Conan?'

'Yes, my lord?' The groom gave him a wary look.

'Conan, I am a knight, not a lord.' *A landless knight. I would give my eye teeth for a manor half the size of St Méen. And she tosses it away as though it were a trinket bought at a fair.*

'Yes, sir, my apologies.'

Realising that Conan was eyeing him as though he feared he might bite, Arthur shook his head and raked his hand through his hair. 'Hell burn it, Conan, ignore me. I'm bad company today.'

Conan studied him for a moment and nodded. 'That's all right, sir. Likely the journey back to Champagne's preying on your mind?'

Arthur swept the brush across Steel's flanks and grunted.

'Can't be pleasant, travelling that far at this time of year,' Conan went on. 'Must be hard to leave the comforts of Fontaine.'

Arthur gripped the brush till his knuckles showed white and forced lightness into his voice. 'I shall be glad to see home.'

He couldn't understand it, but the words stuck in his throat, like a lie. Suddenly chill, he stared blindly at Steel. It was a lie. He had no desire to return to Troyes, not if Clare was to stay in Fontaine.

He wanted her with him—he wanted her at his side, where she belonged.

Mon Dieu, what the devil was the matter with him? Clare didn't belong to him. Yes, he had bedded her, but that didn't give him rights over her. She was just a girl, a pretty girl whose eagerness to bed him had been a rare delight. A rare and transient delight. He mustn't allow desire for more of the same to turn him from his duty to the Guardians. Besides, there were plenty of pretty girls in Troyes, he would simply find another.

His mouth twisted. As soon as the thaw came, he would be on his way. Tempted though he was by the idea of lingering, he had to get back. If the Veronese was operating in Troyes, Count Henry must be told. The Guardians must step up patrols, they must increase their range. It was his duty to rid Champagne of the slavers.

There were other reasons for Arthur to leave as soon as possible. Clare elicited oddly possessive feelings in him, feelings that for her sake, he would never act on. She had told him that she would never marry, but her change of fortune would inevitably lead to a change of heart. Lady Clare de Fontaine would marry, and she would marry well. The field must be left clear, so that when a suitable man appeared Clare could make the dynastic marriage that she surely deserved.

'The wind's lost that raw edge,' he muttered, scowling through the doorway.

'Aye, sir, the thaw's not far off. You'll be back in Champagne before you know it.'

Winter kept its grip on the Brocéliande for another week, but eventually the day dawned when the roads were passable. Beneath a light dusting of frost, the sap was rising. Buds swelled on the trees. Green shoots poked through the snow like tiny spears.

The weather wasn't the only thing telling Arthur it was time to go. After a shaky start, Clare and her adopted sister looked set to become friends. This was due in no little part to Count Myrrdin, whose face lit like a beacon whenever he saw them talking to each other. At first, the girls' unlikely friendship was probably founded on little more than the fact that they both wanted to please Count Myrrdin, but their friendship would, Arthur was sure, evolve into something more solid.

How could the Countess fail to appreciate Clare's thoughtfulness in riding out to St Méen to reassure her of her father's love? How could she fail to appreciate Clare's generosity in allowing her to keep the manor?

Clare de Fontaine was thoughtful; she was tactful and generous. She had all the qualities needed to make a fine chatelaine for her father's castle and it would not be long before she herself realised it.

On the day of his departure, Arthur waited until everyone had broken their fast before approaching her to make his farewell. Servants had cleared away the last of the crumbs as he glanced at Ivo. 'Are you packed up and ready to go, lad?'

'Yes, sir.'

Arthur jerked his head towards the main door. 'Go and ready the horses, I'll join you shortly.'

Clare was standing near the dais, examining a tablecloth with two maidservants. Today, her gown was the colour of a June sky and her veil was so light that it seemed to be fashioned from gossamer. She looked calm. Poised. And born to her role as Count Myrrdin's heiress.

Feeling as though he had taken a dagger to the heart, Arthur stepped forwards. 'My lady? A word, if you please.'

The women pushed past him with the cloth and then Arthur was looking into those rare and beautiful eyes. His guts twisted as he realised it was probably the last time he would do so.

Her eyelashes lowered. 'You're leaving,' she said, voice flat. 'You're leaving this morning.'

'I… Yes.' Suddenly tongue-tied, it was all he could manage.

Arthur had had a little speech planned. He had planned to tell her that she was going to make a fine lady, a lady any lord would be proud to marry. He had planned to tell her that she need have no fears for her father's wits—any man who could manipulate his daughters into befriending each other in such trying circumstances could hardly be wanting in wits. He planned to say... oh, countless things, but he was conscious of the women bustling from the hall; of a group of soldiers warming their backs at the fire; of Ivo waiting for him in the stable. Regret was a cold hand squeezing his insides. 'There is no time.'

She smiled. 'You return to your duties in Troyes.'

'Yes, my lady.'

She offered him her hand in the grand manner. It was slim and delicate, faintly red and chapped with too much work, but the scars of her harsh past were fading. Arthur kissed it and forced a smile. 'I am happy you have found your home, my lady.'

'Thank you for bringing me to Brittany, sir. I realise it was a great inconvenience.' Her lips curved and, briefly, heart-stoppingly, her eyes danced. 'At least for the most part.'

'Not at all,' he said, pressing her fingers in a small, secret caress. Her comment was a timely reminder that, tongue-tied or not, there was something he must say before he left. Conscious they were not alone, he leaned as close as he dare, and lowered his voice. 'You will let me know if there are any consequences from our stay at the monastery.'

Her brow wrinkled. 'Consequences?' Her cheeks went pink. 'Oh. No, sir, there are no consequences.'

'You are certain?'

'Quite certain.'

A cold wave washed over him. It wasn't disappointment, but it felt remarkably like it. Keeping his expression under a tight rein, he looked guardedly at her. 'You will be happy here, I think.' *I hope.*

Slender fingers tightened on his. 'Sir, you have been a good friend and I am truly sorry to bid you farewell. Please remember you are always welcome at Fontaine. We would be honoured to see you at any time.'

'Thank you, my lady. For my part, I should like you to know that if you ever need my help, you must not hesitate to send for me.'

'My thanks.' With a shy smile and a self-conscious glance at the soldiers by the fireplace, she withdrew her hand from his. 'Farewell, Sir Arthur. Godspeed.'

'Farewell, Lady Clare.'

Chapter Thirteen

Clare kept her gaze on Arthur's broad back as he strode down the hall. She felt as though she had turned to stone. When he snatched his green cloak from a trestle and flung it about his shoulders, she had to clench her fists to stop herself running after him. Her eyelids prickled.

By the fire, a soldier sniggered.

'My lady?'

Clare started. Her maidservant was back, the tablecloth folded over her arm.

'My lady, what else would you like us to do?'

Clare opened her mouth and shut it with a snap. There was room in her for only one thought. *Arthur is leaving.*

'Later, Jan, later,' she muttered. Picking up her skirts, she left the hall. As soon as the door shut behind her, she flew to the tower stairs. Up she went, up past her bedchamber, through the door at the top and out on to the battlements.

A keen westerly was whistling through the crenels and the sky was a patchwork of blue, white and grey. It would rain later. Wrapping her veil about her neck, Clare found a spot where she had clear sight of the gatehouse and the road out of Brittany.

She didn't have long to wait. The brisk clopping of hoofs announced his departure. She saw a splash of green and the guards saluting. Ivo was at his side. Everything looked small. The unicorn on his shield caught the light and the hard shine of his helmet. She couldn't see his face. Or his eyes. *That man wears a small silver pendant about his neck.*

Clare gripped the parapet, choked with an emotion she had no business feeling, let alone naming. An emotion that was alien to her.

No, that was wrong, she couldn't delude herself. The feeling blocking her throat wasn't entirely alien. She had felt it in some small measure for Geoffrey, and for Nicola and Nell. She was beginning to feel it for her father. Love. It seemed that what she felt for Sir Arthur Ferrer was similar. Could this be love? Could it?

Blinded by tears, she watched him ride through the gatehouse and on to the road. The icicles hanging from the battlements were melting—

messy dark splotches were eating into the snow heaped against the walls.

Is this love? She wanted to call him back and feel those strong arms close about her. She wanted—

Behind her, the tower door grated and Count Myrrdin stepped through. The wind was whisking through his hair and beard.

'He's gone, then?'

Heart too full to speak, Clare gripped the battlements and managed a nod.

'Humph. Thought that boy would stay.' Mismatched eyes peered closely at her.

Her father looked distressed. Clare wasn't used to being on the receiving end of someone else's concern and she didn't want him upset. She forced words to her lips. 'Sir Arthur is sworn to Count Henry of Champagne.'

Her father made a dismissive gesture. 'The man's not a serf. Thought you'd find a reason to keep him.'

Blinking away her tears, she stared at the road that led up through the forest and out of Brittany. Everywhere snow was turning to slush. The three horses—they were taking Swift back to Count Henry—were leaving muddy tracks in their wake. When the rain came, Arthur and Ivo would be riding through a sea of mud.

Her father shifted and gave an odd laugh. 'You think I didn't notice, but I know.'

Despite the wind, Clare's cheeks burned. 'Know what?'

'You dote on that man.'

'Papa!' Her throat closed. 'I do not.'

Her father harrumphed, and the lines round his eyes crinkled. 'Don't lie to me, my girl. I am not the most talkative of men, but I observe many things and you are sweet on that man.' He patted her hand. 'He is certainly sweet on you.'

Her heart jumped in her breast. 'He is?'

The white head dipped. 'I was half-expecting him to ask permission to court you.'

Her father was studying her with such intensity that Clare began to think that she had been mistaken in concluding that age had weakened his mind. 'I do like him, Papa,' she surprised herself by admitting. 'But I have no wish to marry.'

Her father grunted, his gaze going out over the battlements. The wind toyed with his hair. It looked like a messy white cloud. Arthur and Ivo were trotting into the trees. One moment Clare could see the unicorn on its green shield and the next all she could see was tree trunks and a criss-cross of bare branches. A rook cawed. In the unknown depths of the forest, she heard the drumming of a woodpecker.

He has gone.

'You need to marry, Clare. Had you asked me, I would have accepted him, but I have to say I am relieved you did not.'

'You are relieved? Why?'

'You will need a good steward when I am gone. And whilst I grant you that Arthur Ferrer makes a fine knight, I hear his stewardship of Ravenshold was less than exemplary.'

She stopped breathing. 'Papa?'

'Ravenshold was in a state of ruin at the end of his tenure. The castle was derelict.'

Clare stared at the gap in the trees, at the muddy tracks in the snow, at the snow-frosted branches. 'Ravenshold was derelict?' *That cannot be true. Arthur is diligent. Careful and thorough in all things. Precise.* 'Papa, who told you this?'

'It's common knowledge, apparently. And whilst I would deny you nothing, I would wish for a careful steward for Fontaine. The land is everything, my dear—it's all about the land.' He smiled, and patted her hand. 'Don't fret, I shall find a good steward. Someone you will like. And you needn't fear I shall rush you into it. You won't have to marry until you are ready.'

Clare's stomach felt hollow. She didn't want her kind, eccentric father to find her a husband. And he was wrong about Arthur. Very wrong. *Arthur? A bad steward? Impossible.*

She held his gaze. 'You gave no sign of having misgivings about Sir Arthur, Papa. Why didn't you mention this earlier?'

Count Myrrdin's eyes lost their sharp intensity.

'I…I…' His expression clouded, his face was the image of confusion. 'I…I forgot.'

'You forgot?'

'I was thinking about something Father Alar has told me.'

'Papa?'

His fingers tightened on hers. 'When you arrived at Fontaine and there was no doubt as to your lineage, I asked Father Alar to make enquiries in the village. I wanted to know what happened after your birth.'

The wind tugged at her veil. It was trying to unwind it from her neck. 'You've learned something?'

'A little. It touches on a confession Father Alar heard years ago. As you will know, confessions are entirely private, but, given the circumstances and the length of time that has elapsed since the confession, Father Alar felt he could reveal what was said. A villager confessed that her sister had stolen a baby girl. The woman was ill, grieving after the death of her child.'

'She stole me?'

'And she fled Fontaine. The sister never saw her again, so the trail soon goes cold. We shall have to imagine that the woman went to Apulia and took you with her.'

A grey cloud was drifting over the castle. Clare watched it pass, thinking quickly. *I was stolen by a grieving woman who then ran away from*

Fontaine. How did I fall into the hands of the slavers? How?

'The woman was unbalanced, Papa?'

'It seems so. I expect the nurse panicked when you were taken—she must have put Francesca in your place.' He cleared his throat. 'Father Alar swears he had no confessions from the nurse, so that is pure speculation.'

'Does he know where Francesca came from?'

'Sadly, no.'

Clare would have liked to have told Arthur what the priest had revealed. It didn't explain exactly how she'd fallen into the hands of the slavers, none the less, Arthur was the only person who knew she had been enslaved and she would have liked to have discussed it with him.

Had the woman died on the road? If she had been ill, she might have been reduced to beggary. *The woman might have been forced to sell me to the slavers in exchange for food. It could have happened at any point between here and Apulia.*

With an abstracted nod and a vague smile, Count Myrrdin released Clare's hand and gazed out over his domain. His nose was red and the skin about his eyes was lined and wrinkled. His hands were heavily veined and mottled with cold. Clare caught her breath. Her father was an old man—he should be wearing his cloak.

She linked arms with him. 'Papa, where's your cloak?'

'One of the dogs ate it?'

'Papa?' Goosebumps ran over her skin. It looked as though her father's period of lucidity was ended. She'd learn no more about her infancy today.

'I have no idea, my dear. None whatsoever.'

'Come along, Papa, we need to go into the warmth.'

As the thaw set in, the highway turned to mud. It splattered up the horses' legs, and covered their flanks. Arthur's grey stallion was no more—Steel had been transformed into a dappled creature he no longer recognised. Ivo's cloak was spotted with brown and Arthur's was no better. Mud coated their boots.

And the rain! It hammered into their faces with such determination Arthur could almost believe a malevolent spirit was at work. From top to toe, both he and Ivo were sodden. His sword was doubtless rusting in its sheath. He glanced at his shield, half-expecting to find his device had been washed away. But, no, the unicorn on the shield was unchanged, a flare of white in a world of mud and rain.

Arthur grimaced at Ivo. Despite the rain, he'd driven them hard. And fast. He'd hoped that focusing on the journey would stop him thinking about Clare.

It hadn't worked. He missed her with his every

breath. Which was odd, since towards the end of his time at Fontaine, he hadn't spent much time with her. But he'd known she was nearby. He'd known what she was doing—sometimes she would be talking to her father in the hall. At others, she'd be checking on supplies for the kitchen or sitting in the solar with Francesca, learning a new stitch. Once, Arthur had heard her asking the priest if he would care to teach her to read and write. And at those times, even though Arthur hadn't been with her, he'd liked knowing where she was. But now...

He tried to keep his mind occupied. He told himself to think about the slavers and how he might find them. He told himself to think about what he would say when he spoke to Count Henry.

Nothing worked. He felt as though he'd lost part of himself. It was an unfamiliar feeling and he didn't like it. So he'd driven himself—and poor Ivo—harder than usual.

Days had passed and they had made good time.

'You've done well, Ivo. Despite the conditions, we've covered some ground today.'

'When shall we reach Troyes, sir?'

'We've entered Champagne. With luck we'll be back at the barracks tomorrow.'

'That's good to hear.'

'Are you warm enough, lad? We can't have you getting ill again.'

'I'm fine, sir.'

The gloom was thickening. Behind the clouds, the sun was sinking. Ahead, a handful of lights glimmered.

'Dieu merci,' Arthur muttered. 'Thank God.'

'Sir?'

'Village ahead. We'll seek shelter at an inn and dry out.'

They trotted briskly into the inn yard. A girl was running hither and yon, chasing after a bedraggled chicken, which must have escaped the coop. A couple of horsemen with a pony and cart were on the point of leaving. They looked like merchants. Poor devils, they must be planning to ride through the night. The lead man was swathed in a voluminous cloak. His torch sputtered and hissed in the rain. The torch wouldn't last long and Arthur's heart went out to them even as something about them caught his attention. Something about them jarred.

Uneasy for no reason that he could put his finger on, he watched them ride out. The rider with the torch went first, the man leading the pony and cart followed. Arthur found himself studying the cart. It looked like a thousand other merchants' carts and to be riding in daylight in this season was bad enough. But night riding? If they were merchants, wouldn't their goods be soaked by journey's end?

Arthur addressed the second rider as the cart

trundled by. 'Good evening. Filthy night for a journey. I hope you've not far to go.'

The man grunted. 'Not far.' He wouldn't meet Arthur's eyes.

The cart's wheels churned through the mud. The cart wasn't full. There were two or three misshapen bundles in the back and several coils of rope that looked like snakes. The bundles had, in fact, been heavily wrapped, so with luck the contents would survive the downpour. They must be valuable to make it worth setting out on such a night. Likely they were delivering a special order for a local lord.

Shaking his head at the hoops ordinary folk must jump through to earn a crust, Arthur turned back to the yard. Yellow light streamed through the stable door—a couple of grooms were in there, waiting out the wet. 'There's a welcome sight,' he said, smiling at Ivo.

'Indeed, sir.'

Head down against the rain, Arthur was guiding Steel towards the light when a choked squeak reached him. It came from behind and was immediately followed by a dull thump and another of those squeaks. He swung round, his gaze instinctively going to the cart rattling into the night.

A dumpy shadow shifted in the back. 'My knight! My knight!'

Arthur's blood chilled. That was a child's

voice—a voice so high and thin, no amount of rain would muffle it.

'My knight! Help! *Help!*'

Wheeling round, Arthur looked at the grooms. 'Fetch help, there's trouble.'

The grooms goggled. 'Trouble, sir?'

'Move!'

One groom dashed for the inn and the other snatched up a pitchfork. 'I'm with you, sir.'

'Good man.' Arthur spurred after the cart, sword in hand. 'Ivo, *à moi!*' His hood fell back, and the skies emptied.

Chaos. Mud flew every which way. The shadow in the back of the cart resolved into the shape of a little girl.

'My knight! Sir Arthur!'

The child was screaming, as though for her life. There was no doubt that she knew him, but her hair was so matted and tangled, and her face so smeared with dirt it took a moment to place her.

'My knight! Sir Arthur!'

'Nell?'

There was no time for more than a glance. *Mon Dieu*, a gag hung loose about the child's neck, but it was Nell and no mistake. Her hands were bound.

The torchbearer made a snarling sound and lobbed the torch at Arthur—sparks flew as it flamed towards him. Steel whinnied and danced sideways. Then came sounds that needed no interpretation...the thunder of hoofbeats as Ivo drew alongside him; the hiss of Ivo drawing his sword; the squelching footsteps of the groom ploughing through the mud.

The light from the inn strengthened. There were shouts and commotion as the other groom raised the alarm. Out of the corner of his eye, the thin silver line that was Ivo's sword wavered and dipped.

'Steady, lad,' Arthur said. 'Remember the drill.' Only one of the two men presented a threat—the man who had flung that torch. The other was too slow. His face was round as a full moon, his mouth hanging agape. 'Lead rider's mine. You watch the other.'

He dug in his spurs and Steel surged forwards.

His man was riding straight at him. He was sloppy, all over the place. He had such poor control it was a wonder he kept his seat. His spurs were gouging into his horse's sides with more energy than sense and, to cap matters off, he was pulling on his reins as though he wanted to bring his mount to a standstill.

'Conflicting signals,' Arthur muttered. He felt sorry for the horse. Lord, the man's cloak was flapping like a loose sail in a storm and his whole body shifted as he waved his sword.

They met in a clash and Arthur's opponent rushed on, carried by momentum. Steel spun round. They engaged briefly in a second pass and again at a third. The rain sluiced down. It was no contest, but by some miracle his man stayed seated, slashing and chopping with such little finesse, Arthur wouldn't have been surprised to see him maim his own horse. Arthur was content to bide his time. His chance would come and soon. The man had been ill-trained, if at all.

The opening came without warning. An inept lunge had his foe lose a stirrup. Another had him lurching to the side. He lost grip of his sword— a deadly silver stripe spiralled into the dark. The man thumped into the mud. His horse bolted.

Arthur flung himself off Steel and rested the point of his sword on the man's throat. 'Yield?'

'Aye, hell burn you, I yield.'

The man's accent was unfamiliar, he was not a Champenois. Arthur's skin prickled. Could this be Lorenzo da Verona? Clare's voice resonated in his mind…*there are slavers in Troyes. Slavers. He is known as the Veronese…*

Could this be the man who had precipitated Clare's flight from Troyes?

The groom with the pitchfork ran up, an excited crowd at his heels. Ivo was back by the cart, surrounded by more folk from the inn. His squire had done well—the other fellow was also at sword-point. And Nell? Nell was shivering on the back of the cart and alongside her three—no, *four* bedraggled waifs clung to the cart's handrail. *Mon Dieu*, if this was slavery, these men had much to answer for. Count Henry would tear his hair out when he heard. Slavery in Champagne.

'Sir Arthur!' the children shouted and drummed their feet. 'Sir Arthur!'

Arthur looked at the groom, and jerked his head at the man in the mud. 'Tie him up. Let's get everyone into the dry.'

'I have him, sir,' the groom said.

Four children shivered by the inn fire, rubbing at wrists and ankles reddened by ropes. Arthur sat on a bench with Nell on his lap and tried to comfort her as, one by one, the innkeeper's wife hustled the children behind a curtain screen to whisk off their damp, dirty clothes. Maidservants ran in and out with a succession of washbowls.

Other customers were murmuring quietly to one another, shooting occasional glances towards the fire and the screens. The children's plight had shocked everyone. At the far end of the inn, the two men were bound hand and foot and roped to a post. To be safe, Arthur had given Ivo and the grooms the task of guarding them.

'I've plenty of tunics my boys have outgrown,' the innkeeper's wife said, as she drew the smallest boy behind the screen. 'They're slightly moth-eaten in places, but they're clean and dry.'

'This is very good of you,' Arthur said.

The woman vanished behind the screen and,

above the crackling of the fire, Arthur could hear her sympathetic clucking. 'You poor lamb, that's a big bruise. My, you're a brave one. Here, this salve will make it better. Do you want to put it on, or shall I?'

Gently, Arthur chafed Nell's wrists. He couldn't get at her fingers because she was clinging to him like a limpet to a rock, but she was permitting him to touch her wrists. Her face was buried in his tunic. Slavers. Would the children remember this in later years? Dear God, he hoped not, but they were certainly old enough.

This must have been Clare's fate.

Except that Clare had been younger. A baby. There were no babies here today, but that little boy—he must be what, two years of age?

The landlord emerged through the door from the kitchen. 'Excuse me, sir, you asked about food. We've ham-and-pea broth and plenty of bread. There's cold chicken and spiced apple pie.'

'Thank you, landlord, they should enjoy that. Let them have whatever they want. I'll pay.'

'Very good, sir.'

Bread and soup was set on a trestle. Arthur stroked Nell's damp, tangled hair and turned her face to his. 'Nell, are you hungry?'

She gave him a watery smile and nodded.

'What happened, Nell? Why aren't you in Troyes?'

The smile faded. Nell shook her head and her eyes filled. '*Maman, Maman...*' Her voice broke.

Arthur's heart turned to lead. Nicola must have died. 'Something has happened to Nicola?'

Nell gulped. 'She's *very* poorly. She got worse after Clare left. And then those men came, they were asking about Clare.'

'What are their names, Nell, do you know?'

Nell sniffed and shook her head. 'They hit me.' She paused. 'They hit the others, too. They are bad, bad men.'

'They won't hit you again,' Arthur said, firmly. 'Tomorrow we shall take them to Count Henry and he will see that they are punished.'

Nell stuck her thumb into her mouth. Her dirty, mud-splattered thumb. Warily, for he was afraid of startling her, Arthur pulled it out of her mouth. 'It's time to see about dry clothes for you, too.' He shifted and grimaced. 'You're all damp. And then you must eat.'

Nell sent the slavers an anxious look. 'What if they escape? They'll come and get me.'

'No, they won't. Tomorrow they are meeting Count Henry.'

A mud-streaked face looked up at him. 'They're going to prison?'

'Most likely.'

'And you will take me home?'

A lock of damp hair had fallen over her eyes, Arthur stroked it back. 'Of course.' He set her on her feet and turned her towards the screen where the landlord's wife was waiting with an outstretched hand. 'Time to get you properly dry.'

As Nell submitted herself to the innkeeper's wife, she looked back and a smile trembled into being. 'I prayed for you to come, Sir Arthur.'

Arthur's chest constricted.

Whilst the innkeeper's wife measured Nell against a frayed brown tunic, Nell's eyes held his. 'Sir Arthur?'

'Hmm?'

'Did you find Clare?'

'Yes.'

'I knew you would!' Nell's smile was dazzling. 'Where is she?'

'Clare's living in Brittany, with her father.'

Nell's eyes filled with questions.

'Come, child, behind that curtain with you,' the innkeeper's wife said. 'You can catch up with your news later.'

Nodding, Nell ducked behind the screen.

The next day, Arthur led a somewhat ramshackle cavalcade through the Paris Gate and into Troyes. Sergeant Hubert was on duty at the castle drawbridge. As the sergeant saluted, his eyes bulged as he took in the cart, the children, the prisoners, and the makeshift guard that Arthur had cobbled together that morning. A guard that

was comprised of Ivo and two raw conscripts—
the grooms from the inn.

'Captain Ferrer, is that you, sir?' the sergeant
asked, glancing briefly at the unicorn on Arthur's
shield before returning his puzzled gaze to the
cart.

Arthur pushed back his visor and grinned.

'Welcome home, sir.'

'My thanks. Sergeant, is Count Henry in residence?'

'Yes, sir.'

'Send word to him at once, would you? I need
to speak to him as soon as possible. Please tell
him it's a matter of some urgency.'

Arthur was ushered directly to the solar, where
Count Henry was sitting before a sea of parchments, dictating to a scribe. Count Henry dis-
missed the scribe with an airy wave of his hand.
'We shall finish this later, Piers.'

'Very good, my lord.'

Count Henry came to grasp Arthur's hand.
'Captain! Thank God you're home. I take it you're
ready to resume your duties with the Guardians?'

The Count's smile was as warm as ever and it
went some way to dispelling any concern Arthur
might have had that Sir Raphael of Reims might
oust him as Captain.

'Yes, my lord.' Arthur was conscious of a faint
feeling of bafflement. Of disappointment. Hav-

ing Count Henry confirm that Sir Raphael was not going to replace him should surely lift his spirits more than this? 'Sir Raphael performed well, my lord?'

'Adequately. The boy's a trifle green, Captain, as I am sure you suspected, but he handled the responsibility better than I hoped. Notwithstanding, I'm glad to have you back, as I will explain in due course. All went well in Brittany?'

'Very well, *mon seigneur*.' Arthur launched into a brief account of Clare's unexpected rise in status. When he had finished, Count Henry was frowning.

'Captain, you say Count Myrrdin has accepted this girl as his legitimate daughter?'

'Without question. Apparently Clare—*Lady* Clare—resembles Countess Mathilde so closely there can be no doubt.' He shrugged. 'My lord, not only does Lady Clare have Count Myrrdin's eyes, what I didn't realise when we set out was that she also has Countess Mathilde's hair and build. Everyone at Fontaine remarked on the likeness from the moment she rode into the bailey.'

'Good Lord. And what about Countess Francesca? How do matters stand with her?'

'Count Myrrdin accepts her as his adopted daughter, my lord. He loves her, but he has declared Lady Clare his heiress.'

Count Henry rubbed his cheek and took a thoughtful turn about the solar. 'Countess Francesca will not find this easy to digest, although she will keep her title, thanks to her marriage to the Comte des Iles.' He looked across, eyes sharp. 'Count Tristan is proud, he married the Countess for Fontaine—he's been acting as Myrrdin's steward for years. I'm curious, Captain, as to how Count Tristan reacted to Lady Clare's good fortune?'

Arthur spread his hands. 'I cannot say, my lord. The Count of the Isles wasn't at Fontaine, he's attending the young Duchess in Rennes.'

Count Henry grimaced. 'What a tangle. It might have been better if Lady Clare had been illegitimate.'

Arthur found himself springing to Clare's defence. 'I can't agree with you there, my lord. Thanks to her resemblance to Countess Mathilde, Count Myrrdin is delighted to have found her.'

Although perhaps, if Clare had been illegitimate, I might have asked her to marry me again and she might eventually have seen her way to accepting me. The thought had flashed through Arthur's mind before he could stop it. It was unsettling. It made his guts churn and he couldn't work out why. Arthur had been landless when he met Clare and he was still landless. If she had never known her true lineage, would she have come to accept him? Would she?

'Yes, but think, Captain,' Count Henry was saying, 'the ramifications of this are... Lord, what a mess. What happened, do you know? How could Myrrdin have lost his daughter in the first place? Did he suspect nothing?'

'In my view, Count Myrrdin has long suspected that Countess Francesca was not his child.' Arthur held Count Henry's gaze and picked his words with care. Clare had sworn him to secrecy on the matter of her enslavement, and he wasn't about to betray her. He would say as little as possible. 'Count Myrrdin seems to believe Lady Clare was snatched from her cradle shortly after her birth. He was making enquiries when I left, but as to whether he will learn anything, I cannot say.' He took a deep breath. '*Mon seigneur*, turning closer to home, I have to report that last night my squire and I had an extremely unpleasant *contretemps* with a couple of felons. More precisely, with a couple of slavers.'

'Slavers?' Count Henry's eyebrows snapped together. 'Now there's a coincidence. Sir Raphael has been running to me with the most unsavoury rumours.'

'Concerning slavers?'

Count Henry nodded. 'It's the main reason I'm glad you're back. Sir Raphael is far too credulous—someone's spreading rumours about child slavery and the man believes them. He insists slavers have been at work in Troyes. In Troyes. It's unthinkable, of course, but Sir Raphael is so convinced, he almost had me believing him.

'He brought a woman to see me—she was completely hysterical. Babbling about a missing child. Missing? I told her the child had most likely run away, and what's more—'

Arthur shook his head. 'Count Henry, I regret to inform you that Sir Raphael has hit on the truth—slavers have indeed been at work in Troyes.'

Count Henry stared. 'Not you, too? Captain, I was confident you would put an end to this nonsense.' He plucked a scroll out of the mess on the table and waved it under Arthur's nose. The scroll was weighed down with blue seals and beribboned in yellow. Arthur recognised it as a trade charter. 'Troyes is the safest town in Champagne. It has to be. What will happen to our reputation as a centre for the fairs, if merchants cannot trade here and know they are secure? I have been in correspondence with King Louis on the subject, but—'

'My lord, slavers have definitely been operating in the town. And the proof has currently been placed under guard in the castle lock-up.'

'You have proof?' Ashen-faced, Count Henry dropped the trade charter next to a heap of tally sticks. 'I think, Captain Ferrer, you must tell me everything.'

By the time supper was over, Arthur must have repeated his tale a dozen times. It had been hard keeping Clare's name out of it, and he regretted not being able to mention her involvement. When the Veronese and his henchman came to trial it would undoubtedly help if Lady Clare de Fontaine were to testify against them. Her word would have more weight than any defence they might muster. But if Clare couldn't even confess her past to Count Myrrdin, she was surely never going to overcome her dread of testifying in Count Henry's court.

Arthur couldn't blame her. Until she had reached Brittany her life had been one ordeal after another. She had suffered enough and, if it helped her, he would spare her more trouble. She had honoured him with her trust when she had told him about the slavers. He wasn't about to throw that away.

So, Arthur had told the tale a dozen times and had kept his lips firmly sealed about Lady Clare de Fontaine's involvement with the slavers. As for the Veronese, he and his henchman were firmly lodged in Count Henry's prison and there they would stay until the trial.

Nell had been placed in the care of one of Countess Marie's ladies and it was full dark before Arthur found space to take her home. As soon as he could, he went to the ladies' solar to collect her. Shortly afterwards, he was striding through the narrow streets with Nell dancing at his side.

Doors and shutters were edged with light. The air was crisp, and filled with the smell of cooking fires, of baking bread and roasting meat.

'Aimée lives there,' Nell said, pointing at one of the tall, wooden houses. 'She and Clare are friends. When Clare comes back, you'll see.'

Arthur didn't have the heart to tell the child that it was unlikely that Clare would return, so he murmured something non-committal, and they crossed the street to Nicola's house.

It was in darkness. Here, there was no telltale light creeping round the door, not so much as a sliver squeezing past the shutters. Arthur gave a shutter a gentle tug. It remained firm. Locked tight. He tipped his head and listened. Not a sound. No one was living here. Which could only mean one thing…

His throat closed. Nell was an orphan.

Nell skipped blithely to the door. As she reached for the latch, Arthur snatched her into his arms and swung her about.

'Nell? I should like to meet Aimée. Which house did you say was hers?'

'I want to see Mama first.'

A wave of something perilously close to panic swept through him. Nicola was dead, he knew it. Arthur would rather charge full tilt into a mêlée than deal with a grieving child. He looked helplessly at her. What should he say? What should he do?

'My knight?' To his astonishment, Nell laid her hand against his cheek. 'Don't be sad, we can see Aimée in a minute. I just want to see Mama first.'

A lump the size of a hen's egg was jammed in his throat. Arthur swallowed—it seemed there was no escape. Lord, he'd rather deal with slavers...

'Nell.' He hugged her to him. 'Nell, I think we might have to be very brave...'

The child's eyes gleamed in the light from a nearby torch. Her expression had sobered. It was the sort of expression one usually saw on someone four times her age. She looked remarkably wise. And immeasurably sad.

'I know that. Before the bad man stole me, Mama told me that she might have to go away. She said she was dying.'

Arthur's eyes smarted and he had to clear his throat before he could speak. 'Mama told you she was dying?'

Nell nodded, and that impossibly small, comforting hand went on patting his cheek. 'Yes. And sometimes, I heard Mama talking about it with Clare. About what would happen to me after Mama was gone.'

Sniffing, Nell stared mournfully at the door. A large tear gleamed silver as it trailed down her cheek. 'Sir Arthur, you needn't worry about me. If something has happened to Mama, Clare will come. I know she will, she promised.'

Chapter Fourteen

'Lady Clare?'

The Captain of Count Myrrdin's guard caught her as she was about to enter the stables. Only yesterday, Clare's father had given her a bay mare and she was keen to try out her paces. She wasn't going to make the mistake of naming her too quickly—Swift had been a ridiculous name for that slug of a pony that she'd borrowed for her journey here. It seemed that Sir Arthur Ferrer had done more than teach her to ride, he had instilled in her his love of horses. The bay was a beauty and she must have the right name.

'Captain?'

The Captain held out a scroll. 'My lady, an envoy has ridden in from Troyes. He brought letters with him. This one's for you.'

'Thank you, Captain.' Clare took the scroll

and stared blankly at it. The letters on the outside meant nothing to her—she hadn't begun her
reading lessons yet—they were simply brown
scribbles that looked as though they represented
a series of waves. Could those marks really mean
something? There was a green seal with a knight
on it. It reminded her of the lead token that had
given entry to the Twelfth Night Joust. It seemed
a lifetime ago.

She fingered the seal, and her heart thumped
against her ribs. *Arthur. Arthur has written to me.*
She could think of no reason why he should do
so, but green was his colour…

'Who sent this, do you know?'

The Captain shrugged. 'My apologies, my
lady, the envoy didn't say who the letter was from.
Is there anything else?'

'Thank you, Captain, that will be all.'

Why has Arthur written to me?

Holy Mother, she missed that man. She'd
scarcely slept since he'd ridden out of Fontaine
and her nights had become a tedious succession
of empty hells. Longing, she had discovered, was
akin to hunger, gnawing at her, incessant. Clare
felt lonely. And she had learned a new meaning for
misery. Misery was not knowing what Arthur was
doing, it was not knowing whether he was happy
or not. Had he visited that girl—Gabrielle—in the
Black Boar?

In bed in her tower room, Clare would curl up

in a ball and try to push the loneliness away. But the loneliness wouldn't leave her, nor the longing, nor the emptiness. How could she be lonely when for the first time in her life she was with her real family? She was surrounded by people who were genuinely concerned for her—her father loved her, her sister had become a friend, she liked her maid…

It seemed ungrateful to feel such misery.

The bay mare forgotten, Clare went to find Francesca.

She found her hunched over a trestle in the solar, sketching a design for a wall hanging on to a length of cloth. Her fingertips were black with charcoal.

Clare opened without preamble. 'Francesca, can you read?'

'Yes, indeed. Why?'

'A letter has arrived from Champagne.' As Clare broke the seal, the green knight cracked in two. She stared at it in dismay. 'Oh, no!'

'What's the matter? Clare?'

'The knight—oh, never mind. Here, I'd like you to read this to me.' Clare bit her lip. Her stomach was tying itself into knots. If the letter was from Arthur, she would prefer to digest the contents in privacy, but someone had to read it to her and Francesca seemed the safest choice. Arthur knew she couldn't read and she was sure

a chivalrous knight like Arthur wouldn't dream
of referring to what had passed between them at
the monastery—none the less, it would make her
uncomfortable showing it to her father. And she
couldn't ask Father Alar!

Francesca dusted charcoal from her fingers
and took the roll of parchment.

'It's from Sir Arthur,' she said, giving Clare a
measuring glance. 'But I suspect you know that
already.'

'I wasn't certain.' Impatience was building up
inside her, the knots were tightening.

'Goodness, Clare, it's very long.'

'Francesca, *what does he say?*'

Lifting an eyebrow at her tone, Francesca
began to read.

*Lady Clare. Right worshipful lady, greet-
ings. I pray that you, Count Myrrdin and
Countess Francesca are in full health.*

*Much as I regret it, I fear this letter will
bring you much sadness and some anger. In
brief, Ivo and I were half a day's ride from
Troyes when we were hailed by Nicola's
daughter, Nell. It happened as we arrived
at an inn where we intended to pass the night.
Nell had been taken by slavers, who had put
her in a cart with some other children. Nell
recognised my voice and managed to attract
our attention—*

Francesca broke off with a gasp. 'Slavers?'

Clare's nails dug into her palms. 'Holy Mother, Francesca, *read on*!'

Eyes wide, Francesca bent over the parchment.

With the aid of some grooms and a number of villagers, we captured the slavers and freed the children. You must not worry about Nell, she is safe in Troyes. The other children have been returned to their families, and the slavers are in Count Henry's custody awaiting trial. My lady, you may be interested to hear that one of them is known as 'the Veronese'.

Count Henry has put out a call for further witnesses. Stories have been circulating that the old trade routes may have been used by slavers for years. As you might imagine, he is anxious to meet anyone who could throw more light on this. Unfortunately, we know of no one who might help, but the Count would be delighted if someone were to step forwards. Whether that will happen or not is in God's hands, but one thing is certain, these men will come to trial. I am sure you will join me in praying that justice is done.

Nell asks after you constantly. She has asked me to inform you that Nicola has died...

Francesca paused a second time, Clare felt the weight of her gaze on her, then she sighed and resumed reading.

Nell is a brave and wise child, and she has been remarkably resilient in the face of her mother's death. She asked if she could come and live with me. I have explained that the Troyes barracks are no place for a small girl and she seems to understand this. She is presently living with Aimée across the street from her old house. Countess Isobel d'Aveyron has offered to foster her, but Nell told me that she is happier living in a familiar place with people she knows. She wants for nothing and asks after you often.

Nell was under the impression that you would come for her. I have explained that your home is now in Brittany and she understands, but she was insistent that I write to tell you about Nicola.

Should you wish to send a message back to Troyes, concerning Nell, or indeed on any other subject that may please you, I pray that you send word back with the envoy who brought this letter.

I remain your humble servant and friend. Each day I pray that all God's blessings may be yours.

Arthur Ferrer

'That's it. My goodness, what news,' Francesca said, staring at the letter with round eyes. 'Is Nicola the woman you lived with in Troyes?'

'Yes, her death is not unexpected, she had been barely clinging to life for over a year. But the child, oh, Lord...'

Clare's mind was a jumble, some thoughts were painful—*Nicola has died...Nell is on her own...Slavers...the Veronese.* Other thoughts made her nervous and jittery—*Arthur prays for me every day. And he has kept my secret, as he swore he would. It would surely have advanced him in the eyes of Count Henry if he had revealed that I might be the witness Count Henry is looking for, yet he has not done so. He has kept his word.*

Francesca touched her arm. 'Clare, you're white as milk, you need to sit down. I am sorry about your friend Nicola.'

'She was a kind, good woman.' Eyes prickling, Clare took the parchment, blinking rapidly to bring the squiggly lines back into focus. They were strongly formed in brown ink. Had Arthur paid for a scribe? Or had he written this himself? 'Are these marks at the bottom his name?'

Francesca smiled and pointed. 'Yes, that larger mark is the "A", the first letter of his name, the rest follows. "Arthur Ferrer".'

'Careful, Francesca, your finger's dirty, you're marking it.'

'You love him.'

Though Francesca spoke softly, the words hung in the air. *You love him.*

Clare couldn't move. She opened her mouth to deny it and closed it again. *You love him.* It sounded like the truth and it felt like the truth.

'Love,' she murmured. 'Is that the reason for this aching sense of loneliness, even though I am not alone? I feel empty inside. Is that the reason I haven't slept since he left?'

Francesca squeezed her hand and sighed. 'That's love.'

Love. I love him.

'I wasn't sure. I thought—' Clare shrugged, even as the solar shimmered behind a sudden rush of tears. 'I am not used to love, you see. I was beginning to understand that what I feel for Nicola and Nell is love. Its hurts to know that Nicola has died.'

'I'm sure it does. Clare, there are many kinds of love.' With a glance at the solar door, Francesca lowered her voice. 'If you want him, you will have to fight for him.'

'What do you mean?'

'It won't be long before Papa finds you a husband. He was speaking of it again the other day.'

'*No!* I told Papa I had no wish to marry.'

'Clare, you cannot escape it. As his legitimate daughter you *must* marry.'

'I cannot!' Clare would never forget the way her master had lorded it over his wife in Apulia.

Ugly memories rushed back at her. The beatings.
The echoes of her mistress's stifled screams were
as chilling today as they had been when the beatings had taken place. Clare thought of the veils
her mistress had worn, not for modesty, but to
hide the bruises. 'I have seen at close hand how
marriage can turn a husband into a demon.'

'A demon?' Francesca glanced frowningly
at the letter. 'I doubt Sir Arthur is a demon. A
demon would never have taken such care with
someone else's child—'

'He is good with Nell,' Clare said. 'I saw that
for myself back in Troyes. And of course I realise
that Sir Arthur would never treat me badly. But I
am wary of marriage.'

'Go on...'

Clare pursed her lips and pushed back the
memories. 'Francesca, I have status here. And
freedom such as I never dreamed was possible,
particularly for a woman. I don't want to give
that up.'

'I don't see why you should have to give anything up,' Francesca said. 'Love should strengthen
you, not weaken you. If you and Sir Arthur love
each other—'

'You're jumping to conclusions. I have no idea
what Arthur thinks of me.'

Francesca gripped her hand. 'He is fond of you,
I am sure. He is certainly attracted to you. You
must have noticed.'

Wiping her eyes, Clare hoped Francesca didn't mark the flare of hot colour in her cheeks. *He was certainly attracted in the monastery.* 'He asked me to marry him.'

'He did?' Francesca's fingers tightened on hers. 'When? What did you say?'

Clare bit her lip. 'It was on our journey here. I refused him.'

'Do you love him?'

Clare nodded. 'Very much. And I think I loved him then, only I didn't realise.' She returned the pressure on her fingers. 'Francesca, I have been such a fool. I thought… I didn't know much about love. Until lately my experience of it has been somewhat…meagre.'

'Did Sir Arthur mention marriage again after you arrived here?'

Clare stared at the name scrawled at the bottom of the letter. She had no idea if her love was reciprocated. Arthur had never mentioned love and he had ridden away without a backward look. It seemed likely that he had offered her marriage at St Peter's out of a misplaced sense of chivalry. He had taken her maidenhead and his code dictated that he must ask for her hand. And she had refused him.

'He endorsed what you and Father have told me, that I must marry. He didn't repeat his offer.'

'No, he wouldn't. Too proud, I expect.'

'Too proud?'

'Clare, before you reached Fontaine, Sir Arthur thought you were illegitimate. That changed when you arrived. He wouldn't presume to offer for you knowing your true lineage. He would realise that Papa would want you to make a dynastic marriage.'

'He did say something of that nature.'

'He cares about you.' Francesca plucked the scroll out of her hand. 'Look at this. He opens with "right worshipful lady". Clare, that is not a common mode of address.'

'Is it not? Francesca, a large part of my life was spent in Apulia, some nuances of the language escape me.'

'Believe me, "right worshipful lady" is a phrase used only by the closest of friends. And look here…' a charcoal-smudged finger stabbed at the parchment '…he prays for you each day. Clare, you can't let the man rot in Troyes. Not when you are looking at this letter as though it were the Holy Grail. What are you going to do?'

Clare held out her hand for the letter and looked Francesca square in the eye. 'I made a promise when I was living in Troyes.'

'Oh?'

'I said I would look after Nell when Nicola's time came. I must honour that promise.'

'You're returning to Troyes?'

'If Papa agrees.' She paused, staring at the bottom of the scroll where Arthur had written his name. 'I also need to speak to Papa about my marriage.'

'Your marriage? But didn't you say—?'

'Papa mentioned that he might consider Arthur for my husband and I need to see if he's of the same mind.' Clare's pulse quickened. It wouldn't be easy, her father was changeable. And what if Arthur no longer wanted her?

I ought to tell Arthur about the charges that were laid against me in Apulia. If I am considering marrying the man, he should know everything about me.

'Arthur did like me,' she murmured, meeting her sister's gaze. *And I pray he will continue to do so when he learns the truth.* 'Francesca, if liking exists, do you think that love might follow?'

'I certainly think it's worth a try. You have to marry someone—why not try for the man you love?'

Clare straightened her back. 'You're right, I shall speak to Papa without delay. However, whatever he decides, I will be going to Troyes, I have to see Nell.'

'If you'd care to take a companion, I'd love to come with you. I've always wanted to see Champagne. My husband has a manor outside Provins. We could visit it.'

'I'd welcome your company. Though I should warn you, the way is long and arduous.'

Francesca smiled. 'Not with a guide and a large escort. So, that's settled. And on our way, you can tell me about your life in Apulia. I am curious to know how it is that you don't recognise love when it is staring you in the face. You've been keeping things from me and I don't like it.'

Clare held her hand out for the scroll, smoothed out the creases and rolled it up. *Am I doing the right thing? How will Arthur react when I tell him about Sandro?*

Francesca was watching her, an impish glint in her eyes. 'By the way, Clare, next time you get a *billet-doux*, if you want to open it without destroying the seal, you might try sliding a hot knife under it.'

'A *billet-doux*?'

'That, Clare, is a love letter, and that is what this is, a love letter.'

Hope flaring in her breast, Clare looked at the letter and wondered. A love letter? Maybe. But what Francesca didn't know was what Arthur had *not* said in his letter.

Arthur wants me to testify against the Veronese. He knows it's the last thing I want to do, but this letter is his tactful way of letting me know...

Clare couldn't testify. If she did, every noble in the land would come to hear that Count Myrrdin's daughter had spent most of her life as a slave. She simply couldn't shame her father in that way.

Be that as it may, if Count Myrrdin agreed to accept Arthur as her husband, she would have two reasons for returning to Troyes. She would be returning with a proposition for Sir Arthur Ferrer. The outcome of that would be in God's hands and it had no bearing on her other reason, which was that she must honour the promise she had made to Nell. She would offer Nell a home at Fontaine.

She was not returning to testify against the Veronese. She was not.

Count Myrrdin insisted that his daughters took a respectable escort with them on their journey to the Champagne Court. His idea of a respectable escort turned out to consist of two of his household knights with their squires, six men-at-arms, two serving men as well as his daughters' maids. The women, including the two maids, rode astride. Along the way, the party attracted no little attention. In the villages, people stopped to stare. Gaggles of children ran along the road after them, laughing and giggling as they held up food in hope of selling it—their mother's best almond cake, a wheaten loaf sweetened with honey and raisins, a round of goat's cheese…

After living in the shadows for so long, Clare felt awkward being the focus of all eyes. However, after handing a penny to a gap-toothed girl in exchange for a wheaten loaf and receiving a broad grin along with loaf, she was pleased to find she was enjoying herself.

When she had left Troyes at the turn of the year, she had done so hastily, a shabby runaway who had begged a ride on the back of a merchant's cart. It was hard to credit the transformation that had taken place in the past few months. It was Lent and here she was, returning as Count Myrrdin's legitimate daughter! She had a loving, if eccentric, father and an adopted sister who each day was becoming more and more of a friend. Strangest of all, she was an heiress who, by her father's order, must travel with an escort so grand it drew all eyes.

They reached Troyes towards the end of an afternoon of a hard spring frost, a frost that made the budding shrubs glitter with white. The cold bit sharply through gloves and boots. As the city drew near, Clare could see the guards on the walls—their faces were lost in the mist of their breath.

Entering by the Auxerre Gate, Count Myrrdin's daughters and their train were soon riding through the grain market.

Clare's gaze was pulled to the Black Boar on the other side of the square. On account of the chill, there were no girls sitting on the bench outside it, but shrieks of feminine laughter were gusting through the louvres along with the smoke.

It was none of Clare's business, but that didn't stop the thoughts jumping into her head. *Is Gabrielle working there today? Has Arthur visited her?*

'What is that place?' Francesca asked, her saddle creaking as she turned to see what Clare was looking at.

'It's just an inn popular with soldiers from the garrison,' Clare murmured.

On their travels, Clare had allowed herself to open up to Francesca, who had become something of a confidante. She had told Francesca the truth of her life in Apulia, even of the shame of her enslavement, on condition that Francesca never revealed it to their father.

'It's your story,' Francesca had said. 'You will tell him when you are ready, I am sure.'

'I couldn't do that, Papa would be shamed!'

'Nonsense, it wasn't your fault. Does Sir Arthur know?'

Clare had grimaced. 'He knows most of it.' And soon she must tell him about the crime she had been accused of in Apulia. Attempted murder. She was learning to put her trust in others, particularly in Arthur, but was this too large and shameful a secret? Charges had been laid against her. *I stabbed a man and almost killed him.*

Worry gnawed away at her. *How will Arthur react when I tell him?*

Smiling brightly, she pointed ahead down the Rue de l'Epicerie. 'If we follow this street, we should reach a bridge over a canal. The palace is on the other side of the bridge.'

Count Myrrdin had only agreed to his daughters taking the journey provided that they were lodged in Count Henry's palace. They carried letters from Count Myrrdin to Count Henry, everything had been arranged. Almost everything. Clare's stomach tightened. She wasn't sure how Count Henry would react to one particular request, which had been dispatched by special messenger some days before they had set out.

Her father had read the letter to Clare before he had affixed his seal to it, and the contents were never out of her mind. Her father had written to Count Henry asking that, if Sir Arthur was agreeable, Count Henry would release him from his oath of fealty and permit him to return to Fontaine with Clare.

Clare had found herself praying more fervently with each passing mile. *Dear Lord, let Arthur accept me. Let him learn to love me.*

And now with Count Henry's palace but a few streets away, she would soon be learning the Count's decision.

Would Arthur be waiting to greet her? She mustn't expect it, he would surely be in the barracks with his men and the other Guardians. As she recalled, the barracks were behind the old Roman walls inside Troyes Castle, quite separate from the palace. In any case, her meeting with Arthur ought to wait.

Duty—and the promise she had made to Nell—must come first.

They rode towards the canal with Clare flanked on one side by her sister, and on the other by Sir Denis. Her status wasn't the only thing that had changed since she was last in Troyes. She glanced warmly at her sister. She had gained some far more important riches along the way. 'Francesca, it seems hard to believe, but I had no friends and no family until I came to Champagne. Now I am blessed with both. First there was Geoffrey—'

'The knight who found you and brought you to Troyes?'

Clare nodded. 'And then there was Nicola and Nell, and then Aimée...'

'You can't forget Sir Arthur,' Francesca said, giving her an arch look.

Clare felt herself blush. 'I have a father and—' she reached across and gripped Francesca's hand '—a sister.'

Francesca might not be her sister by blood, but Clare liked her so much she had soon forgotten it. They were sisters in every way that mattered. On the road to Troyes, Clare hadn't been the only one to have opened her heart. Francesca had repaid the compliment by opening hers, too.

Clare almost wished she hadn't. It had been

uncomfortable learning that Francesca's greatest fear was that her husband, Count Tristan, might seek an annulment when he learned that his countess was no longer an heiress. It preyed on her mind. It would be unbearable if her homecoming should result in the destruction of Francesca's marriage.

When Clare had ridden out to St Méen to speak to Francesca, she had feared that her sister must hate her, but she had been thinking wholly about the inheritance that she had snatched from her grasp. Not once had she thought that the poor girl might be worrying herself sick over her marriage. Francesca had to be mistaken about Count Tristan, she had to be…

Where is he? Count Tristan must have heard about my arrival in Fontaine. Why has he stayed away? If nothing else, he should have come to Fontaine to reassure Francesca that all will be well. Where is he?

Clare released Francesca's hand, guiding the bay mare—she had named her Copper—past three nuns walking arm in arm down the centre of the street. 'Francesca?'

'Hmm?'

'I am sure you are wrong about your husband,' Clare said softly. 'You have been married for how long?'

'Two years.'

'By now Count Tristan must have learned to appreciate you. He cannot fail to love you.'

Francesca looked swiftly away, but not before Clare had seen the glitter of tears in her eyes. 'You are kind to say so.'

'Sir Arthur! She's here!' Ivo hurtled into the armoury and skidded to a halt. 'She's reached the palace!'

Arthur returned the spear he had been examining to its rack and fought to keep his expression as bland as possible. His heartbeat had picked up, but it wouldn't do for Sir Raphael to notice.

'A moment, Ivo.' He turned back to Sir Raphael. 'We need to order a few dozen more spears if the city walls are to remain properly manned. I favour giving the commission to Isodore. Any objection? Perhaps you have someone else in mind, someone who might forge better steel?'

He braced himself to receive a sly comment about his father being an armourer, but Sir Raphael simply smiled and shook his head. 'I agree with you, Captain, Isodore's the best man for the job.'

'Very well.' Arthur smiled a dismissal. 'You may place the order with him.'

He waited until Sir Raphael had left the armoury before turning to Ivo.

'When did she ride in?'

'Not half an hour since. She's brought her sister with her and an escort fit for a princess.'

Arthur strode to the door. He'd not had a moment's peace since Count Henry had casually mentioned that Lady Clare was coming to stay at his court. He'd been telling himself that Clare was coming to see how Nell was faring. He'd been telling himself that it was far too late for her to have discovered that their time together had resulted in a child. The idea that Clare might after all be bearing his child brought a smile to his face. It was possible, but not likely. His smile faded. She had already told him that that was not the case.

He'd also been telling himself that it was even more unlikely that she had come to testify against the Veronese and his accomplice. Although Count Henry did seem inordinately pleased about her visit...

One question pushed his speculations aside. *Is Nell the only reason Clare is in Troyes?* He had to find out. Immediately. Because whilst these weeks without her had been nothing less than hell, they had helped him come to a realisation.

He loved her. Life without her was quite simply no life at all. He loved her and they belonged together.

Whatever Clare's reason for returning to Troyes, it was most fortuitous. If she hadn't come back, he would have had to ride back to Fontaine to ask for her hand again. Never mind the difference in their status, she was the only woman for him. She felt something for him, he hoped it was more than liking, but he couldn't be sure. However, she had only given her body to one man. Him. There was hope.

Never mind that Clare had reservations about marriage, he would help her overcome them. *I love her. I will not lose her.* His parents had never married and his father had lived to regret it. Arthur wasn't about to make the same mistake.

Chapter Fifteen

Wryly aware that a man had no business doing his courting in his chain mail, Arthur had paused briefly at the barracks to remove it and don a green tunic that was far less martial. As he buckled his sword-belt over the tunic, he could hardly believe what he was doing. He was about to ask Clare to marry him. Again. Somewhat bemused, he shook his head. It was something he had never thought to do once, never mind twice…

The apartment in the palace that Count Henry had set aside for Lady Clare de Fontaine and her sister was easy to find, but when Arthur had got there he was told that the ladies had gone into the town. A lesser woman might be resting after the rigours of the journey. Not Clare. However, he knew exactly where she would be.

Leaving the palace, he had gone directly to

Aimée's house. Sure enough, standing like sentinels either side of the door, were two of Count Myrrdin's men. Arthur recognised them from Fontaine.

'Good evening, Sergeant,' he said, knocking on the door.

The sergeant nodded. 'Good evening, Sir Arthur.'

A small cooking fire flared on the hearth. Tallow candles guttered as Arthur ducked his head under the wooden lintel and went in. Clare was sitting on a wall bench with Nell on her knee. There were others in the room. Arthur found himself giving Aimée and Countess Francesca cursory nods, but he only truly saw Clare. She was richly attired in a topaz-coloured gown. Her veil looked light as gossamer. She looked well. Very well for a woman who had ridden halfway across Christendom.

Her eyes widened. 'Sir Arthur! I didn't expect to see you so soon.'

'My lady.' He bowed his head, astonished to discover that he seemed to have lost the use of his tongue. He felt unusually self-conscious. Unusually unsure of his ground. He searched her face, mind racing. *Has she missed me as much as I missed her?* He wanted to snatch her into his arms and kiss her senseless—not being able to do so was nothing less than torture. Above all, he wanted her to acknowledge what they must both know. *We belong together.*

Nell pushed off Clare's knee and danced over to touch his hand. He was rather startled to re-alise he had curled it into a fist. Relaxing, he let the child take it.

'Sir Arthur, my knight,' Nell said, swinging his hand to and fro. 'Welcome.'

'*Holà*, Nell.' Arthur was unable to tear his gaze from Clare's. He thought he could see faint smudges beneath those extraordinary eyes, but the candlelight was jumping around almost as much as Nell. 'I...' he cleared his throat, and tried to ignore the heavy thump of his heart '...Lady Clare, if I may, I need to speak to you.'

'Please, sir....' she gestured about the room and her veil trembled '...we are among friends.'

The Countess gave a swift head-shake. 'Clare, I think Sir Arthur does not wish for an audience.' With a smile, she pushed to her feet and held out her hand for Nell. 'Come, Nell, you were going to show me your old house. Aimée, you have the key, I believe. Will you come with us?'

There was a flurry of activity while Aimée hunted for the key and the women found their cloaks. Then the door opened, the candlelight dipped, and he and Clare were alone.

Arthur took a step towards the bench and found the use of his tongue. 'All is well in Fontaine?' He could feel the warmth of the cooking fire on the back of his calves.

'Thank you, yes.'

'And your father? You were concerned for him, as I recall.'

'Papa is as he was. He has good days...' her chest heaved '...others are not so good.'

Her eyes glowed in the reflected light of the fire. Arthur's mind seemed to seize up. He took another step nearer and reached for her wrist. 'Clare...' he was astonished to hear his voice break '...Clare, for God's sake, come here.'

He tugged at her wrist and she came easily to her feet. Dimly, his mind registered that he hadn't had to give her more than a slight pull. It was as though she had been waiting for him to pull her body to his. And then she was in his arms, turning her face to his. As he touched his lips to hers, triumph flooded through him. The sense of rightness had his knees buckling.

'Clare.' He cupped her cheek with his hand, pushing the veil aside so he could slide his fingers into that bright beauty that was her hair. Her eyes had darkened, her cheeks were pink. And he couldn't seem to say anything save her name. 'Clare.'

'Arthur...' She took his shoulders firmly, slid a hand round his neck and held him close.

The kiss drew out. The sweet smell of femininity—of Clare—surrounded him, transporting him back to the dormitory where he had made her his. Clare was giving his lower lip small, biting kisses. And his upper lip. She caught his tongue lightly between her teeth and pressed her body closer. Arthur had been holding himself in check since the moment their eyes had met and his restraint was weakening—the dark pulse of desire was throbbing insistently through every vein.

Arthur groaned. He could no longer remember why it had been so important to see her. There was something…something important he must say…no, something he must ask…

'Lord, Clare.' His breathing was quick and uneven, and the sound of her breathy little gasps was an invitation to sin. Acting on instinct, he backed her up against the wall by the door, relearning the delicious curve of her buttocks beneath his palm, relishing the softness of her breasts through the stuff of her gown.

Reaching for her hem, he had dragged the topaz-coloured gown—it had the feel of silk— halfway up her thighs, when he came back to himself. *We cannot, not here—the others may return. And her father's guards are on the other side of that door.*

'Clare. *Ma mie.*' Silk rustled as Arthur released her gown. Retreating an inch, he rested his forehead against hers and gave her a rueful grin. 'This must wait. There is something I have to say first.'

'Oh?' Dreamy eyes—one grey, one green— had his mind blurring. He gritted his teeth.

'Clare, I need to ask…' She looked up at him, tongue moistening her lips. Her chest heaved and it didn't help when Arthur's gaze caught on the faint outline of her nipples. The throbbing in his loins was intense. Inescapable. 'It's important.'

'Mmm?'

'Clare, you refused me before, but you must see that I have to ask you again. I am hoping that this time you will see your way to changing your mind. Marry me. Please.'

She went very still. Arthur held his breath. His chest was aching. The feeling of triumph was hard to hang on to. Torture, this was torture. When her hands fell from his shoulders and she stepped away from him, his heart clenched. She had withdrawn back into herself, he could see it, and her face had emptied of colour.

She is going to refuse me.

Clare blinked up at him in surprise. Happiness flooded through every vein. *Arthur still wants me.* He hadn't mentioned love, but that might come in time. *Arthur has asked me to marry him.*

However, there should be no secrets between man and wife. This was the moment to confess that charges had been laid against her in Apulia. Yes, Arthur was Captain of the Guardians, but he would surely protect her. The charges were false, and he would believe her. *I trust this man.*

Lord, let him believe me. She straightened her skirts and clasped her hands in front of her. She squared her shoulders.

Clare looked as though she was about to be executed.

Arthur's heart fell to his boots. She was going to refuse him—she was about to tell him that her father had found her a great lord.

'Arthur, there's something I must say to you fir—'

'Clare, you must agree—we belong together.'

She smiled. 'Won't you hear me out?'

The old insecurities rushed back at him. He wasn't sure he wanted to hear her out. Lord, but she looked perfect as Lady Clare de Fontaine. She took his breath away. Standing in the dim light filtering through the shutters, her topaz gown had the shimmer of gold. *She might be a fairy queen. She is far, far above me. I am baseborn, and she is Count Myrrdin's legitimate daughter.* He didn't want to hear her list the differences between them, he'd been hearing them all his life, and he knew them by heart.

'My apologies if I've spoken out of turn.' His voice was icy. 'I shall not ask you again.'

White teeth sank into her lower lip. 'Arthur? Whatever's the matter?'

He gripped his sword hilt. There was a bitter taste at the back of his throat. It struck him that at this moment he would rather be anywhere but here in Aimée's house with Clare. But however disappointed he was personally, he couldn't forget he was Captain of the Guardians. Duty demanded that he asked for help regarding the slavers. 'I was wondering if you'd changed your mind about testifying against the Veronese.'

'Arthur?' Her hand went to her throat. She seemed slow to catch his meaning. 'You expect me to speak in court?'

'It would be a great help if you did.'

She shook her head. 'Not that, Arthur. I can't.'

Clare had known Arthur wanted her to testify. None the less, it was galling to have him raise the subject so soon after making his proposal. *Did he think that I'd change my mind if we were betrothed? Was that why he asked me to marry him?*

Doubts swirled through her mind. If he had asked for her hand purely to get her to testify, what hope did she have of gaining his acceptance when he learned about Sandro? His icy voice echoed in her ears. *I've spoken out of turn, I shall not ask you again.*

Her refusal to testify was clearly a bitter disappointment and he was making no bones about it. His face, which had been so open whilst they'd kissed, was closed. Hard.

He won't hurt me. Clare knew that Arthur would never hurt her, however disappointed he was. *Arthur, I am sorry.* She spoke the words in her mind, as loudly as she could, willing him to understand. There was no way she could go into court and testify before the world.

'Arthur, let me explain why I can't testify.'

'I don't need chapter and verse. I merely need your answer.'

'I can't.' And there was no way she could explain if he wouldn't hear her out. *There's a price on my head in Apulia. I'm wanted for attempted murder and I don't want the world to know.*

'Very well.' His voice was clipped. 'I shan't ask again.'

Clare managed a weak smile. It wasn't returned and her skin seemed to shrink. She hated letting him down, but what choice had she? She couldn't testify. Francesca seemed to believe that her father would accept her enslavement, but Clare wasn't convinced. 'When does Count Henry sit in judgement?'

'In three days' time.'

Clare rubbed her arms. She felt cold, very cold. Were her feelings for him so transparent that he thought a kiss would bend her to his will? How embarrassing. She moved to the fire, but she had gone numb to her core and could feel no heat. 'I trust it will go well. Arthur, I'm truly sorry I can't testify, I realise your position in Troyes would be strengthened if you secured a noble witness, but I can't do it.'

He gave her a bleak look. 'I understand your difficulties, my lady.'

My lady. She felt empty inside. Arthur would surely forgive her in a moment or two. He would forget his disappointment, smile at her again, and he would remember he wanted to marry her.

She looked hopefully at him, but his face was stony. Distant. She felt shaky inside.

'Arthur—*sir*—would my testimony really make such a difference?'

His nod was curt. 'Reports are trickling in from towns along the trade routes. My lady, they bear out what happened to you. Slavery has been going on for some time—in Brittany, in Champagne, in France. Sad to say, many nobles have taken the view that slavery is confined to the lower orders. They don't think it's in their interests to eradicate it.'

'They've been turning a blind eye?' It was her turn to frown. 'But this is dreadful, Arthur. The lords cannot want to lose their vassals.'

Dark eyes bored into her. 'The slavers have been clever, restricting themselves to abducting one or two from each town or village. Usually, they took children. If it became known that Count Myrrdin's daughter had fallen prey to them, I am certain attitudes might begin to change. However, I respect your feelings concerning testifying.' He inclined his head. 'And now, if you would excuse me, my lady, I must return to my duties.'

Clare nodded and he reached for the door latch.

'Arthur, I am sorry to fail you in this, but it's good to see you again. Thank you for caring for Nell.'

He turned and looked back, lips twisting. 'You are welcome, my lady. You have everything you need at the palace?'

'Thank you, yes.'

He bowed. 'Then shall I bid you good day.'

As soon as the door shut behind him, Clare wanted to call him back. She wanted to feel those strong, careful arms close tightly about her. And most of all she wanted to see him smile at her in the tender way he had smiled at her earlier.

Arthur said he understood her refusal to testify, but that was clearly a lie. Her refusal had driven him away. She hugged herself and stared into the fire. Golden flames fluttered like knights' pennons. Her throat ached. Her eyes stung.

If only he'd listened. Had that been so much to ask?

Was this how it was going to end after all that warmth and tenderness? With Arthur saying farewell in so cold and distant a fashion?

She clenched her jaw. She'd hoped for so much more.

It can't end like this, I won't let it!

If her testimony meant that much to him, she was going to have to be stronger than she had been in her life. Francesca was in the right—she was going to have to fight for him. She was going to have to speak out in Count Henry's court.

She's rejected me again. I shall have to forget her.

Arthur shouldered his way past Count Myrrdin's guards without giving them so much as a nod. He strode straight for the castle. The stables. He would ride. Riding settled him, and if he had to ride until midnight to ease the ache in his guts, then so be it.

He threw the saddle on Steel, barked at the guards on the Preize Gate to allow him through, and was cantering down the road before the bell for Vespers rang out from the Cathedral.

She won't have me. Why? She flings herself into my arms, responds to my kisses with an eagerness that matches mine, yet when I ask her to marry me she looks at me as though I had asked her to walk through fire.

Had her father found her a husband? It was possible. If Count Myrrdin had found her a husband, he was likely to be cut of a similar cloth to Count Tristan des Iles. He would have lands and revenues in his own name, and noble blood in his veins. The illegitimate son of an armourer wasn't fit to be her husband—he'd been insane to think they might have a future together.

The sky was a black canopy lit by stars and the moon was so bright it made a white snake of the road. There was enough light for Arthur to give Steel his head. They thundered over the ground, storming past a mill and a scattering of outlying cottages. The ridges and furrows of the peasants' field strips were stripy with moonlight, black and silver like the markings on Tristan le Beau's shield.

She won't have me.

Arthur scowled into the night. What he couldn't fathom was the ease with which she had come into his arms. The apparent hunger of her response. Clare would never respond to a man in such a way if she didn't want him. And she certainly shouldn't have allowed him to kiss her if her father had chosen her husband.

Women! Would he ever understand them?

He wouldn't ask her again.

In the half-light, trees cast eerie shadows. Arthur drove Steel in a wide loop until his stride began to shorten, then he allowed the pace to slacken and directed him towards the Paris Gate.

His time with Clare had been a dream, a beautiful dream, and he wanted to be able to recall it with pleasure. He shouldn't sour his memory with bitterness because his dream of marriage had been a delusion.

He gritted his teeth. He was honest enough to realise that some anger remained. *I could help her, if she would but let me.* He wasn't such a bad match. He had several years' experience act-

ing as Count Lucien's steward at Ravenshold and
had kept the estate going in the teeth of Count
Lucien's absence and Countess Morwenna's ill
health. It hadn't been easy given the restrictions
Count Lucien had placed upon him, but at the
end of his time there, the lands had been bringing in more revenues than they had done when
Lucien's father had been Count d'Aveyron. And
his lord had been satisfied enough to recommend
him to Count Henry.

Lights were beginning to spark on the horizon,
Arthur could see the dark line that was the city
wall, and the flare of torches at the Paris Gate.

Clare would need help in the days and months
to come and he knew he could give it. People
would expect much of her. Would they give her
time to adjust to the changes? He sighed. They
would have to. He was confident she wouldn't
fail, but he wished he could have been at her side.
He ached.

'It is not to be.' Clare—and her father—had
other plans.

His mind a haze of confusion, anger and misery, Arthur shouted for the guards to open the
gate. He rode on until, with a jolt, he saw the
Black Boar. Lights winked behind the shutters.
Gabrielle. *Gabrielle.* Everything came sharply,
painfully, into focus. His guts twisted.

Time was when a visit to the Black Boar—
and to Gabrielle—would have eased most ills.

Not tonight. Swearing under his breath, Arthur realised that his old remedy had lost its efficacy, possibly for all time. He rode on, towards his pallet in the barracks.

'Won't you tell me what's worrying you?' Francesca asked, as they reached the top of the winding stair that led into the apartment. 'You scarcely ate enough to keep a mouse alive.'

They had taken supper in the hall of Count Henry's palace. Clare hadn't seen Arthur, but then she hadn't looked for him. The Captain of the Guardian Knights would surely eat in the hall in Troyes Castle, or else at the barracks.

'I wasn't hungry.'

The walls in the apartment were covered with hangings of various woodland scenes. Clare's gaze lingered on a white unicorn—it had been garlanded with flowers and a ring of girls with linked hands were dancing around it.

'You look like misery itself. Clare, what's wrong? What did Sir Arthur have to say?'

'He asked for my help and I refused him.'

'What on earth did he want?'

'He wants me to testify when the slavers come to trial. He doesn't expect it, but he wants it.' Clare sighed. She'd decided not to mention Arthur's proposal of marriage. It would prompt a flood of questions she wasn't prepared to answer until after the trial. 'My refusal caused great offence.'

Francesca went to the window seat, dragged a cushion to the floor in front of the fire and sank on to it. She patted the cushion in invitation and Clare went to join her.

'It would help Arthur if I testified,' Clare said. 'He would win favour with his lord.'

Francesca looked pensive. 'I think Sir Arthur already has Count Henry's favour, he wouldn't be his Captain otherwise. And I hear that his previous lord, Lucien d'Aveyron, rated him highly.'

'Oh?' Clare's interest quickened. 'Papa told me that Ravenshold—Count Lucien's Champagne holding—was derelict at the end of Arthur's tenure. I knew Papa must be mistaken and it's good to hear you confirm it.'

Francesca gave her a knowing smile. 'You're going to testify.'

'Yes.' Colour rising, Clare stared at the unicorn on the wall hanging. 'But there's something—something unpleasant—that may come to light when I do. That's what's been holding me back. It's bound to change the way people think about me. Papa will be shocked. You will be, too…'

'That sounds worrying. What is it?'

Clare hesitated. 'It…it's something I have done. And…oh, Francesca, I couldn't bear to lose your regard.' *And if I lost Arthur's regard it would be even worse. It turns me inside out to see that*

I have disappointed him. How much worse will it be if I lose his regard permanently?

Francesca looked steadily at her. 'I can't believe you can have done anything that would make me hate you.' Her mouth went up at one side and she took Clare's hand. 'Surely you know that? You deprived me of a county and our friendship still blossomed.'

Clare drew back, sharply. 'Have I been mistaken in you? I thought you had forgiven me. Please say you have. I couldn't bear to think otherwise.'

'Don't be a goose. I was angry at first, naturally. But I was upset about the wrong things. The important things are these…Papa loves me…I have gained a sister.' Francesca gave her hand a warm squeeze. 'And, quite frankly, the idea of coming to blows with Tristan over the best way to run Fontaine filled me with horror.'

Clare's eyes widened. 'You would have come to blows?'

'If you'd met Tristan, you'd know what I mean. Tristan has…strong views. And very set ideas as to how a county should be run. Clare, traditions in Fontaine go back for years, Tristan might not have respected them. I am happy to hand Fontaine over to you. Besides, Tristan has enough land of his own. You may have Fontaine, with my blessing.'

'Truly?'

'Truly. Clare, I've learned to love you. Whatever you're hiding, our friendship will withstand it. And as for Papa—already he adores you. He will stand by you.'

Clare's eyes filled. 'You can't know how much I value your goodwill.'

'Clare?'

'Hmm?'

'Won't you tell me what it is that you have done? You might find it helps.'

Firmly, Clare shook her head. 'You'll find out soon enough.'

Henry, Count of Champagne, was in the habit of dispensing justice from a painted and cushioned throne that stood high on the dais in the great hall of Troyes Castle.

Court was in session as Clare arrived. Francesca and Sir Denis accompanied her and she paused in the doorway to take stock, gripping the skirts of her simple grey gown as though her life depended on it. She had chosen to dress modestly for the hearing. Her hair was covered by a plain white veil.

Lest anyone should be in any doubt as to Count Henry's authority, the colours of Champagne— blue, silver and gold—were emblazoned on a pair of tasselled standards hanging behind him. Heavy wooden beams arched overhead. One side of the roof was busy with the colours of Count

Henry's household knights and the facing rafters were bright with those of his Guardians. A fiery dragon glared at the black head of a wolf; a silver fish fluttered before a green tree...

Benches were filled with noblemen in lavishly embroidered tunics. A row of liveried pages lined the walls, and a troop of knights stood at the ready, hands on their sword hilts. Clare found herself seeking out one man—Captain Arthur Ferrer.

The Captain was on his feet near his lord's right hand, reading from a parchment. Formally attired with a green surcoat over his chain mail, he stood out on account of his height. The unicorn on his tunic must have been sewn with silver thread, for it sparkled when he moved.

Arthur's dark head was turned towards two men standing in fetters before the court. One of them was immediately recognisable as the Veronese. Clare reached for Francesca, but in truth she was astonished at how little she needed her support. Shouldn't the sight of the Veronese send her heart to her throat? Shouldn't she be breaking out in a cold sweat? Neither of these things was happening. Her mind felt cool and calm. Clear. She glanced towards Arthur who, reading from the parchment, had yet to notice her. No matter. She knew what she had to do.

'These men stand accused of abduction and slavery,' Arthur was saying. He ran through a list of indictments which included kidnapping, theft, breaking the peace and using violence against Count Henry's officers on the Count's highway. 'My lord, a number of witnesses are prepared to attest to the fact that children were snatched from the streets of Troyes.' He paused. 'Unfortunately, we have no proof as to what would have been their fate had they not been rescued. None the less, it is my firm belief that these men are slavers.' A choked oath came from the Veronese, but Arthur swept on. 'It is also my belief that the children were to have been taken to Verona and they would eventually have ended up as slaves.'

A ripple of shock ran round the hall.

'You're lying!' The Veronese glared balefully at Arthur. 'Where's your proof?'

'Why else steal children?' Arthur asked, his mouth a grim line. 'You were transporting them from Champagne to sell them abroad as slaves.'

The Veronese sneered. 'This is a tissue of lies. Has anyone been enslaved? Where are your witnesses?'

Holding Francesca's arm, Clare moved slowly into the hall. Arthur had seen her. She felt the weight of his gaze, but forced herself to focus on Count Henry. At the foot of the dais, she and her sister sank into deep curtsies.

'Countess Francesca, Lady Clare,' Count Henry inclined his head at them. 'As you see, court is in session. Do you care to watch?'

Clare had spoken with Count Henry a number

of times since her return to Troyes. Naturally, she had wanted to meet Arthur's liege lord, but far more importantly she had wanted to sound him out on his reaction to the letter her father had sent him from Brittany. She liked the Count very much, even though he had refused to be drawn on whether or not he would permit Arthur to leave his service.

'Thank you, my lord.' Clare drew in a breath. 'But if it pleases you, I have something to add which may alter the course of proceedings. I do not come to watch, I come to give evidence.'

A surprised murmuring broke out, then faded.

'Please, my lady, continue.'

'Count Henry, I believe I am the witness Sir Arthur has been looking for.' She allowed herself a brief glance in Arthur's direction and saw a welter of emotions flicker across those lean features. Confusion…pride…triumph…

Count Henry drew his head back. '*You*, my lady?'

Clare lifted her chin. Her hands were shaking, but her calm had not deserted her. 'Count Henry,' she said, pleased at the strength in her voice even as she pointed rather shakily at the Veronese, 'that man is a slaver. I have watched him sell many poor souls into slavery.'

The Veronese began to splutter. 'She's lying!'

Vaguely, Clare was conscious of Arthur moving to stand at her side. 'Bravo, my lady.' His murmur was soft and for her ears alone. 'Bravo.'

The Count looked at her. 'My lady...?'

Clare took another deep breath and it all tumbled out. From her first memory in Apulia; to the beatings her mistress had received from her husband; to the slaves who were worked half to death on her master's estate...

Count Henry interrupted her. 'Where did you say these things took place?'

'I ended up in Apulia, my lord. Near Trani.'

'She's lying, the bitch is lying!' the Veronese choked out. 'I come from Verona and even an idiot would know that Verona is miles from Trani.'

'The trade routes extend a long way, my lord,' Clare said, quietly.

'She's lying!'

Arthur fixed him with a look. 'It is you who are the liar in this hall.'

'The bitch is the liar, you can't believe a word she says! She's the one who should be on trial, not me. There's a price on her head. In Apulia that woman—' chains chinked as the Veronese pointed at her '—is wanted for attempted murder. Attempted murder, do you hear me? She—'

'Silence!' A ripple ran round the assembly as Count Henry pushed to his feet. 'You are speaking to Lady Clare de Fontaine, the daughter of Count Myrrdin of Brittany.'

The Veronese blanched. 'Count Myrrdin's daughter?'

'Just so.' Count Henry gestured at a guard. 'Sergeant, take these men back to the dungeon. These proceedings will continue later.' Turning to Clare, he offered her his arm. 'Lady Clare, if you would be so good as to accompany me to the solar, I should be grateful for your counsel.'

Clare put her hand on Count Henry's sleeve. 'It will be my pleasure, my lord.'

'This way if you please.' Count Henry led her towards the stairs and lowered his voice. 'I would hear your full testimony before coming to judgement. And I will do so in private. Sir Arthur, would you care to accompany us?'

Chapter Sixteen

Arthur watched the gentle sway of Clare's hips as she mounted the turning stairs ahead of him. He was stunned by her bravery—bravery he recognised as being of the highest order. If his men faced their foes—their fears—with such courage, Champagne would be cleared of outlaws in a trice.

Clare stood accused of attempted murder. It was incredible. Unbelievable. She would never murder anyone. And yet…learning that charges had been laid against her in Apulia explained so much. She had anticipated what would happen when she faced the Veronese—she had been reluctant to testify because she knew what would be hurled in her face. Attempted murder—*Mon Dieu*!

Not once since he had known her had he seen her do anything remotely cruel. She was the soul of kindness. She had cared for Nicola and Nell, and her warm heart had won over her sister in the most trying of circumstances…

Clare? A murderess? Impossible. He wouldn't want to marry a woman who—

His breath caught. Was this what she had been trying to tell him at Aimée's house? Dark accusations had been laid against her. He racked his brains to remember exactly what she'd said.

I asked her to marry me and she said…no, she didn't actually say anything…

She'd looked startled. And desperately worried. She'd been trying to tell him about the charges, she'd wanted him to know. Yes, that fitted. Clare hadn't been brought up a lady, but she had her own code of honour—she wouldn't be able to accept him without telling him everything.

Mon Dieu. No wonder she'd been digging her heels in about appearing in court. She'd known exactly what the Veronese would say. If only he'd listened.

Arthur followed Clare and the Count into the solar and latched the door. He felt dreadful. Guilty. *I should have heard her out.*

'Clare?' He managed a quiet aside as they moved to the fire. 'I failed you, and I want you to know how sorry I am.'

She looked at him, her expression arrested. 'You failed me?'

'You knew what would happen if you appeared in court. You knew what the slaver would say.'

Her throat worked and she nodded.

'You must have been eaten up with worry for months.'

'Years.'

Arthur clenched his jaw. The fear that she might at any moment be caught and dragged back to the scene of her slavery must have weighed on her like a millstone. He should have been there to support her—instead, he had tried to browbeat the poor woman into testifying.

Guilt was tearing him apart. He'd failed her. Walking into that court had been the last thing she'd wanted to do and yet she had done it. Why? Because he'd asked her? Her appearance in court must count for something, he would hang on to that. He loved this woman and it was beginning to look as though she had faced her fears for him. He would win her yet.

It was undeniably cheering to learn that the root of her reluctance to testify had been fear of what the Veronese might reveal. She dreaded losing everything she had won since arriving in Champagne. The urge to reassure her was over-powering.

'Clare, you'll never have to answer that charge in Apulia. I won't permit it. And I am certain both your father and Count Henry will agree. The accusation is unfounded, I'm sure.'

Clare was looking at the floor, twisting her hands together. It struck him that the grey gown and white veil gave her the look of a nun. He couldn't see her face, only the top of her veil. He stared at her, aching to gather her in his arms and kiss away her distress.

Those extraordinary eyes lifted. Even painted with fire glow, her face was haggard. Bloodless. 'Sir Arthur, I am afraid the accusation is true.'

Impossible.

Her bottom lip was quivering and Arthur had to tighten his jaw to stop himself from reaching out to her.

'The accusation is true?' Count Henry said, soberly.

It was the Count's tone that got through to him. Incredibly, Clare had admitted that the Veronese had spoken the truth.

'Impossible,' Arthur heard himself say. 'It's impossible.'

Count Henry held up his hand. 'A moment, Captain. Lady Clare?'

Clare nodded and twisted her hands—twisting, always twisting. Arthur enfolded them in his. They felt like ice.

She gave a faint smile, stared at their linked hands and started to speak. 'I was a maidservant for many years. My master and mistress had a son, Sandro. When I was a child, Sandro tormented me almost every day, it was his favourite game. As I grew older, the game changed. Sandro made it plain that he wanted to do more than torment me. He watched me and followed me about. One day, when I was running an errand for my mistress in the village, he grabbed me and dragged me into a nearby copse. He intended to…to force himself on me. He pushed me to the ground and tore my gown. He had his hand over my mouth and I couldn't breathe. And then…and then…' she gave a choked sob '…my fingers closed on the hilt of his dagger. I couldn't breathe and everything was going black. Blackness. Just blackness—'

'Jesu, Clare—'

'Let her finish, Captain.'

Anger balled in Arthur's chest, but he managed to nod. 'My apologies.'

'When I came back to myself, Sandro was pinning me down. He was unconscious.' Huge eyes met Arthur's. 'I struggled out from under him and there was blood everywhere. My clothes… his tunic. It was Sandro's blood, not mine. I must have stabbed him. I don't remember doing it, but I must have done. I stabbed him.'

Arthur could stand it no longer. He hauled her fully into his arms. When she sagged against him, curling her fingers into his surcoat, something within him eased.

'Arthur, I never wanted to kill him, I just wanted him to leave me alone.'

Arthur swallowed. '*Attempted* murder,' he said slowly, looking over her veiled head at Count Henry. 'The Veronese spoke of attempted murder, my lord, and that is not the same as murder.'

'Indeed it is not,' Count Henry replied, face stern. 'Lady Clare, a charge of attempted murder means that your master's son lives.'

A tear hung on Clare's eyelashes. She took a deep, shuddering breath. 'I just wanted him to stop, I never meant to wound him.'

Arthur cupped her face with his hand and, before he knew it, he had pressed a kiss to her forehead. Was it his imagination or had she leaned into him a moment ago? Nevertheless, he shifted, putting space between them. This woman had yet to accept him. He mustn't presume that because she had been prepared to stand up in court, she had changed her mind about marrying him.

'Of course not, you were defending yourself against rape.' Over her head, Arthur held Count Henry's gaze. 'My lord, the charges against Lady Clare do not bear scrutiny.'

'I agree. I wouldn't trust the Veronese if he were the last man on earth. Those poor children. And to think this traffic in misery has been going on for years.' Count Henry made a disgusted sound. 'Lady Clare, I should like to offer my heartfelt thanks for your testimony.'

'You are welcome, my lord.' Clare looked towards the door. 'Shall the court be reconvening?'

'Not today. And please don't concern yourself about attending again in person. If you would be kind enough to dictate your written testimony to a scribe, Sir Arthur and I will witness it. That should suffice.'

Colour rushed into Clare's cheeks. 'You believe me,' she said, eyes shining. 'You *both* believe me.'

Arthur's heart twisted. That simple statement—*you believe me*—revealed more than anything the horrors of Clare's past. He took her hand and smiled down at her. 'We believe you.'

Clare smiled shyly back and her fingers curled around his. Arthur loved her smile and it seemed an age since he had seen it. It was so shy, so… hopeful? Hopeful? His pulse began to pound. When she smiled, she had the most kissable mouth in Champagne…

Count Henry coughed. 'Lady Clare, I am sure Count Myrrdin would wish me to spare you further sight of the Veronese. If I may, I shall join you in the palace apartment tomorrow morning after you have broken your fast. I shall bring a scribe with me. He can note down the details of your formal testimony.'

'Yes, my lord.'

Halfway to the door, the Count paused. 'Lady Clare?'

'My lord?'

'Concerning your father's petition…'

She seemed to freeze. 'My lord?'

Count Henry's eyes rested briefly on Arthur before returning to Clare. 'My lady, you might care to know that I have at last had word from my overlord, King Louis. He has agreed to your father's request.' The Count tucked his thumb into his belt. 'Further, since you have spent many years abroad, perhaps I should remind you that King Henry of England is overlord of Brittany—you will also need his agreement. And the agreement of the man in question, of course.'

'Petition? What petition?' Arthur said, frowning. But Clare was busy giving his liege lord one of her shy smiles and didn't seem to have heard. Then the click of the door latch caught his attention. Count Henry had gone.

'What the devil was that about?' he demanded. 'And why has he rushed off? I should have thought he'd want your testimony as quickly as possible.'

This time the shy, tremulous smile was for him. It tugged at his heart.

'I believe the Count is giving us a chance to renew our acquaintance.'

'To renew our acquaintance? Clare?'

Her eyelashes drifted down. 'Arthur, he knows that I…that you…that we…' Under the grey cloth of that nun-like gown, her breasts rose and fell. 'Arthur, I didn't just come for Nell. Before I left Brittany I did something extremely unladylike.'

'You did?'

She bit her lip, her very kissable lip. 'You recall how eager my father was to choose me a husband?'

Arthur stopped breathing. 'Yes?'

She shrugged. 'After you left, Papa and I aired our views on marriage many times. As a result of those discussions, Papa sent a petition to Count Henry.'

Arthur's fingers tightened on hers. 'A petition concerning your future husband?'

She nodded and glanced away. 'If he will have me. He is presently sworn to Count Henry. My father asked that the Count release him from his duties in Troyes.'

His duties in Troyes. Arthur's spirits lifted. So that was why Count Henry had left them alone…

Clare had asked for him, and Count Henry… *Dieu merci*, it looked as though the Count approved of the match.

Arthur wiped his face clear of expression and watched her like a hawk. She was trying to hide her feelings, but that shy, hopeful look was very much in evidence. None the less, he wasn't about to betray his eagerness, scarred as he was by her refusal at St Peter's and by that misunderstanding at Aimée's. A man liked to make sure of his ground before entering the lists against uncertain odds.

The white veil quivered and her breath was choppy. She was nervous.

'"*If he will have me?*"' Arthur repeated, forcing himself to release her hands. 'Is this man not in agreement?'

'He—' twin spots of crimson appeared on her cheeks '—he…has not yet been told.'

'I hope he's worthy of you.'

'He is…oh, he is far, far above me.'

Arthur waited, unable to draw breath. A log shifted in the hearth, and footsteps sounded out in the stairwell—someone was coming down from the tower above. After they had passed the solar door, Arthur said, 'And…?'

She was playing with the edge of the white veil, crumpling the fabric. 'Arthur, stop teasing. You know I must marry and you must know I cannot marry anyone but you.'

Arthur's heart soared, but he kept a tight rein on his expression. 'You wish to marry me?'

She released the veil and stared at him. 'Yes!'

He leaned in and her breath warmed his cheek. 'Why?'

'I can't marry a stranger.'

'Better the devil you know, eh?'

Her eyebrows snapped together. 'In this case, yes. You are my anchor. You have been since you came after me and found me outside that inn.' Her chin lifted. 'I wanted to tell you all this when we were at Aimée's.'

'Clare, I am truly sorry I wouldn't let you speak.' He gave her a wry smile. 'I am listening now...'

'If I can't marry you, I won't marry anyone. I told Papa as much. Luckily he has agreed, though at first he was doubtful.'

'Oh?'

She made a dismissive gesture. 'He was concerned about your skills as a steward—the word was that Ravenshold was falling into ruin at the end of your tenure.'

Arthur grimaced, though the rumours didn't surprise him. Ravenshold had been derelict when he'd left to join the Guardians, but he hadn't been responsible. Only a handful of people knew the truth of what had happened there. One day, he hoped to tell her the whole. 'That didn't worry you?'

Clare shook her head, and her veil swirled about her. 'A rumour like that? How could it? You are the most honourable and diligent of men.' She hesitated. 'Papa remained unconvinced—I believe he made mention of Ravenshold in his letter to Count Henry.'

'Do I take it from that mysterious exchange a moment ago, that Count Henry has written back to him?'

She nodded. 'He's explained that you were following Count Lucien's orders in Ravenshold. Arthur, both Count Lucien and Count Henry have said they are certain you would make a competent steward for Fontaine. And now King Louis has approved our marriage.' Those rare and beautiful eyes looked shyly at him. 'Well, sir, what do you say? Do we petition King Henry of England and seek his approval, too?'

Arthur felt his lips curve. 'It is most unusual for a lady to proposition a man in this way.'

'Well, as you must remember, sir, I am no lady.' When Arthur would have protested, she gave him a sad smile. 'I've not had the right upbringing. Part of me will always be a slave.'

He gripped her arms. 'Never say that. *Never.*'

'It's the truth.' She shrugged. 'May I have your answer?'

'My lady…Clare, the man you marry will become Count of Fontaine. Are you sure you don't want a man with noble blood in his veins?' He grimaced. 'Someone who will listen to you when you try to confide in him?'

She gave him a slow smile. 'My mind is fixed on a knight, on Count Henry's Captain. And…' she lifted an eyebrow '…he listens more than most men.'

'*Mon Dieu*, I'm not even legitimate.'

'So much the better, in many ways neither am I.'

'What can you mean? *Ma mie*, the world knows you are legitimate.'

'Arthur, don't you see? I was brought up as a

slave, part of me will always be a slave. I *need* you. You may not have been born into the nobility and you may not be legitimate, but so much the better. You know the way of the world and you've learned the rules. You've learned to succeed, notwithstanding your background.'

'You need me.' His voice was flat. She needed him. Was it unreasonable of him to want more?

Eyes bright, she gripped his arm. 'I need you to help me when I make mistakes. I'm an outsider, you're not. I need you at my side, to explain when I find this new world confusing. Which…' her gentle smile warmed his toes '…is quite often, I fear. I am hoping to hear you say that you need me as much as I need you.'

'You refused me before.'

'At the monastery.' She sighed. 'How I have come to regret that. I was ignorant. I couldn't recognise love when it was staring me in the face.'

Arthur took in a breath and pulled her tight against him. As she swayed towards him, a strand of auburn hair caught the light. Her waist was made for holding and her scent, warm and feminine, filled the air. He cleared his throat. 'Love?'

Hand on his surcoat, she lowered her eyelashes. In another woman, Arthur would have said the gesture was flirtatious, but Clare didn't flirt. She slid her palm up and down in a way that made his skin heat even though he had chain mail beneath his surcoat. Lord, he just had to think about her fingers on him and his flesh heated.

'Love. I love you, Arthur. And I am sorry it has taken me so long to know it.'

'Clare, I…' His voice was husky, and in any case words seemed inadequate, so he tilted her head and his mouth found hers. Soft. Warm. Loving. He heard a murmur of pleasure. Hers. His. Their tongues duelled and fire streaked to his loins. He was sliding his hand down the magical curve that was her body, fitting her to him, wishing she could feel the swiftness with which she inflamed him, when he realised that there was more to resolve. A small but persistent doubt niggled at the back of his mind.

Reluctantly, he raised his head. Dazed grey and green eyes smiled into his. 'Where are you going? Come back.'

'In a moment. I want you to know how much I regret not listening to you at Aimée's.'

A line appeared between her eyebrows. She was toying with his ear, making it burn. 'It was upsetting, but perhaps it was just as well.'

'Oh?'

Small fingers curled into his surcoat, and her eyes held his. 'After you left Aimée's, I felt terrible. I could see my refusal to testify had disappointed you.' She wrapped her arms about him and hugged him. 'I couldn't bear to think I'd let you down, so I changed my mind. My love for you gave me the strength to come forwards.' Her smile was wry. 'There, you have found me out. I feared the loss of your goodwill more than I feared appearing in court. And thank God for it, because justice will be served when Count Henry gives judgement.' Her voice changed, faltered. 'You know everything now. You will have me, won't you?'

'I'll have you.' He smiled down at her. It was as though a weight had lifted from him. He could no longer feel the drag of his chain mail. 'Though why I should agree to marry an unladylike wench who asks me to marry her, I'll never know.'

'It's because you love me.'

He looked into those remarkable eyes and grinned. 'How could I possible love a woman who insults me as you do?'

'Do I?'

'At that dreadful inn, you said I looked like a gargoyle.'

Her eyes sparkled. 'I thought you would have forgotten that.'

He put his hand on his heart. 'I treasure every word you ever said to me.'

She peeped up at him from beneath her eyelashes, making him realise that, once again, he had misjudged her. Clare could flirt. With him. 'Good,' she said, softly. 'Then tell me you love me. Arthur?'

He leaned his forehead against hers. 'I love

you, Clare. I will love you all your days. I will cherish you and—'

She slid her hands up his chest, pulling at his surcoat. Her brow darkened as she felt the chain mail beneath it. 'Do you think Count Henry has given orders for us not to be disturbed?'

It was easy to follow the train of her thoughts— the darkening of her eyes had Arthur's loins throbbing unbearably. Biting back a smile, he glanced about him. The cushioned window seat looked a likely spot, although it was a trifle narrow. 'That would be most unladylike.'

'Would it? Oh dear.' Gripping his hand, she towed him to the window seat. 'Never mind. You can finish teaching me how to be a lady later. First, I must help you disrobe. That chain mail is not appropriate for what I have in mind—'

Voices in the stairwell had Arthur's head turning sharply towards the door. '*Ma mie*, I think it might be better if I escort you back to your chambers in the palace. Ivo can stand guard for us. We shall be more at ease—'

She gave him a look. Her colour was high and there was a determined light in her eyes. 'Arthur, I haven't been at ease since you left Fontaine. In truth, I haven't been *at ease* since we left the monastery. I need you. Now.'

With a laugh, he slid his hand round her neck and shook his head.

She frowned. 'What?'

'That gown makes you look like a nun, but your behaviour—not that I'm complaining, mind.' He reached for her veil, searching for hairpins. 'Lord, I hate these things.'

'Veils?'

'They hide your hair.' As the white veil pooled on the floor, he felt nimble fingers working on the buckle of his sword-belt.

'For myself,' she murmured, 'I am not so fond of chain mail. The first thing you must teach me is how to get it off you. Later, we can go back to the apartment—the bed is as soft as swansdown. And very large. You'll want to try it.'

Arthur grinned. 'Count Henry would be appalled if he could hear you. Lady Clare de Fontaine ought not to behave in this manner. We are not yet marr—'

She shook her head at him, smile warm. 'You can teach me the other rules later. For now, there are far more important things to learn.'

'My lady, I am yours to command.'

* * * * *

A sneaky peek at next month...

HISTORICAL

IGNITE YOUR IMAGINATION, STEP INTO THE PAST...

My wish list for next month's titles...

In stores from 7th February 2014:

☐ Portrait of a Scandal – Annie Burrows

☐ Drawn to Lord Ravenscar – Anne Herries

☐ Lady Beneath the Veil – Sarah Mallory

☐ To Tempt a Viking – Michelle Willingham

☐ Mistress Masquerade – Juliet Landon

☐ The Major's Wife – Lauri Robinson

Available at WHSmith, Tesco, Asda, Eason, Amazon and Apple

Just can't wait?

0114/04

The Regency Ballroom Collection

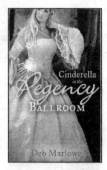

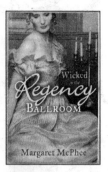

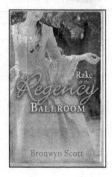

A twelve-book collection led by Louise Allen
and written by the top authors and rising
stars of historical romance!

Classic tales of scandal and seduction in
the Regency ballroom

**Take your place on the ballroom floor now, at:
www.millsandboon.co.uk**

0214/MB458

Join the Mills & Boon Book Club

Subscribe to **Historical** today for 3, 6 or 12 months and you could **save over £50!**

We'll also treat you to these fabulous extras:

- **FREE L'Occitane gift set worth £10**
- **FREE home delivery**
- **Rewards scheme, exclusive offers…and much more!**

Subscribe now and save over £50
www.millsandboon.co.uk/subscribeme

SUBS/OFFER/H1

Discover more romance at

www.millsandboon.co.uk

- ❤ WIN great prizes in our exclusive competitions

- ❤ BUY new titles before they hit the shops

- ❤ BROWSE new books and REVIEW your favourites

- ❤ SAVE on new books with the Mills & Boon® Bookclub™

- ❤ DISCOVER new authors

PLUS, to chat about your favourite reads, get the latest news and find special offers:

- 📘 Find us on facebook.com/millsandboon

- 🐦 Follow us on twitter.com/millsandboonuk

- ❤ Sign up to our newsletter at millsandboon.co.uk